Shel

"You better _____ _____ _____ _____ ill sets in."

She was a c_____ _____ _____ _____ nd red, her eyes wide with indignant anger. He found himself hard-pressed not to laugh. "So you'd rather catch your death." He shook his head in amazement. "You know I've seen you in less, darlin'."

Her cheeks flamed, and her hazel eyes sparked fire. Grudgingly she reached up under her soggy skirts and peeled off the wet stockings, almost slapped him in the face with them, then tossed them over the chair. She might be angry, but she was no fool. She had no desire to catch her death. "There," she snapped, turning. "Happy now?"

"Not quite." He inclined his head. "Skirts, too."

"In a pig's eye!" she exclaimed.

Weston sighed heavily. "You can take them off yourself, or I can do it for you. What'll it be, Lizzy?"

Stories of Love on the Great Lakes
From Berkley Publishing

TWILIGHT MIST
by Ann Justice

TEMPEST WATERS
by Nancy Gideon

SECRET SHORES
by Kelly Ferjutz

SUMMER STORM
by Teresa Warfield

LOVER'S COVE
by Jo Anne Cassity

LOVER'S COVE

JO ANNE CASSITY

BERKLEY BOOKS, NEW YORK

LOVER'S COVE

A Berkley Book / published by arrangement with
the author

PRINTING HISTORY
Berkley edition / October 1993

ISBN: 0-425-13821-6

A BERKLEY BOOK ® TM 757,375
Berkley Books are published by The Berkley Publishing Group,
200 Madison Avenue, New York, New York 10016.
The name "BERKLEY" and the "B" logo
are trademarks belonging to Berkley Publishing Corporation.

PRINTED IN THE UNITED STATES OF AMERICA

10 9 8 7 6 5 4 3 2 1

For the two men in my life:
my husband, Russ,
and my son, John.
I love you guys.

Acknowledgments

With sincere gratitude, I would like to mention the following people and organizations:

The Toronto Historical Board and Marine Museum—for all the time they spent helping me locate and verify my research, as well as for their patience in answering my countless questions. My thanks go out to all: Richard Stromberg, John Summers, Catherine Anderson, and Lisa Brazier.

Judith Stern, my editor—for believing in this writer and for the wonderful opportunity to write this story.

Tammy Mackey—my only sister, my very first reader—I love you, Tammy.

Carole Byrnes—fellow writer, faithful friend—as well as my very favorite librarian. Thanks, Carole.

Paulette Brewster—fellow writer, dear friend. I couldn't have done this one without you, Paulette. May God bless and keep you always, and may we never forget William Ernest Henley's words.

Josephine Jessie Lambert—my mother, who taught me not only to read, but to love the words I read.

And to my Lord and Savior, Jesus Christ—without whom I could write nothing.

Jo Anne Cassity
Niles, Ohio
February, 1993

CHAPTER
1

Toronto, Ontario, Canada—early June, 1885

Weston Munroe stretched out on the grassy slope.

With a sense of deep satisfaction he watched the last of the crimson-tinged shadows melt into the shimmering waters of Lake Ontario. Leaning back on one elbow, he bent one knee and relaxed, and in the final violet moments of dusk, far away from the reaches of the gaslit city, he enjoyed the soft summer breeze.

Along with a calming chorus of crickets, a gentle wind played throughout the full, leafy tops of the trees like the sweetest of melodies, cooling the air, becoming a most fitting epitaph to a warm June day.

He gazed down at the placid silver surface of the moonlit waters, watched the shadows play around him, and realized he'd missed his home much more than he'd ever thought possible. This land was beautiful, this lake an endless, iridescent carpet stretching out to surround the islands that graced its surface.

"Shining waters," he said with respect. The Iroquois

knew what they were doing when they'd named these
waters.

He reached into his shirt pocket and withdrew a cigar.
He bit off the end and spit it out, then struck a match
and lit the cigar, savoring the flavor with slow deliberateness.

Alone with only his memories and the fireflies flitting
around him, he grew pensive and quiet for some time,
until below him on the beach a movement to his left
caught his eye. He squinted. Through the shadows he
watched with interest as the familiar slim silhouette of a
woman came into view. Her movements loose and fluid,
she ran along the edge of the water, unbuttoning her
clothing, then casting off each piece to a dry spot higher
along the shore. Down to only brief white undergarments, she stopped, turned to face the water, and allowed
the waves to lap her bare ankles, while she reached up
and took the pins from her hair. A dark tumble of auburn
hair fell down her back to her slender waist. She pushed
her fingers through the waves to loosen the tangles, then
shook the heavy mass back from her shoulders. The light
of the moon turned her hair to a shimmer of red fire.

Weston smiled. A story Benjamin—the ageless lighthouse keeper—had once told him came to mind, an old
legend about sailors saved by beautiful mermaids who
lived deep within the water's depths. Now that she'd
grown up, Weston thought this young woman fit the
description perfectly.

He smiled, remembering Benjamin with affection.
Benjamin, with his endless stories of shipwrecks and
mysterious Iroquoian legends. Some stories had been
so frightening that Weston and his older brother, Aaron,
had lain awake in fear many a night. But not this girl.

He looked across the beach toward the Gibraltar Point

Lighthouse. It stood still and silent, an ancient soldier with glowing eyes, guarding this land and lake as it had for as long as Weston could remember.

As he refocused his attention on the young woman below, nostalgia swept him.

Elizabeth McRaney. His Lizzy Beth.

So she still came here.

But in the five years he'd been away, she'd done some growing up. Still, he would have recognized that hair anywhere. Even as a freckle-faced tomboy, she had had beautiful hair. He could see now that she was no longer the skinny girl he remembered from their youth.

He wondered with a sudden pang of jealousy if Aaron had ever seen her like this, her hair loose, her spirit free. No, he thought, abruptly abandoning the idea. Of course he hadn't. Aaron was too much of a gentleman to sit up on a rise, encased in darkness, and watch a lady undress.

But Weston wasn't.

After all, he was the one who used to sneak out to meet her in the shadows of the moonlight, and together they would swim the dark waters of the lake and pretend to be pirates with treasures to hunt and seas to conquer. Later, when she'd reached fifteen and he eighteen, they'd begun to play other, more intense games.

He wondered if she ever thought about those times. She'd just begun to develop into a young woman. But he had already become a young man and knew that their nightly meetings, though innocent as they'd always been in the past, could no longer continue along that path. They had to come to an end.

He savored the taste of his cigar, enjoying the sight below him.

Elizabeth bent forward at the waist. She reached downward, scooped water into her hands, then held them up as though in worship to the star-studded sky and let the water trickle down her sides.

Her eyes drifted shut. Ohhhh . . . Being outdoors felt so good.

Poor Papa, she thought and experienced a sharp twinge of guilt. He would be most disappointed if he knew she was out here again.

Ah, well . . . He'd fallen asleep hours ago. He'd not catch her this night.

An old memory surfaced, bringing with it a momentary sting of embarrassment. He'd caught her once, many years ago. He'd caught her with Weston Munroe, many years ago, after a night such as this . . .

She closed her eyes and saw Weston as he'd been that night, standing tall and proud in the silver beams of the moon's rays.

She wrapped her arms around her waist and hugged herself tight and remembered, once again, how his hands had felt upon her skin—warm and strong and wonderfully young and impatient.

Lord, but she'd loved him.

Her heart contracted with pain. The bastard! The lying snake! The bloody cur! How could she have ever believed he'd keep his word?

I'll be back, Beth. I promise. I'll come back for you.

Five years later, his words, useless memories indeed, still rang like empty, resounding bells in her ears.

She shivered, then contemptuously spat onto the smooth surface of the water. If she ever laid eyes on him again, lady or no, she'd throw a punch he'd not soon forget. Who better to land one on than the one who'd taught her such skills?

She swallowed the tightness in her throat, angry at its presence.

She hated Weston Munroe.

She hated him almost as much as she hated Captain Edward Braxton—the man she held responsible for the loss of her mother.

But, she admitted with frank honesty as a bevy of memories assaulted her, there wasn't a man in all Toronto who could out-swim, out-dance, out-skate, out-fight, out-scull or out-log Weston Munroe. He'd been the best at almost everything he'd done. He'd been her ideal. As a child, she'd worshiped him. As a budding woman of fifteen, she'd loved him.

Her mind conjured up his image once again. She saw him with the sun glinting off his white-blond hair and wicked laughter gleaming in his blue, blue eyes.

And she remembered his mouth and the way his lips were curved and the way they felt, warm and wet, when he'd kissed her.

Damn him! She slapped at the surface of the water with both hands, causing a spray to shoot high into the air.

Scowling, she pushed a strand of wet hair back from her face and gazed up at the glowing, opalescent disk of the moon. He'd ruined her for anyone else. No other man's kisses had ever moved her like that again. Not even Aaron's.

Guilt coursed through her at that reminder, and she promised herself for the hundredth time that she would be a good wife to Aaron once they were married. She would make her father proud. For once in her life, instead of being the rebel, she would be like her sister, Abigail, and do the proper thing. She would be a lady.

As though to wash the memories of Weston away, she dove deep into the water, disappearing beneath its cool, healing depths.

Weston stood and stretched lazily. Watching her, the temptation became too great, and he grinned and dropped his cigar, then ground it under the heel of his boot. Slowly he unbuttoned his shirt, peeled it off, and dropped it to the ground below, then hopped on each foot as he pulled off his boots. Without further hesitation he headed down toward the shore, his grin widening.

Elizabeth stayed beneath the water for as long as possible, then broke the surface with a small gasp, drawing air deep into her deprived lungs. The breeze felt almost cold upon her scalp and shoulders, but the coolness of the air didn't disturb her. A shallow ripple along the surface of the water several feet away caught her attention.

Cautiously she approached it, thinking of fish. Big fish! Sucker fish!

From out of the past came memories accompanied by childish voices. "Watch out for the sucker fish, Lizzy Beth," Weston called out and laughed, while Elizabeth struggled to fight her way to shore. "They'll suck your toes off!"

Fighting against the weight of her petticoats as they wrapped around her legs, she'd turned. "Sometimes I hate you, Weston Munroe," she'd snapped over her shoulder at the boy behind her.

"How bad do you hate me, Beth?" Weston's question had followed, his eyes glinting mischief. "How bad?"

Another ripple pulled her back to the present. No, she thought with a grimace, fish wouldn't come this close. And there were no such things as sucker fish. There never had been. The ripple was probably just the current.

So don't be such a coward, Beth! she told herself with disgust. *For heaven's sake, there's nothing out here but you, the wind, the stars, and the moon.* And a few old tired memories.

If there was anything Elizabeth McRaney despised, it was a coward.

Then something brushed against her bare ankles.

Before she could scream, her feet jerked from beneath her, and she plunged down into a dark whirlpool of water. She thrashed violently, trying to find her footing, struggling to right herself and escape whatever it was that had hauled her down into the frightening depths.

Then, as suddenly as she'd been toppled, she was righted. But the monster who pulled her up and lifted her onto her feet had two strong hands. And his laughter rang out, deep and throaty, into the hollow quiet of the night.

She came up coughing, choking on the mouthful of water she'd inhaled when she'd first gone under.

Instant anger flared through her like hot lightning.

A long time had passed since she last heard that laughter, but she knew it well. Though the tone and timber were slightly different, without a doubt she knew not only the laughter, but to whom it belonged.

Her hair obscured her vision, hanging in front of her eyes like a mass of stringy, dark red seaweed. She flung it from her face, slapping it back, furious and embarrassed at her weakness. She plunked her hands upon her hips and stared into the laughing blue eyes of her tormentor.

"Damn you, Weston Munroe!" she shrieked, her voice shrill with the remnants of her panic. "You lowdown black-hearted son of a bloody—" She drew back her arm and swung, aiming a punch at his head.

Quick as always, he dodged her attack, catching her tiny wrist with one hand, her waist with the other.

"Whoaaaaa," he said, still laughing. "Is this how ye say hello, Lizzy Beth?"

Fury rose in Elizabeth's heart. Five years. Five years without so much as a blasted letter. The bastard! She ripped her hand from his grasp and, before he could stop her, slapped him.

Hard.

His head snapped to the side, but the irritating smile never left his face. He lifted his hand and tenderly massaged his jaw. "Damn it all if ye haven't grown up pretty, Beth," he said softly, while he looked her up and down, his eyes warm with appreciation.

She stared at him in frozen wonder, stunned by his brashness.

But despite all her anger, despite all her inner turmoil, she couldn't help but notice he was still beautiful, blond and beautiful. He was bigger than she remembered, thicker through the chest, a few inches taller, his arms more muscular, his biceps bulging. And his voice—different somehow, smoother and deeper, with a certain inflection in his speech that had not been there in the past.

Gazing at him, she realized he was a man fully grown. She experienced an instant intuitive warning.

"Sometimes I hate you, Weston Munroe!" Her hazel eyes blazed. Incensed, she spun, dismissed him, and fought her way toward shore, her undergarments clinging to her body, outlining all the hollow places she used to secretly wish were fuller.

He pushed his way through the water behind her. Reaching her, he grabbed her arm and spun her around to face him. Once again she swung wildly. "Hey!" He ducked quickly, just in time to miss another well-aimed punch. "Is this any way to treat your future brother-in-law?" he asked with laughter in his voice.

Silence.

They stared at each other. The smile faded from his face. The reality of the words he'd spoken hit them both.

Her throat tightened and closed.

His chest hurt, suddenly feeling heavy and leaden.

She stared into his eyes—eyes that had grown dark and solemn—and experienced a rush of that old familiar yearning.

"I hate you, Weston Munroe," she whispered fervently. Tears sprang to her eyes, clouding her vision, burning her throat. "I really do."

He moved closer, his body almost touching hers. "Do ye, Beth?" he asked in a soft voice. "How bad do ye hate me?"

She didn't answer him, unwilling as she was to hear the lack of conviction in her own voice.

His hand came up and touched her shoulder lightly. With slow deliberateness, it rode upward, beneath her hair, to cup the back of her neck. Then he did what he longed to do, had longed to do since the day he'd left: He gently pulled her head into the curve of his shoulder.

Her eyes sank shut. He was warm and wet and achingly familiar, and to her dismay she fit against him now as perfectly as she had those many years ago.

"Why didn't you come back?" Her voice was a choked whisper. "Why didn't you write to me, Wes?"

He shrugged slightly and shook his head, having no worthy excuse to offer her. "I don't know, Beth. I really don't. I guess . . . I thought . . . it would be better for ye if I left ye alone after . . . And then the years just seemed to—"

"But you promised, and I waited. I waited for so long . . ."

He was quiet for a moment, wracked with guilt for having hurt her. "I never forgot ye, Beth," he whispered earnestly. He bent his head, and his lips grazed her forehead. "Not ever."

She squeezed her lids together, feeling her stomach turn into a vault of liquid heat. For a few precious moments, she gave up the battle and allowed herself to forget that she was soon to be engaged to his brother.

But she was never one to be lost in hope-filled fantasies. Her sanity quickly returned, and with it the anger of betrayal.

She jerked away from him with a strength characteristic of the old McRaney will, and with the palms of both hands she shoved against his wide chest with all her might, to send him flailing back into the water. "Well," she spat, all softness fading from her eyes, "I sure as hell forgot you, Weston Munroe. I forgot about you years ago."

Before he could right himself and reach for her again, she turned and plowed her way through the water.

"Dammit, Beth! Wait!" he called after her.

But Elizabeth ignored him. She was through waiting for Weston Munroe.

Reaching the shore, she ran along the grassy edge, plucking up her clothing as though the Devil himself breathed fire upon the back of her neck.

Then, without a backward glance, she disappeared into the unforgiving blackness of the night.

A medley of church bells rang out into the early morning air. Elizabeth moaned and turned onto her side, pulling the light coverlet up over her head as though to shut the world out for just a little while longer.

"Come on, Beth. Time to get up." Her sister's soft voice blended with the bells, reminding Elizabeth of how beautiful Abigail's voice was when she sang. Nothing like her own, which sounded more like a choked bull-frog than anything even vaguely resembling a human being.

"You know how disappointed Papa gets if he has to wait too long for us."

Yawning, Elizabeth flopped over onto her back again. Yes, she knew. Only too well. After all, she'd been disappointing Papa all of her life.

She pried open one eyelid and searched the room for her sister. Sunlight spilled through the paned glass, filling the room with a golden brightness that hurt her eyes. Sunday already. She ground the heels of her hands into her eyes.

Damnation!

She hoped Papa wasn't going to preach again the sermon about having a meek and humble spirit. She was sure he'd designed and perfected that one especially for her benefit.

She lay on her back, trying to focus her thoughts while her gaze took in the comfortable surroundings of the room she shared with her sister. Simple, clean, white lace curtains hung in front of the window. Stirred by the breeze that came in off the lake, they fluttered outward in gentle invitation.

Except for an oval braided rug that lay in the center of the room, between the two beds, the floor was bare. But the smooth wooden surface shone with a luster from the recent polishing she and Abigail had given it. And the walls, oh, they were especially pretty, covered with the delicate flowered paper their mother had ordered for them from New York City so many, many years ago.

Elizabeth lay languidly, putting off the inevitable moment when she would have to rise. Yet something nagged at the back of her mind. Something was amiss, but her brain, still clouded by the haze of sleep, couldn't bring it to the surface.

And then it hit her with the force of a thunderclap.

Weston Munroe was back!

Hells bells! She snapped up in bed, her hands flying to cheeks that suddenly felt hot.

"Wes is back," she whispered, her eyes seeking Abigail's.

Abigail stood in front of the oak-framed, floor-length mirror, putting the last pins in her dark, glossy, upswept hair.

Their eyes met in the mirror. "Weston Munroe?" Confused, she inclined her head.

"Of course, Weston Munroe!" Elizabeth answered shortly.

Abigail turned and smoothed her dress down over well-rounded hips. Worried, her gray eyes opened wide. "Are you quite sure?"

Elizabeth's gaze flicked away guiltily. "Yes. I saw him . . . last night at the lake . . ."

"Oh, Beth, no . . ."

"I didn't know he was back." Elizabeth hurried to defend herself. "I didn't know he was ever coming back. I quit hoping a long time ago."

Abigail crossed the room to stand before her sister. Though Elizabeth was fifteen months her elder, there were times when Abigail, with her calm, steady, dependable temperament, was much more Elizabeth's friend than her younger sister. "It's all right, sweeting. I know you didn't." Abigail's voice was gentle, her smile tolerant and understanding, so like their mother's had been.

Elizabeth swung her legs over the edge of the bed and stood, her white nightgown slipping to the floor around her ankles. "Ab, what am I gonna do?" she asked in a voice uncharacteristically uncertain and frightened.

Abigail sighed, then took a deep breath. "Oh, Beth . . . I don't know . . ."

Downstairs, from the front of the house, their father's voice boomed up to them, interrupting Abigail's response. "Elizabeth! Abigail! Come now. We'll be late."

"Just a few more minutes, Papa," Abigail called out. With determination squaring her jaw, she grasped Elizabeth's hand and said, "For now, you're going to get dressed and come to church with me and Papa. Then we'll worry about Weston Munroe."

Weston stretched his long legs out under the pew in front of him and pulled at his necktie. Blasted things, anyway! He was sure they were created by some perverse individual with the sole intention of torturing a man to death by slow strangulation.

He scowled, stole a glance to his left, and caught his mother watching him. She tightened her brow in disapproval, trying to appear intimidating, but somehow her round, peachy cheeks and bright blue eyes belied her efforts. He winked and flashed her his most beguiling smile, deepening the dimple in his cheek, charming her as he had for twenty-three years.

Sarah Munroe blushed, and her eyes grew gentle. "You're incorrigible, Weston," she reproved softly. "But I'm so glad you've come home. We've missed you."

He reached over and took her plump hand in his own and squeezed gently, experiencing a deep swell of affection for her. "It's good to be home, Mama."

"You'll stay, won't you?"

He nodded. "For a while." He grinned. "I've missed my best girl, ye know."

And he had.

After all, it was mostly for her sake he'd come home. And it was only for her sake he sat in the family pew, in Reverend McRaney's staunch Methodist church, amid the flutter of gossip and speculation, while he weathered his father's silent disapproval.

Everitt Munroe had never forgiven him for running off as he had. And since his stroke, which he'd suffered during the last year of Weston's absence, he'd become even more adamant about Weston taking his position in the family business. He wanted him to stay at home, like his older brother, Aaron, and his younger brother, Daniel, and learn the financial aspects of Munroe Shipping.

But Weston wanted more.

He wanted not only to transport passengers and cargo. He wanted to build the ships to do it. There was a new age sweeping the land. He could feel it, and he wanted to become a part of it. The age of schooners was fast coming to an end; the change to iron and steel was well under way. In every port he'd docked, every country he'd passed through, he'd studied the new designs. Excitement igniting, he'd learned that the Canadian Pacific Railway Company felt the lakes were ready for vessels comparable in size to the oceangoing type. Such vessels would enhance their passenger service. He agreed and wanted to be among those who would dare to build them.

As people filed into the church, flocking to their customary seats, Weston's attention was diverted from his thoughts. A soft hum spread throughout the small auditorium. He allowed his gaze to travel the room.

It was a modest building by Toronto's standards—a plain, common-looking brick structure with pews that were simple, but strong and serviceable. At the front of the auditorium sat several benches for the choir. Between the benches, on a slightly raised platform, the reverend's podium stood. The only ornamentation to relieve the painful severity of the church's plainness were the windows. They were a colorful array of designs and images pressed upon expensive stained glass.

There were, of course, larger, more lavish houses of worship on Richmond Street. But Reverend McRaney's Methodist church was one of the most respected fundamentalist parsonages in the city, and so Weston's family, along with a large number of their acquaintances, remained fiercely loyal to this establishment.

Weston watched with barely concealed amusement as Mrs. Caufield waddled up the aisle to her designated pew. Her small, sharp eyes scanned the perimeters of the room, first left, then right, making sure she mentally gauged who was present and who was not, so she would be able to pass on the information to her ladies circle. Then they could lament the hopelessly lost souls of the wicked tardy.

Weston coughed while swallowing a chuckle. Mrs. Caufield and her ladies had been lamenting his soul for years. His only regret was that because of him, they had lamented Beth's, also.

Glancing to his right, he noticed his suppressed chuckle had drawn his brother's attention. Aaron raised his sandy-brown brows in question. Weston tamped down the urge to do something wild and shocking as he would have done ten years ago. Back then, Aaron might have shared in his devilry and later his punishment.

Now . . . well, time and distance had changed things between them.

And Aaron planned to marry Beth.

Weston inclined his head in Mrs. Caufield's direction. "She hasn't changed a bit, I see."

Aaron's serious expression lightened somewhat, and he smiled, remembering some of the shared escapades he, Weston, Elizabeth, and a few others of their circle used to have. "No . . ." His voice was thoughtful and quiet. "I suppose there are some things that never change."

A murmur from across the aisle pulled Weston's attention away from Aaron.

Their younger brother, Daniel, scooted into the pew and flopped down beside their father. Catching Weston's eye, Daniel smiled a reckless, happy, fifteen-year-old smile very reminiscent of Weston's own at that age.

Amused, Weston shook his head, then turned slightly in his seat, arching his neck to watch the remainder of the church fill, as the last of the bells pealed, ushering in the few remaining stragglers.

Then he saw her.

CHAPTER
2

Beth hurried down the aisle toward the front pew, her gait a little too long and leggy to ever be considered totally feminine. But dressed in a proper, pleated Victorian blouse of creamy white, tucked neatly into the waistband of a matching bustled skirt, reaching discreetly to her ankles, Elizabeth McRaney was almost the perfect picture of propriety. Other than her stride, the only thing that belied the impression was the somewhat haphazard condition of her hair. Forever wild, it defied all efforts to remain atop her head. The heavy mass, which had been coerced into a knot, had loosened and now sat slightly off center, like some misplaced doorknob atop her head. Several wisps and tendrils had escaped and encircled her face. She pushed impatiently at a strand that caught in the side of her mouth, drew her brows together tightly in agitation, and turned to whisper something to her sister.

Weston grinned, imagining the words she'd used while struggling with her hair that morning.

He willed her eyes to his, but she ignored him, passing by his family with only a brief nod to Aaron and a warm smile to his mother.

Weston tamped down a twinge of disappointment.

Forget it, Munroe. She's gonna marry your brother. Now stay away from her before ye have some real problems to contend with.

He angled a glance at Aaron, who stared after her, the longing evident upon his face. An image of them together flitted through Weston's mind. He fought down a sharp, unfamiliar pang of jealousy and diverted his gaze to the front of the auditorium.

Reverend McRaney strode to his place at the podium. He was a short, square, burly man in his late forties, with a thick thatch of dark brown hair slightly streaked with gray, a serious manner that sometimes belied a rather dry sense of humor, and kind gray eyes that commanded respect from all who knew him.

With a deep authoritative voice, he asked the congregation to stand, then led them in prayer. When finished, he began a hymn and was immediately joined by the choir and congregation.

Aaron Munroe turned and studied his younger brother while they sang. He felt an uncomfortable twinge of disquiet. Recklessly handsome, Weston had always turned heads. And though four years younger, Weston had been first at everything.

Even with Elizabeth.

But, Aaron reminded himself, Elizabeth was going to marry him, not Weston.

Feeling his brother's gaze on him, Weston turned. Their eyes met, Weston's questioning, Aaron's uncertain. Two brothers, each so different. One loved the busy docks he'd sought out throughout his boyhood; the other loved the books and figures that brought commerce to those docks.

They held each other's gaze for several moments, then both looked away, but Weston felt a heavy weight spread across his chest.

He searched the row of bodies standing at the front pew, found the back of a creamy white blouse, and knew a deep sadness.

I never should have come home, he thought, feeling strangely disconnected. *I don't belong here anymore.*

The singing ended, and the reverend followed with another prayer. All heads bowed.

All but Weston's.

From the safety of his position, he studied Elizabeth covertly. With her head bowed obediently, he could see the graceful line of her neck, the smooth curve of her right cheek. Her hands rested on the back of the pew in front of her. She stood motionless, but as Weston watched, he spotted the forefinger on her right hand methodically picking at the cuticle around her thumbnail, a nervous habit she'd always had.

There was a time he'd teased her about it.

Elizabeth tried her best to concentrate on her father's voice. "For only in you are we able to find peace and forgiveness. Dear Father in Heaven, grant us the wisdom to seek your face. Keep us from the temptations of this world . . ."

She stared unseeing at her hands, her chin pressed tightly to her chest.

Don't look at him. She pinched her eyes shut tight. *Don't you dare look at him, Elizabeth McRaney!*

But slowly, as though magnetized, her head turned just a little.

Her eyes mere slits, she peeked sideways. Her eyes flew open; her brows dropped like bat wings.

Blast him!

His eyes were wide open, looking straight at her. But his expression appeared solemn, almost sad. For a second, it caught her off guard, and her eyes softened.

So she hadn't forgotten him either, Weston thought with satisfaction. No matter what she said, she remembered. Slowly a self-satisfied smile stretched across his face.

Her eyes immediately iced over. She threw him her most venomous glare.

As though thoroughly enjoying her contempt, he grinned wickedly and wiggled his eyebrows up and down in a gesture that used to send her into uncontrollable fits of laughter.

Heat sprung to her cheeks.

"Amen." Reverend McRaney quietly ended the prayer.

Elizabeth's head whipped forward so fast she created a breeze. Quite certain everyone in the auditorium had heard the noisy snap of her neck, she reddened further. Cursing Weston with all the colorful expletives he'd ever taught her, she wished herself a thousand miles away from him and his pubescent games.

He'd not grown up at all in five years! Not one wit!

Willing her heart to quiet its thudding, she once again tried to concentrate on her father's words.

The sermon was not overly long. But its focus was, as Elizabeth had feared, humility, godliness, and purity— subjects very dear to the reverend's heart.

I'm sorry, Papa. I'm sorry, she thought, her own heart heavy. She wanted nothing more than to please him, to bring him happiness. He'd had so much sadness in his lifetime . . . No one knew that better than she. And he deserved so much better. As her eyes found her father's face, she silently vowed, as she'd done so many times before, *I'll try harder, Papa. I promise.*

When the service ended, Elizabeth patted Abigail's hand, excused herself, and slipped out of the pew. Halfway to the door, she was caught by her best friend, Gabrielle, who grabbed her arm and whispered breathlessly, "Did you see who's here!"

Elizabeth threw Gabrielle an impatient glare and refused to slow her stride. "Who?"

Gabrielle widened her already immense green eyes in exaggerated wonder. "Who! Gracious, Elizabeth, are you blind?"

Elizabeth ignored her shocked expression. Gabrielle tended to be overly dramatic.

But Gabrielle wasn't about to be thwarted. "You know exactly who! Weston Munroe, that's who!"

"So," Elizabeth said dully, then turned an unusually sweet smile toward the pew that held Mrs. Caufield and her ladies, their eyes and ears strategically aimed at the two girls as they passed by.

The old crows, Elizabeth thought and inwardly seethed. They were probably gossiping about Weston. It angered her no small amount to think of what they were saying. She might be allowed to call him anything she wanted, but as for anyone else having that same right . . .

"So let's go talk to him!" Gabrielle's shorter legs pumped to keep pace beside Elizabeth.

"No." The words were a deliberate hiss.

"No!" Gabrielle practically screeched in horror.

Elizabeth thought the girl about to swoon.

"Oh, surely you can't be serious!"

"Quite," Elizabeth said calmly between clenched teeth. "I'm going to say hello to a few friends and then I'm going home. It's my turn to fix dinner this afternoon, and I have nothing whatsoever to say to Weston Munroe.

But you go ahead." She shrugged carelessly. "No one's stopping you."

"Ohhhh, Elizabeth, pleeeeze, please come with me. You know him ever so much better than I do. After all, he is Aaron's brother, and you and he were practically inseparable as children. You know, he was good-looking before, but he's absolutely wonderful-looking now, and tall, gosh, he's so tall, and did you see those eyes? Gracious, but I don't remember them being that blue, do you, Elizabeth? Do you remember them being that blue?"

Elizabeth's legs churned even faster, perversely pleased that Gabrielle, with her blond curls bobbing wildly upon her shoulders, was growing winded.

But breathless as she was, Gabrielle continued to hound Elizabeth, following her out into the churchyard, talking so fast that Elizabeth thought she might trip on her tongue instead of her feet.

And although Elizabeth was terribly fond of Gabrielle, at that moment she wished her friend would indeed trip, and silence her endless chatter.

When at last Elizabeth did stop beneath the shelter of a huge maple, Gabrielle careened into Elizabeth's bustle, almost toppling the two of them. Righting herself, Gabrielle clasped her hands together in ecstasy, turned her elbows outward, stretched her arms upward, and cocked her perfectly pert nose toward the faultless Sunday sky. "Ohhhhh, I think I'm in love, Elizabeth. This time I really, really do!"

Elizabeth moaned and fought the urge to roll her eyes in disgust. Not again. Gabrielle was always in love. She'd been in love with David Latham last week and the week before that it had been ... Mmmm, who had it been? There simply weren't enough men in Toronto to keep Gabrielle in love forever.

And now Weston.

Ugh! Well, she could have him. They deserved each other. Maybe Gabrielle would talk him to death, while he bored her to death with his insufferable sense of humor.

Elizabeth crossed her arms over her chest and tried to force her thoughts into more charitable forms.

More often than not she truly loved Gabrielle St. Clair. They'd been friends since they were old enough to walk. They made an odd pairing: Elizabeth was taller, thinner, athletic by nature, her auburn hair and hazel eyes her most striking features; whereas Gabrielle was not likely to strain herself by any physical activity. Small and curvy, she didn't need to. With her ample breasts, honey-blond hair, and immense green eyes, there was many a smitten swain who would gladly do her bidding for her.

But Elizabeth had never really minded Gabrielle's breathless feminine antics. For beneath all the senseless flutter, Elizabeth knew there resided a heart of gold. For wasn't it Gabrielle who'd comforted her when they'd learned of her mother's accident, when they'd learned Catherine McRaney would never return home to her husband and two little girls?

But if Elizabeth were to be totally honest with herself, she would have had to admit there were also times when she resented Gabrielle.

She resented the fact that she was fortunate enough to have a mother to cook her meals, wash her clothes, clean her house, and, most of all, to talk to. She resented the fact that the most Gabrielle ever had to worry about was what color dress to wear to the next Sunday service; or who was to accompany her to the next picnic at Hanlan's

Point; or whether her golden hair had grown darker this past year, now that she was no longer in her teens; or who she was madly in love with this week and whether he loved her, too.

Elizabeth resented the fact that Gabrielle didn't have to look into her father's eyes and see the loneliness hidden there or feel the pain he disguised so well.

But Elizabeth saw it and felt it and knew its source. And sometimes, in the wee, lonely hours of the night, the knowledge was a terrible burden to bear. One she would have gladly shared with her sister. One she would have gladly shared with anyone.

If only she could.

Reverend Tristan McRaney smiled and clasped each outstretched hand warmly. "Good to see you, Jim. How's the missus?"

With a smile big enough to make his thin face disappear, Jim Reed replied, "She's better, Reverend. Much better. But don't you quit praying now. It's been a long, cold winter, and Bessie's still fightin' that consumption."

Tristan shook his head in denial. "Don't you worry now, Jim. We won't give up. You tell her we're thinking of her, you hear?"

Jim nodded and moved on. Other hands reached out; other bits of conversation followed: questions about the health of other members, both absent and present; comments about the weather; suggestions about next week's church picnic; speculation about the return of Weston Munroe.

Weston Munroe.

Tristan continued to smile as his eyes searched out the young man in question. He found him in the center of the churchyard, amid a circle of his old friends—young, gay faces, anxious for news of the distant lands he'd seen, hungry for details about the experiences he'd had.

Ah, yes, young Weston. The sun glinting off his blond hair contrasted well with the deep tan of his face. He was as handsome and sociable as ever, Tristan noted. It was a particular boon to him that he'd always liked the boy. It was a particular source of sadness to him that he felt it necessary to guide his daughter in the direction of the older Munroe boy, despite her earlier feelings for the younger one.

But Tristan knew Weston was not the man for his Elizabeth. No. She would need a steady, serious-minded husband, one who could balance her spirited heart.

He was sure of this.

From out of the past an image surfaced. A wave of nostalgia swept him, accompanied by the old, old, familiar grief.

His eyes sought out his daughters. He found them among a cluster of girls beneath the outspread branches of the largest maple tree in the churchyard: Abigail, small and round, with soft gray eyes, delicate, pretty features, and neat, dark chestnut hair; Elizabeth, tall and willow-slim, her glorious auburn hair caught up in a reckless knot atop her head, her features a bit too strong to be considered fashionably beautiful.

Yes, Abigail was the daughter every man would wish for. Kind and compassionate, calm and selfless, she'd never tested or tried him.

But Elizabeth, ah . . . well . . . He sighed and locked his hands in front of his frock.

Elizabeth was his heart.

Elizabeth was the very image of her mother, with wide hazel eyes that were expressive and intelligent, but could also turn to fire and ice whenever she wished, and a tongue that could not be bound. *"But the tongue can no man tame." James 3:8.* The reverend smiled. The Almighty must have been thinking of his Elizabeth when He instructed James to pen that verse, for even as a young child, she'd had a vocabulary that could burn the ears off a seasoned sailor.

But there in the benevolence of the gentle June sun, Tristan McRaney was sure no man alive had ever been blessed with more beautiful offspring, and he silently thanked God for his wife—his beautiful Catherine— even though she'd only been his for such a very short time.

Oh, yes, there had been pain. There still was. There always would be.

But my . . . oh my, he thought, remembering. He wouldn't have missed the dance with her for anything in the world . . .

She laid her palm gently against the small boy's hot, dry cheek, and furrowed her brow with worry. "Maybe I shouldn't go tonight, Mrs. O'Rourke. I want to be here if he should wake."

A large woman, with cheeks the hue of autumn apples and hair as white as fresh Christmas snow, shook her head vehemently. "Now, Mary Grace," she argued, her Irish brogue thick and pronounced, "you needn't do that, darlin'. There's nothin' more you can do for him. You go along now and take your walk. I'll stay with the boy."

Mary Grace stared down at the wasted body of the sick child and knew a deep sadness. In the months that he'd been a resident at the Hospital for Sick Children, she'd watched him grow weaker and weaker with each passing day, the illness he bore steadily eating away at his tiny frame.

He was dying.

And she knew the hapless grief of one who would gladly take his suffering upon herself if only she were able.

Her throat tightened into a burning knot, and her eyes stung. She pressed her lids together tightly, but despite her most stalwart efforts, a small sob escaped from her throat.

The older woman rose from the chair. Her arthritic joints aching, she ambled across the room. Reaching the younger woman's side, she embraced her, patting her back with soothing tenderness. "Ah, now, Mary Grace. Don't you cry, child. Don't cry. We've done all we can, and we've got to trust the good Lord to do his part now." Mrs. O'Rourke pulled a snowy white handkerchief from her apron pocket and pressed it into Mary Grace's hand. "If He wants the child with him, there's nothin' more we can do but be glad for the peace He'll give him. At least the boy won't be sufferin' any longer."

"I know . . . I know . . . But it's so hard." Mary Grace swallowed thickly. "He's so little . . . so little. Not much older than Jacob was . . ." Her voice broke, and she rose, turning into the ample arms of Mrs. O'Rourke.

"Ah, Mary . . . it's all right, child. It's all right."

When her tears had ceased, Mary Grace kissed the older woman's cheek. She turned and bent over the child's bed, pressing her lips to the little boy's pale forehead. Then she left the room to return to her own— a small, spare cubicle she was allowed as a hospital employee.

The room contained a narrow bed, a china wash-stand and basin, a serviceable bureau, and one luxury:

a floor-length mirror hung in a lovely oak frame. She had purchased it herself—in memory of another time, another life, the woman she'd been. She washed her face and tidied her heavy hair, securing it into a simple knot at the base of her slender neck. Then she surveyed her appearance in the mirror, meticulously smoothing imaginary wrinkles from her best black silk dress.

She flicked a piece of lint from her sleeve and drew in a deep breath, repeating the endless Sunday evening rituals she had followed for so many long years.

She wanted to look presentable even though the ones for whom she would look presentable would never see her. One more glance, one more pat, one more brush, and she turned, took the hat with the black silk veil from the post above her bed and put it on, covering her hair, obscuring her face.

Then without a backward glance, she retrieved her reticule from the bureau and left the silent room, the closing of the door a resounding, empty echo, ringing out into the quiet of yet another solitary Sunday night.

A familiar lone wraith in black, she walked the cedar-paved streets of Toronto. And as the purple wings of twilight fell, with the gaslights flickering, she made her way down Elizabeth Street, her heels clicking softly, her pace never faltering.

After all, she knew her route well.

She traveled it every Sunday night, of every week, of every month, except for the few short summer months the children's home was moved from their cramped quarters on Elizabeth Street to the Lakeside Home on the west end of the island, not far from the Gibraltar Point Lighthouse.

She thought it most kind of the city officials to magnanimously donate the land as the summer accommodation for the Hospital for Sick Children. The little ones, so long prisoners of their rooms and beds, enjoyed lying on the broad veranda and watching the boats go by.

So tonight would be her last outing for the space of those summer months.

Reaching Queen Street, she bore right, followed a left onto Simcoe and finally a right onto Richmond, her destination a familiar Methodist church.

Once there, beneath the protection of the trees that hid her and the veil covering her once glorious auburn hair, she waited . . .

CHAPTER

3

Elizabeth was especially proud of her home.

Although not overly large, it was a lovely white-washed Victorian structure, complete with dormers, a gracious front porch, and spooled railings. It sat at the end of Queen Street, east of Ashbride's Bay, on a flat piece of land surrounded by a variety of shade trees, a little ways removed from the red brick homes of her neighbors.

The inside of the house was bright and cheery, the furniture tasteful and attractive, the draperies and wallpaper light and airy—a remaining legacy of the woman who had taken such delight in decorating the home her husband had had built for her. But the piece that had brought the family the most enjoyment was the piano. Papa said his wife had been particularly proud of it, even though it was a somewhat cumbersome object. She'd used it to display her vast array of cherished framed photographs. Now her daughters enjoyed it, finding as they did that it added another dimension to an evening spent with members of their crowd. For although the reverend was a strict parent, he did not wish his daughters to be lonely. As long as the young men and women who gathered in his home were willing to conduct themselves within the realms of social decency, he was quite willing to have them.

Elizabeth strongly suspected that the sounds of piano music, mixing with that of youthful laughter, somehow eased his own loneliness a bit.

As for the location of their home, she knew her father could have requested a house closer to his parish. But he was a quiet man and wished his home removed as far as possible from the hubbub of the city's activities, to a more placid, less hurried place. He said his young wife had agreed wholeheartedly, wanting space for her flower and vegetable gardens, room for her children to play, and plenty of fresh air, which swept freely into the windows, coaxed by the breezes coming in off the nearby lake.

Elizabeth let the door slam shut behind her, clumped down the wide porch steps, and crossed the dew-stained grass. She loaded the last of the picnic baskets into the buggy and paused despondently.

The horse whinnied and shied, lifted his glossy head into the air, snorted his impatience, then thumped his hoof on the ground twice, signaling his desire for her attention.

"I know, Henry," she said quietly, walking to his side. "I wish I didn't have to go, either." She reached out and stroked his flank affectionately, then tipped her face upward to drink in the warmth of the sun's rays, hoping the brightness would somehow seep into her heart and dissipate the uneasiness she felt about the day ahead.

The sky was clear and a sharp blue, the air fresh and sweet, perfect for a picnic by the water. They were off to Hanlan's Point on Toronto Island, the community's favorite picnic site. Not only did it offer its visitors a welcome respite from the summer's heat and humidity, but it was easily reached by boat from the mainland.

And, of course, it was a wonderful location for a sculling match to be held.

Elizabeth knew without being told that Weston would be a participant in the match today.

She wished she could have begged off the day's festivities, but Papa had insisted that they all needed the outing. They'd been spending entirely too much time at home, he'd said in a voice that would tolerate no argument.

Elizabeth sighed softly and laid her cheek against the horse's warm side. She recalled the night she learned of Weston's return. How easy it was to remember the texture and warmth of his bare chest beneath her cheek. A familiar heat began to build within. Her eyes drifted shut.

A week had passed since then. A week of avoiding Aaron. A week of trying to quell old memories, temptations, and longings. A week of dream-riddled sleep, that offered no peace or hope of rest. A week of total and complete confusion.

From out of the past came the memory of another summer day, bringing with it the image of a younger Weston. Once again she felt his warm exploratory hands upon her bare skin, touching her where no other had ever dared, in ways no other had touched her since.

The sound of her own voice, young and scared and trusting, drifted through her mind. "Do you think we'll die from doing this, Wes?" she'd asked in her innocence. Her blouse and undergarment were pushed off her shoulders and lay scrunched around her waist. She clasped him tight to her naked chest, pressing her cheek against the hard ridge of his shoulder. "Mrs. Caufield says people who do things like this before they're married could die."

"Aw, Beth, Mrs. Caufield is an old crow. We won't die," he'd answered, kissing her over and over again, his mouth hot and wet and wild, his oar-roughened hands gentle upon her budding breasts. And then he'd broken away and grinned down at her wickedly. "But, hell, Lizzy, it might be worth it if we did." She'd giggled then, her worries eased, while he resumed his study of her anatomy and took her lower lip gently between his teeth.

"Wes . . ."

"Mm-hm?" His tongue traced the outer shape of her lips. "Like this," he said softly, his eyes dancing with merriment, while he gently urged her to follow his lead.

She blushed, but ever his eager pupil, she complied, losing herself in him and his silken touch. In time, she pulled back slightly and tried again. "Wes . . ."

"Mm-hm?"

"Is this . . . what we're doing . . . right now . . . ," she questioned hesitantly, gazing up into his beloved blue eyes. "Is this what makes babies?"

He grew immediately still, then lifted himself off her and rested his weight upon his elbows. With a knuckle he traced the curve of her cheek and kissed the tip of her nose lightly. "No, Lizzy . . ." His expression grew serious, his eyes gentle. "There's more. Much more."

"Are you sure?"

"Yes."

"But how do you know for sure?"

His face had reddened slightly, and he'd shrugged. He'd bent his head then, kissed the hollow of her throat, and simply said, "I just know, that's all."

A noise from behind signaled Abigail's approach. Elizabeth's eyelids snapped open. She lifted her head and abruptly abandoned the useless memory to the past where it belonged.

"Do we have everything?" Abigail asked, her eyes widening in surprise as they traveled over her sister's dress.

Turning, Elizabeth nodded, forced a tight smile, then gave Henry one last pat before moving around the buggy and agilely hoisting herself up into the rear seat. "Yes, everything except Papa."

"He's coming," Abigail said. Holding her parasol in one hand, she caught her skirts and climbed into the seat beside Elizabeth. "He said he'd only be another minute." She arranged her pretty blue-silk skirts neatly beneath her, positioned her bustle more comfortably, then snapped her matching parasol open to shield her fair skin from the sun.

Turning her attention to their gentle surroundings, Elizabeth lapsed into a pensive silence. She focused her eyes on the poplar-lined street while she tried to force her mind to concentrate on something other than the day's festivities.

Her sister provided the means by asking, "How's Benjamin? You haven't mentioned him in quite some time."

"Oh, he's fine," Elizabeth answered, glad for the diversion. "At least he was last time I saw him, which was a couple of weeks ago. I'll need to take the ferry out to see him soon." Then she smiled and whispered conspiratorially, "I did hear Eli's still jumping the evening ferry to come over and raid Mrs. Spencer's chicken coops."

"Oh, no." Abigail covered her mouth and giggled.

Elizabeth nodded. "I don't know what Benjamin's going to do with that dog. He denies Eli would ever do such a dastardly thing."

The two women laughed, knowing very well Eli was the worst chicken thief in all of Canada. Imagining Benjamin's affected indignation, they laughed all the harder.

After a few moments, their chuckles faded into silence once again.

But Elizabeth's thoughts remained with Benjamin Duncan. She loved the old man dearly. Other than Abigail and Gabrielle St. Clair, he was just about the closest friend she'd ever had. She could tell him most anything. Truth be told, there were things she'd shared with him that she'd never even shared with her sister or Gabrielle.

For besides being her friend, he was her teacher as well. Though she had attended school, as had the other children of the community, she had learned important things from Benjamin that had remained with her. He was the chief of storytellers, a champion spinner of tales. With his quick wit and deep, hearty voice, he could weave almost any knowledge into the kind of story a child would remember forever.

Though an intrinsic member of the community, he lived apart from the crowds by preference, comfortably secluded in his cozy lighthouse with only the call of the seabirds, his countless books, and the steady, faithful companionship of his dog, Eli. But he held a particular sense of pride in the fact that he had witnessed so many changes in this wonderful country. How many times had he recited its history and origin to her? Far, far, too many for her to count.

"It's a grand country, Lizzy," he would say. "You can be proud to be a Canadian. Though we're under British rule, we're a country unto ourselves." And then he would go on to tell her so many other things: that Canada was an infant country—a melting pot for many Europeans seeking new lives in an exciting new land where the opportunities were limitless.

And Elizabeth knew he was right.

Until 1834, Toronto had been known as Yorkville. Then a town of seventy-five hundred, it had proclaimed itself the City of Toronto. The area bordered by Bloor, Bay, Scollard, and Yonge, however, stubbornly persisted in clinging to the old name even while the newly named city grew like a well-watered garden of weeds. In no time at all, it managed to acquire a vast melee of merchants, bankers, and politicians with such buildings as the Metropolitan Methodist Church, the General Post Office, the Government House, and the Union Station, among many other churches, public buildings, houses, factories, and warehouses. Now, barely one hundred years old, it held much of the distinction and old-world culture of its English and French forebears, so evident in the Victorian architecture of its buildings and its clean, neat, cedar-planked streets. But whereas Montreal and Quebec were predominantly French, Toronto was a marvelous medley of cultures.

"Beth." Abigail's voice broke into Elizabeth's thoughts, interrupting the silence. "I hate to ask, but I must. Where in heaven's name did you get that dress?"

Elizabeth's eyebrows rose as she smoothed down the flat, plain collar of her dress.

The garment was ghastly—a dark, drab shade of gray, with no bustle, no shape, and no redeeming qualities whatsoever.

She wore it this day with impish pride.

Keeping her voice low, she leaned toward her sister. "Exactly what is wrong with this dress?"

"Oh, for goodness' sake, Elizabeth," Abigail said gently, her gray eyes mirroring her mortification. "It's about

the homeliest thing I've ever seen. I noticed it the minute
I walked out of the house. I can't imagine why you'd
wear such a thing today of all days."

"Today is the perfect day," Elizabeth remarked curt-
ly.

"But where on earth did you get it?"

Elizabeth turned away, fighting the smile that tugged
at the corners of her mouth. Yes, she thought, beginning
to enjoy herself immensely, this was the perfect dress
to wear today. "I found it upstairs in the trunk. It was
Grandmother Emily's."

Abigail wrinkled her brow in puzzlement. "But why
are you wearing it? It hardly fits you. It's much, much
too large. And it's completely out of style. Grandmother
must have worn it fifty years ago."

Elizabeth shrugged and fixed her sister with a stubborn glare. "Because I want to, that's why."

"Papa won't like it."

"It's comfortable," Elizabeth lied.

"He still won't like it."

"Papa doesn't dress me anymore."

"Oh, Elizabeth, it's truly horrible."

"It's fine!"

Abigail sighed, giving up the fight. "Beth, sometimes
you make me tired."

"Oh, hell's bells, Abigail!" Elizabeth snapped impatiently, her hazel eyes flashing sparks of gold. "If I want
to wear an ugly dress, who's to say I can't? Papa?
Mrs. Caufield? Aaron? Weston? I really don't give a
damn what anyone says!" She crossed her arms over
her chest, set her jaw firmly, and glared straight ahead
at the horse's rump.

Abigail's expression softened. Understanding dawned.
Ah, Weston . . . So that's what this is all about. Out loud

she said, "I suppose everyone will be there today." She watched her sister's guarded expression carefully.

"I suppose." Elizabeth feigned casual disinterest. Pick, pick, pick, the forefinger worked the cuticle.

"Have you seen him since that first night?" Abigail dropped all sense of pretense and got right to the heart of the matter.

Elizabeth shook her head, her facade of unconcern crumbling. She closed her eyes, folded her hands in her lap, and laced her fingers tightly. "No." Her voice was a small whisper.

"Do you think he'll race today?"

Elizabeth nodded. "Most likely."

"I bet if he'd been here five years ago, he could have taken Ned Hanlan," Abigail remarked in an offhanded manner, while studying her nails with intense interest. She cocked her head slightly. "There isn't a better sculler in all the world than Weston. I don't care if Ned did take the championship."

"Hmph!" Elizabeth muttered, turning away, knowing full well that what her sister had said was true. "You'd best not tell Weston that. He's full of himself as it is."

"Oh, Beth," Abigail said, laying a hand on her sister's arm. "Maybe if you could find it in yourself to forgive him, you could deal with the rest of this situation so much better. After all, if you're going to marry Aaron . . ." She hesitated a moment. "Well . . . it would help if you and Wes could be friends once again."

Friends, thought Elizabeth sadly, her heart giving a queer little jerk. *Oh, Abigail. We were so much more than friends. Surely you know that.*

Just then, Reverend McRaney came out of the house. He was dressed in his usual attire: black bowler, black frock coat, black trousers. He smiled as he approached

the buggy. But as he reached it, his gaze came to rest
upon his eldest daughter. The smile on his face died.
Without a word, he set his jaw squarely. In thick silence,
he lifted himself into the seat in front of the two women,
clicked his tongue, gave the reins a sharp snap, and set
the buggy in motion.

"You racing today?" David Latham asked Weston.
They stood side by side, two old friends gazing out
at the sparkling azure water, each comfortable in the
other's company, while gentle waves lapped the shore
just beyond their feet.

"I'm thinking I will." Weston responded noncommittally. "I brought my skiff."

"Do you think you can take the race?"

"Maybe." Weston shrugged. "Who knows? It's been
a long time. Maybe too long."

"Hanlan's good."

"Yes, I know. But so was I." Both men knew that he
had stated the truth, with no reason to boast. Benjamin
had been his teacher, and Weston had developed his skill
as a sculler when he was a very young man. The size
and strength of his arms had helped gain him a favorable
reputation.

Weston turned to his friend and said, "I want to do
it, David!" His voice was impassioned, his eyes bright
with excitement.

Confused, David furrowed his brow. "You mean win
today?"

"No." Weston gestured impatiently. "Yes. But that's
not what I mean. I want to build steamers! I want to
build steamers like the *Algoma*!"

David Latham stared at his friend as though Weston
had lost his mind. He snorted derisively and shook his

head. "Your father will never go for it. Neither will Aaron for that matter. They're not interested in building steamers. They're exporters, not shipbuilders." He straightened his suit coat and pocketed his hands in his proper, conservative trousers. He wished he had worn something more comfortable, as Weston had. The late morning sun glared down mercilessly, promising a very warm day. He stared enviously at the casual rolled-up shirtsleeves and open neckline of his friend's white shirt. No formality there. Just trousers, black suspenders, shirt, and boots, and an "I don't give a damn" attitude.

Weston tugged at the thighs of his trousers, then bent down to pick up a flat rock near his foot. He straightened, dipped at the knees, brought his arm back, then around again, and with a quick snap of his wrist, sent the rock flying, skipping across the placid blue surface of the water. Skip—one, two, three, four, five. Up and down the rock danced upon the sun-kissed water until it finally disappeared with a solid plunk.

"Beat that one," Weston challenged. He hooked his hands on his hips, arched a brow, and angled a sly glance at the smaller man. It was the same look he'd used many a time in the past to accompany the childish words, "Dare you, David. I dare you." Neither the look nor the words had ever failed him in the past. "We could do this together, you and I." His voice was quiet, but they both knew the gauntlet had been thrown.

"Aw, Wes, I don't know . . ." David shook his head again and stared down at the glossy toes of his polished shoes. He bent, picked up a rock, then imitated Weston's previous movements, flinging the rock out onto the surface of the water. Skip—one, two, three. Gone. He pocketed his hands once again and stared dispassionately at the radiating ripples. After a lengthy silence, he said, "It would take a lot of capital . . ."

"We can get the money."

"And time . . ."

"I have the time."

"What the hell do you know about building steamers?"

"Men have been building steamers on the lakes since the *Vadalia* in 1841, David. I'll hire men to design them. In Scotland they're building them, cutting them in two, then sending them here to be reassembled. Why should they build them for us when we can do it ourselves?" Weston countered David's arguments quickly, skillfully. He was a master at the game, and they both knew it. When they were children, Weston had been able to goad David into doing things his own cautious nature never would have allowed him to attempt. David remembered only too well the warm spring day Weston had dared him to jump off the church roof—just to see if he would. David had spent the entire summer mending a broken leg from that venture.

"But schooners are more practical for your father's business. And my father's lumber—"

"My father's business is doing well, but it's stagnant. It's not growing. In a few years, schooners will be obsolete, you'll see." Weston turned an enthusiastic grin on his friend. He punched the air with his fist, spun, and began to pace. "I want to carry passengers, too. Aaron can still have his ships to transport his cargo and your father's lumber, but why not branch out and do more?"

For the next twenty minutes Weston talked and talked and talked. He opened another button on his shirt, ran his hands through his wavy golden hair, and with the skill of an artist, painted an oral picture of the future dynasty they could build.

David looked uncertain, but inside he felt exhilarated. "I don't know," he said slowly, pushing a hand through his short dark hair. But despite his hesitant words, his voice lacked conviction. In a few more minutes Weston would have him hooked. A few more minutes, and he'd be jumping off the roof again.

And, dammit all, Weston knew David would give in.

"I have other backers, too. Men who believe in what I want to do." Weston's eyes danced wickedly. "C'mon, David. Take a chance. I dare ye."

Though David tried to keep a rein on his excitement, his heart leapt at the challenge. Damn Weston Munroe, anyway! He could get more than a broken leg out of this adventure.

"Do we have everything?" Reverend McRaney asked, his eyes still stormy as he took in the rear view of his eldest daughter's plain apparel. Whatever had possessed her to wear that dress, he couldn't guess, but he'd wisely abandoned the idea of an argument with her, knowing that that would be useless. If he had told her he liked her in her yellow taffeta, she'd have worn the green silk. If he had told her he didn't approve of the dress she was wearing, she'd be sure to wear that one in particular to next Sunday's service.

Elizabeth was Elizabeth, and arguing with her was not the solution to any problem.

Along with several other disembarking passengers, the three McRaneys gathered their belongings and made their way down the ramp onto the perfect stretch of beach.

"Hello, Mrs. Warner. It's good to see you," Abigail said politely, passing a small, rotund woman who carried a child on each hip.

"You, too, dear," Mrs. Warner replied with a tired smile, "and Elizabeth, too."

But Elizabeth didn't hear her. Deep in thought, her gaze fixed ahead, she walked several steps in front of her father and Abigail, her stride as long and leggy as ever.

The beaches on Hanlan's Point were indeed beautiful, but no more beautiful than the majestic hotel that graced the island. It stood before her in the distance, a grand, impressive structure, and as always, the sight of it intrigued Elizabeth. With three floors and extensive balconies, Hotel Hanlan beckoned visitors from miles away with its distinct air of grandeur, along with the gracious hospitality it offered.

Its tall, pointed pavilion roofs rose high above the main front of the building, yet it derived much of its character from the timbers that covered its frame, sheathing it in wide boards, with the joints covered by narrow protective strips laid in a grid pattern. The unusual skeletal structure of the building added a graceful lightness to its appearance, creating a particular charm and appeal.

"I spoke to Aaron after the service Thursday evening," Reverend McRaney said to his daughters. "He said he'd meet us here around noon."

Elizabeth remained resentfully silent. *Aaron, Aaron, Aaron,* her mind chanted. Even though she knew it was unfair and felt terribly guilty about it, she didn't want to see Aaron. Her mood plummeted further.

They were not the first of the congregation to arrive. Up ahead, not far from the hotel, on the smooth lawn, under the shady limbs of several large maples, stood a large group of people gathered around the many tables, already laden with food. Breads, meats, fruits, along with an elaborate assortment of tempting desserts, filled the air with a variety of enticing aromas.

Elizabeth's stomach rumbled. Well, she thought, at least that was normal. She was hungry. Her unladylike appetite was at times a particular source of embarrassment to her father and sister.

There was a festive air to the mingling crowd. But that was customary when a sculling match was held.

The excitement added a carnival-like quality to the day.

Ladies strolled around the sculpted grounds, dressed in their pretty Sunday best, their hats trimmed in flowers, their frilly pastel parasols open wide to protect their creamy complexions from the sun. With many of them were their favorite admirers, also dressed in the most respectable finery, their heads covered with straw hats or bowlers.

Elizabeth hadn't brought her parasol.

She'd long ago given up the quest for flawless skin, accepting the inevitable spray of freckles that had splashed across her nose for as long as she could remember.

As she walked among her neighbors, friends, and the other members of her father's congregation, she caught more than her share of speculative glances.

"Reverend McRaney's eldest," she could almost hear them say. "You know, the ill-mannered, undisciplined one."

But she held her head high, her spine as ramrod straight as any queen's, her back so perfectly aligned she looked as though she might snap in two if she tried to bend over.

Still, more than a few raised eyebrows and hushed voices followed her trail. Briefly she wondered what provoked their whispers. Was it her choice of dress, or was it the fact that by now everyone knew Weston Munroe had returned and would be present today?

Then she decided that the reason for the gossip really didn't matter. She'd never cared before. Why should she care now?

Because you're going to marry Aaron, that's why, her conscience answered for her. *And he deserves better than to have his neighbors and friends gossip about his intended.*

Yes, she agreed, a pang of guilt jarring her out of her stubbornness. *He certainly does.*

Almost choking with the effort it cost her, she turned to a small group of women and smiled.

"Elizabeth!" Gabrielle St. Clair captured her attention by calling out to her above the din of voices. "Over here, Elizabeth! Wait!"

Elizabeth turned, spotted her friend, and waved a greeting.

Without a word of apology to the young man who stood at her side, Gabrielle sailed off toward her friend.

He had to be one of Gabrielle's newer conquests, Elizabeth concluded, for she didn't recognize him. She felt a twinge of pity for him, for it was obvious he was trying valiantly to hide his disappointment at his sudden abandonment.

But he needn't have wasted the effort.

Gabrielle had forgotten him the moment she'd left his side.

CHAPTER
4

Gabrielle hurried across the lawn, her ruffled parasol held high before her like some sovereign's scepter, her bustle jiggling slightly with her short, brisk steps. Reaching Elizabeth, she tugged on her friend's sleeve twice. "Wherever have you been all week?" Her voice was shrill with excitement, her cheeks rosy and bright. But as she took in Elizabeth's dress, the smile on her face faded as quickly as a candle in the breeze and was replaced by a genuine look of horror. She pressed the palm of her free hand to her breasts and whispered, "Gracious, Elizabeth, you look like you should be going to a wake, not a picnic! People will think you quite mad!"

Elizabeth shrugged, her expression one of secret amusement. Refusing to comment, she stopped beneath the protective arms of a large tree and set her basket down on the table before her. She withdrew one of the blueberry pies Abigail had baked and placed it on the table's surface.

"I'm happy to see you, too," Elizabeth replied easily, not at all offended by Gabrielle's words. She was used to Gaby's thoughtless statements and knew they were not aimed with any particular malice.

"Oh, I hope there are some interesting people here today," Gabrielle said, then set her mouth into a petulant line, the subject of Elizabeth's dress already forgotten. She hooked a hand on her hip and rolled her big green eyes in exaggerated disgust. "I'm so bored, I could just die. I declare, Elizabeth, I almost wish winter was on its way so we could at least look forward to skating or sledding or planning our Christmas dresses."

"You could always go swimming. I should think it's quite warm enough," Elizabeth suggested, then laughed as her friend's expression grew even more doleful.

"You know I can't swim. Besides, I never really liked the water. It absolutely destroys my hair and dries out my skin."

"What about the man you were talking to a minute ago? I don't believe I've seen him around before. He could offer you a summer diversion."

"Oh, him." Gabrielle waved her hand in the air and sighed. "His name is Franklin Fuller. He recently moved here with his parents from Montreal. He's nice enough, but he's not terribly interesting. His father is in banking, too. Papa does business with him and invited his family to dinner last week. I'll introduce you if you like," she offered casually.

Elizabeth smiled, then shrugged noncommittally. "Well . . . today's match should be fun," she said, still busying herself with emptying the contents of her basket.

Gabrielle gave her a sulky glance from under her long, luscious lashes. "Talking with Weston Munroe would be even more fun." Then, with a note of reproof in her voice, she said, "I still can't believe you wouldn't come with me to speak with him last Sunday. We should have welcomed him home. I'm surprised at you, Elizabeth. After all, it was the proper thing to do."

Elizabeth halted her movements and met Gabrielle's eyes with a bold stare. "When have I ever done the proper thing?"

"True," Gabrielle said, relenting slightly. "But your behavior has mellowed since you've been seeing Aaron."

"You could've welcomed Weston home without me," Elizabeth countered. "Since when did you need my help to speak to a man?"

"This is different, and you know it. Weston always liked you better. You were the one who could climb trees and swim and skate and do all those boy things so much better than I ever could. He never even noticed me back then. But," she said and smoothed the back of her upswept hair, adding with a silky smile, "we aren't children any longer, and I doubt he cares very much about those things now." Then abruptly she changed the subject, launching off in a totally different direction so quickly it made Elizabeth's head spin. "Do you think I look all right in this dress, Elizabeth? Mama says I do, but I don't know . . . I feel sort of plump-looking in it." She laid a hand against the small curve of her stomach. "I'm not as tall as you, you know, and I don't want to look . . . well . . . fat." She whispered the word as though it were the most repulsive obscenity and leaned closer. "Did you see Enid Evans lately? Gracious, but she's gotten round this past year, don't you think? I doubt she'll ever find a husband looking like that."

For the first time Elizabeth felt a prick of genuine jealousy. With new eyes, she saw her friend as most men saw her. She was indeed lovely. In her pink silk dress, with her small, corseted waist, her full, high breasts, and her smooth pale skin, any man in his right mind would have been attracted to her. Soft, voluptuous, womanly—those words came to mind.

Beside her, Elizabeth suddenly felt terribly under-developed, very dull, plain, and extremely young and foolish for ever wearing such an unattractive dress when she had many finer ones at home to choose from.

She dropped her gaze and stared at the ground. She had never wasted time on trying to make herself beautiful; she'd never seen the point. Weston had often said he thought her fine exactly as she was.

But that was a long time ago.

"Ohhhh," Gabrielle said, practically lifting off the ground with excitement, "there's Aaron, Elizabeth!"

Elizabeth spun in the direction Gabrielle pointed.

Aaron walked toward her, the smile on his face eager and warm. He looked as handsome as ever, his short, sandy hair neatly combed, his mustache trimmed to per-fection, his suit neatly pressed, his shoes shiny. She felt an immediate pinch of guilt, knowing that it should be him she thought of, not his brother. He was stable and steady, kind and patient—all the qualities she admired most in a man.

Not at all like Weston.

"Elizabeth, hello," he said, reaching her. He held out his smooth, clean hands.

She complied, lifting her own and offering him a smile laced with genuine affection. He gave her fingers a proper, gentle squeeze then released them.

Though he couldn't have missed her dress, his eyes respectfully focused on her face. "I've missed you," he said. "I would have come by the house to take you out for a ride, but you didn't answer the note I sent home with your father."

His words were not harsh, but somehow Elizabeth sensed the soft accusation that lay concealed within them.

"I'm sorry, Aaron. Really I am. I've been a little busy. The garden . . . the children at church . . ." She left off mid-sentence, feeling the shallow inadequacy of her statements.

Gabrielle unknowingly alleviated her tension by barging into their conversation. "Hello, Aaron." She tipped her head in his direction and moved closer to the couple. "How is your family?"

A strategically placed question, Elizabeth knew.

Aaron turned to Gabrielle. "They're all fine," he said. "Thank you for asking."

"And Weston?" she crooned, her eyes wide with interest. "It must be wo-o-o-nderful to have him home."

Aaron nodded and smiled. "Indeed, it is. We've missed him very much." Aaron's gaze shifted and focused above Elizabeth's shoulder.

She sensed him before she saw him.

A tense anticipation sluiced through her, like the one a flock of birds must feel the moment before they burst out of a field when danger approached.

"Of course they missed me." His voice came from behind her.

She turned to watch his approach, and panic gripped her.

Her heart banged against her chest. A pulse thumped in her head. Her palms grew damp. She cursed herself a thousand times for her reckless stupidity in wanting to goad him by wearing an unattractive dress in the color she knew he hated most.

Her eyes found his. An ache rose within as he closed the few steps between them with the easy saunter she remembered so well.

Her breath caught in her windpipe.

Oh, he was undeniably handsome, a tall golden god.

His clothes were masculine and casual, his hair lighter and slightly longer than his brother's. It fell carelessly forward over one side of his forehead, while in the back it lay on the collar of his white shirt. She knew that hair, the way it felt, the way it curled around her fingers, the way it smelled . . .

His laughing blue eyes rode her up and down, then up and down once again. His eyebrows rose in question; his grin widened, deepening his dimples.

Her fascination abruptly ended, and she longed to kick him.

I see ye dressed for me, Lizzy, his eyes teased.

Damn you, Weston, hers answered.

Then, dismissing her without a word, he turned the full effect of his charming smile on Gabrielle. "How 'bout you, Gaby, did ye miss me?"

Gabrielle blushed and allowed her eyelids to lower enticingly, while Elizabeth thought the poor girl just might start salivating at any moment.

"As a matter of fact," Gabrielle answered, "I was just telling Elizabeth that things haven't been the same without you, Weston. There's no one to give Ned a decent race anymore."

"So I've heard," Weston said, his eyes crinkling at the corners. Without concern for Elizabeth's and Aaron's presence, his gaze stroked Gabrielle's form from top to bottom with slow deliberation. He extended his hand and held her dainty one in his considerably longer than was necessary, while his eyes expressed genuine appreciation for her many finer attributes.

Elizabeth seethed.

Gabrielle preened.

Aaron cleared his throat.

Gabrielle parted her perfect lips provocatively, then hesitated a moment to allow Weston to witness the full effect of her beauty, before breaking the short silence by saying, "You really should stop over sometime soon, Weston. I know Papa would love to hear about your travels."

Weston inclined his head. Understanding her invitation perfectly, he found himself mildly amused. She was a practiced flirt, interested in working her technique on him. With his own gorgeous gaze, he smiled down into her stunning face and made her some tempting offers of his own. "I just might do that sometime."

It was at that moment that Abigail chose to breeze in and interrupt their intimate study of each other. She took Gabrielle's arm, ignoring her protests, and steered her away, claiming that she was quite sure there was a certain young man over near the hotel asking after her.

Elizabeth wanted to kiss her.

"Aaron!" Sarah Munroe called from across the lawn. "Could you help me a moment?"

Aaron waved acquiescence to his mother. To Elizabeth he said, "Excuse me a minute." He looked at Weston and smiled. "Keep her company for me, will you?"

Weston pocketed his hands and fought a pang of guilt. Despite all, his brother trusted him. It was a sobering thought. "Of course," he promised quietly.

Aaron left them alone. An uncomfortable silence fell. Elizabeth moved to the table, picked up the picnic basket, and pretended to busy herself with withdrawing the rest of its contents.

Weston moved in closer.

She looked up at him. Their eyes met, hers cautious, his amused.

He stepped nearer. "Lovely dress ye're wearing, Lizzy," he whispered perversely. He took another step toward her and peeked around at the back of her dress. "Not only is it my favorite color, but ye must have known I never did like those bustles ye women wear. Can't get any idea of what the real thing looks like back there with all that extra padding hiding everything."

Oh, the conceited bore! She wanted to hit him.

He took in her explosive expression, threw back his head, and roared with laughter.

She pinched her eyes shut, inwardly cringing at the sound, knowing everyone within a mile's distance could hear him.

There would be talk tomorrow to be sure.

"Go away, Weston," she hissed, placing herself on the opposite side of the table from him. "I have nothing to say to you!"

"Whatsamatter, Lizzy? Ye can't run away into the night and hide now, can ye?" he goaded. He flattened his broad palms upon the table and leaned in toward her, the muscles in his arms tense beneath the rolled-up sleeves of his shirt. "I guess that means ye're gonna have to talk to me whether ye like it or not."

"I don't have anything to say to you!"

"Ye missed me, Beth, didn't ye?" He wiggled his eyebrows wickedly.

She snorted her disgust, turned her head away, and refused to answer him. Oh, he was an evil man! She pushed a strand of hair away from her face.

He moved around the table and reached for her hand.

She snatched it away so fast she created a blur.

She grabbed for the blueberry pie, her eyes sparking fury. "You'll wear this pie, Weston Munroe. If you touch me again, I swear you will!"

Her threat launched him into another fit of laughter.

She glanced around to see if they had any spectators. Damnation! They did! Mrs. Caufield's biddies watched with rapt interest behind the safety of their fans and handkerchiefs.

"Tell me ye missed me or I'll kiss ye right here in front of everyone," he said, when finally his chuckles had subsided.

Mortified, her eyes nearly popped from their sockets. "You wouldn't dare," she whispered.

"Oh, Lizzy," he threatened softly, "I think ye know me much better than that."

She did. Aware of the dangerous truth of his statement, she turned to him, plunked her hands upon her hips, and gave him her full attention. "All right, Wes. What do you want?"

The merriment in his eyes faded somewhat, and his expression grew serious. But no words came. He felt a hollow moment of indecision. How could he tell her what it was he wanted when he didn't know himself?

She shook her head sadly. "You left . . ."

"Only for a while . . ."

"For much too long."

"I'm home now."

She threw her hands into the air in frustration. "Don't you see, Wes? We can't just pick up where we left off. I'm different now. I've grown up. I'm not the little girl who used to follow you around." She hesitated a moment, swallowing hard. "I'm not the same young woman who loved you." Her eyes grew solemn, her voice gentle. "I'm going to marry Aaron, Weston."

"Are ye?" he questioned, raising a brow.

"Yes." Her answer was a hoarse whisper.

"Why?"

"Because . . ." She swallowed again. "Because I care for him very much."

"But do ye love him, Beth?"

"Yes," she answered a little too quickly. "Yes, of course I do."

Weston shook his head and shut his eyes a moment, surprised at the sharp wave of pain that shot through him. Somehow he hadn't expected those words to hurt quite that much. But they did. A desperate yearning gripped him. He longed to reach for her, to touch her, to hold her, to put his palm against that small, sweet dip at the base of her spine and stroke it the way he used to.

But he couldn't, and he knew it.

She would not welcome his touch any longer. She'd made that very clear.

She belonged to his brother now, and the realization of that truth was the bitterest knowledge he'd ever had to digest.

He opened his eyes. In silence he gazed at her for several minutes. As always, her wild auburn hair was escaping the confines of its off-centered knot. Sweat dotted the freckles on her nose; her dress was the ugliest piece of material he'd ever seen; and her cheeks were growing pinker by the moment.

And he thought her beautiful.

Women like Gabrielle St. Clair might be tempting, but they were shallow, without substance and intensity. In time, they proved boring. They'd never compare to Elizabeth. Beth was special. She always had been.

"Aaron said ye haven't accepted him yet."

"I'm going to."

"When?"

"Soon." She decided suddenly, knowing she must. "Very soon."

For several moments, neither spoke. Around them the steady hum of voices and activity droned on. Lost in their silent world, the two became overwhelmed with thoughts and feelings that could no longer be expressed.

Not today, not ever again.

The seriousness of the moment became too much for Weston. With a lightness he didn't feel, he shrugged, breaking the painful spell. A grin climbed his cheek, and he winked, the old devilry returning. He reached for her hand in a sudden, swift movement.

But she'd anticipated his intent.

Momentarily forgetting their fascinated audience, she spun away from him, picked up the blueberry pie, and flattened it against the stark whiteness of his shirt.

Astonished gasps reverberated around them.

For a second, his smile went slack, his face registering genuine surprise.

Aghast, Elizabeth raised her hands to her face, her pulse thumping wildly in her ears. In a small, strained voice, she groaned, "Oh, dear Lord, what've I done? What've I done?" while blueberry filling and Abigail's carefully designed piecrust continued to plop to the ground at Weston's feet.

Her expression was one of such horrified wonder, Weston thought she might melt into the ground at any moment. He almost felt sorry for her.

Almost.

Taking his finger, he wiped a large chunk of pie away from his top button and plopped it into his mouth. He chewed with exaggerated enjoyment. "Ummmm-mmmm" he said, shaking his head from side to side, "blueberry always was my favorite."

In genuine distress, she swayed from side to side and moaned again, while he thought, *Aw, Lizzy, ye're wrong,*

*darlin'. Ye haven't changed a bit. Ye're the same little
hoyden ye've always been.*

Happier than he'd been in days, he threw back his
head and howled with laughter.

"Please, Aaron . . . not now." Elizabeth turned her
head slightly so that his lips and mustache grazed her
cheek instead of her mouth.

"Then when, Elizabeth? When?"

They sat upon a grassy slope, far away from the tables
of food and the thinning crowd. From their elevated
position, they had a clear view of the lake below and
would be able to see the race quite well. The murmurs
she and Weston had generated had quieted for the time
being, temporarily forgotten in the anticipation of the
race to come. The water below them was calm, but
like a clear blue sky dotted with an abundance of white
clouds, the water's consistent color was interrupted by
the enchanting picture of ladies and gentlemen taking to
a variety of boats to get a better view of the race.

"Soon," she answered softly, turning to him, her gaze
imploring him to understand. "I'm just not ready yet."

She looked up into his compassionate eyes and felt
his disappointment and wished with all her heart she
could love him better. She remembered one cold winter's
day, when she was ten and he seventeen. On their way
home from the schoolhouse, she and Abigail had found
a small, starving sparrow with a broken wing. Elizabeth
had picked it up, determined to take it home and make
it well. Abigail, with her tender heart, had cried a river,
her tears almost freezing to crystals upon her pink, wind-
burned cheeks. Along the way, they'd passed Aaron,
who'd been sent on an errand for his mother. Seeing
Abigail's distress, he'd stopped to ask what was wrong.

When he saw the injured bird, he abandoned the errand and suggested they go to his house, since it was so much closer and the weather so bitter. For the next two hours, on his mother's kitchen table, he patiently worked to set the bird's wing in a makeshift splint.

The bird died shortly after, despite his efforts.

But the memory of that day and Aaron's kindness lived on in Elizabeth's heart.

Aaron released her hand and drew back, stung once again by her rejection. He leaned back on one elbow, bent his leg, and rested his wrist upon his knee. "This is the third time I've asked you to marry me," he stated slowly, thoughtfully. "This is the third time you've told me you would say yes. But when you're ready." He studied her for a long moment, then shook his head. "Elizabeth, I'm not sure you'll ever be ready."

"Oh, Aaron," she said softly, hurting for him, wishing she could say the words he longed to hear. She reached over and laid her palm against his cheek. "I am sorry. It'll be soon, I promise."

Aaron sighed. He turned his attention toward the shore. For several moments, he remained silent, then without looking at her, he asked the question she'd been dreading, "What happened between you and Weston today?"

She gave a small, nervous laugh. It sounded forced even to her own ears. She waved her hand in a careless gesture. "Oh, you know Weston. He likes to provoke me."

Aaron turned to her, his eyes steady upon her face. "About what this time?"

Elizabeth smiled, though guilt flooded her. "My dress." She dropped her gaze to the ground, shrugged, and picked at several blades of grass. "He was teasing me about my dress."

Aaron regarded her in silence for several long seconds.

Elizabeth felt her cheeks grow hot.

"Why did you wear that dress, Elizabeth?" His voice
was low, his manner patient as usual.

Embarrassed, she couldn't look at him. What logical
reason could she give him? What could she say? *I wore
it to irritate your brother, Aaron?* No, she couldn't tell
him that.

Shaking her head, she shrugged again, feeling properly chastened, while her mind worked over a bevy of
senseless explanations.

"They're about ready to start, Aaron!" Daniel Munroe
shouted to his older brother, running up to them, relieving
her of the necessity of an explanation.

She could have hugged him.

Below, the excitement swelled as the scullers gathered
into a group.

Elizabeth watched as Ned Hanlan left his friends and
walked over to where Weston stood. He extended his
hand amiably, and the two shook. Ned pointed to
Weston's stained shirt and hooted. Elizabeth's cheeks
stung with embarrassment. Weston nodded and said
something. Both men laughed like two old friends, then
Hanlan walked away, shaking his head.

A little ways beyond the two men, Gabrielle broke
away from the group gathered nearest the shore. She
whisked her petite form over to Weston's side, then
pulled from her satchel a lace-embroidered handkerchief.
She tipped her head up to him and, with the sweetest of
smiles, offered it to him.

He hesitated a moment and turned in Elizabeth's
direction.

Their eyes met and held across the distance.

Then he pulled his eyes away and fixed them on Gabrielle. Beaming down at her, he accepted her handkerchief and tucked it into the back pocket of his trousers, while Elizabeth looked on, wishing she had the ability to hurl another pie the full distance needed to splatter him again.

CHAPTER
5

Weston drove the blades of his sculls down into the water.

He sat centered in the skiff, his feet pressed firmly against the middle of the stretcher, his heels close together, his toes turned outward at a forty-five-degree angle. Rolling his wrists upward, he raised the blades again, then he turned his wrists, arching them downward to finish the stroke.

He gripped the sculls a little too tightly, causing the muscles in his arms and shoulders to bunch and grow taut with tension.

Damn! He was stiff and out of practice. He'd be sore tomorrow.

But from the waist up, his body swung forward, then back again, keeping his strokes smooth and fluid.

He had long ago mastered the art of feathering the blades, which allowed him to hold to a steady rhythm, propelling his skiff out ahead of most of the other competitors.

The water's crystal surface was peppered with an abundance of skiffs. Like many of the participants,

Weston preferred the familiarity of this small craft for most local matches, though outriggers and the new outriggers with sliding seats proved to be faster and much more sophisticated for more serious matches.

He stared at the skiff out in front.

Hanlan.

He would be tough to beat, Weston acknowledged with grudging respect.

What now, Benjamin? he silently asked, amused by his inability to pull abreast of the leader.

From the recesses of his memory, Benjamin's orders boomed: "Balance, Weston, lad. Remember yer balance. Now bring yer blades down squarely. No, not like that! Squarely! Bring yer elbows in closer to your sides— ye're not a duck flapping yer wings! Loosen up, boy! Ye're too tense! Keep your shoulders and arms loose and don't grip those scull handles so tight!"

Weston relaxed; his strokes became smoother. His skiff skimmed forward.

"Ah, that's right. Now ye have it. Now ye have it. Ye're a natural. A natural."

Weston grinned through the sweat that stung his eyes. As a young man, nothing had warmed him like those well-remembered words of approval. Nothing in all the world.

Across the water, from the comfort of a tall white lighthouse, an old man looked on through his binoculars. He stood on the outside ledge, at the very top of the structure, a silent, thoroughly engrossed observer—the elderly master watching his prized pupil. Beside him sat his companion, a large black dog.

As the old man watched the student make his move, pride swelled within him. He chuckled to himself and thought, yes, he'd always known the boy had what it took. He could've taken Hanlan had he been here five years ago.

He lowered his binoculars for a second, reached down and patted the dog's head affectionately, then returned his attention to the race before him.

From the shore, Elizabeth watched Weston's skiff surge forward. Despite her earlier irritation with him, joy swept her. She felt the old thrill of anticipation rush through her veins, the wonderful heady excitement of watching him in competition, and tamped down the urge to jump into the air, ball her fist, shake it in a most unladylike manner, and scream, "Go, Wes, go!"

At her side stood a sedate but smiling Aaron and an exuberant young Daniel. When Weston's skiff pulled abreast of Hanlan's, Daniel unknowingly satisfied her desire by leaping into the air, spinning around like a sprung cork, and yelling, "Hot damn! Ya got 'im, Wes!" That earned him a sharp look of disapproval from his eldest brother, but a small, secret smile from Elizabeth.

A tense silence hushed the crowd, followed by an expanding ripple of unified cheering, while the two favored contestants eyed each other for the space of several strokes.

Then Weston grinned widely, hoping to break the other man's concentration.

But Hanlan was not so easily distracted and returned Weston's grin with a reckless one of his own, recognizing the familiar tactic only too well.

He had used it to his advantage many a time himself. He was the son of Hotel Hanlan's owner, but more importantly, he was Toronto's champion oarsman.

The citizens of Toronto were extremely proud of him and tended to be a bit smug about it at times. For in all of North America, there were no oarsmen who could compete with him or, for that matter, compete with any of Canada's English scullers. In 1876, Hanlan had become Ontario's champion, and he took the world championship in 1880. He'd consistently defeated all comers everywhere until 1884.

Now, at thirty years old, he was still known worldwide for the ease with which he won and his ability to make his opponents look foolish for even daring to challenge him.

But Weston, with Benjamin's guidance, had observed Hanlan consistently, learning at an early age how to emulate his techniques, both physical and psychological.

"Hey, Hanlan!" Weston yelled between breaths. "Last time I saw Mae she told me ye had a hard time getting it up!"

Hanlan chuckled; his white teeth flashed in the sun. He'd expected no less from Munroe.

As for Mae, everyone in Toronto knew Mae. Even those who didn't frequent her establishment knew she was one of Toronto's most popular and expensive young prostitutes.

But despite Hanlan's amusement, his rhythm remained steady. He grinned back, obviously exhilarated by the prospect of a worthy opponent, and yelled, "That's funny, Munroe! Last time I saw her, she told me you didn't have anything to get up!"

They studied each other for a brief moment, each watching and waiting for the other's reaction.

Then, simultaneously, loud laughter broke from both men.

Their strokes faltered.

From the lighthouse, the old man looked on and grimaced. "All that brawn and no brains, Eli," he muttered to his dog. "Damn young fool won't take this one." Though the race wasn't over, he could easily foresee the outcome from his vantage point. With a heavy sigh of resignation, he lowered his binoculars, turned away, and retreated through the open door, his dog following close at his heels.

In the water, behind the two men, came another skiff, its young sculler much more intent about the outcome of the match. He glanced at neither of his opponents, his attention firmly fixed on the task at hand.

Within seconds, he had them both.

A unified moan reverberated throughout the crowd of spectators, followed by a cresting wave of excitement. The crowd grew jubilant. A new hero was born, the old temporarily forgotten.

Weston and Hanlan looked on, momentarily stunned, then snapped their gazes frontward, promptly turning their attention to the race.

But it was too late.

Their young opponent had seized his opportunity. And though Weston and Hanlan struggled valiantly to regain their positions, they'd lost their advantage to one who'd used their lighthearted jibes and lack of concentration to gain the favored finish.

On shore, Elizabeth sighed, shaking her head in disgust.

Oh, Weston, you idiot, she thought, her frustration rife. She folded her arms across her chest, wanting to hurl curses at him, totally infuriated by his lack of sobriety.

Her mouth pressed into a thin, disapproving line, while she watched Weston and Hanlan reach the shore, grinning like simpleminded fools, not at all distressed by their loss.

As he pulled his boat ashore, Weston's head lifted.

He looked in Elizabeth's direction and found her. Her expression relaxed involuntarily. For a moment, she thought he might wave, and her heart contracted with expectation. But a young man approached him from the left, and Weston turned without acknowledging having seen her.

Swallowing a stinging sense of disappointment, she lifted her chin a notch higher.

With the race over, the multicolored sea of spectator boats turned toward shore, while a thoroughly disappointed Daniel jammed his hand through his wheat-colored hair and strode off muttering adult obscenities under his breath.

Aaron shook his head helplessly and turned to Elizabeth. "I'm going to have to talk to Wes about that boy's vocabulary. Each day he's around him, Daniel sounds more like a sailor and less like a fifteen-year-old boy."

Or maybe . . . exactly like a fifteen-year-old boy, Elizabeth thought silently, remembering Weston and David at that age.

Aaron sighed and smiled. "What do you say we find Abigail and some of the others and play a game of croquet?"

"He could have won, Aaron," Elizabeth said in a small voice without looking at him, her attention still riveted on the shore. "I know he could have."

Aaron took her elbow and squeezed gently. "It's not the winning he loves, Elizabeth. It's the challenge, the competition, the game, the excitement. You know that as well as I do."

After a few moments, she lost Weston's sunlit head among his growing crowd of admirers.

From a small group, farther up the shore, a famili-

ar flash of pink broke loose and sailed in Weston's
direction. After a few seconds, she disappeared into the
crowd, also.

"Yes, I know," Elizabeth said quietly. A keen sense
of isolation gripped her. In earlier times she, too, would
have been at the water's edge, waiting for him to come
in. In earlier times, it would not have mattered to her
whether he'd won or not.

But refusing to give in to the gamut of emotions
threatening to smother her. Instead she turned toward
Aaron, looked up into his kind eyes, and offered him
an overly bright smile. "Yes." She took his proffered
arm. "Let's find Abigail."

"What do ye say, Aaron?" Weston asked his brother
later that evening, while they sat together in their father's
richly furnished study.

"I say you could have won that race, Wes."

Weston shrugged.

"Elizabeth was disappointed."

Weston snorted. She'd been disappointed with him
since he'd returned. Obviously she'd been disappointed
in him before he returned. After all, she was going to
marry his brother. Or so she claimed. Feeling unreasonably affronted, he wondered what had happened to the
saucy, fun-loving girl he'd left behind. He thought about
her recent actions toward him. In the short time he'd
been home, she'd cursed him, slapped him, practically
drowned him, slammed a blueberry pie into his chest,
and dammit if she hadn't hurt his feelings, too, ignoring
him as she had after the match.

Stung by the memory, he folded his arms across his
chest. For all that her antics amused him, he had to admit
she'd become something of a shrew in his absence.

Safely turning his attention back to his brother, he said, "I'm not talking about the race, Aaron, and you know it."

Outside the handsome, vine-covered brick house, the thunder rolled, and the wind picked up force.

Aaron contemplated his response for several long moments, while he rose and poured himself and Weston a small measure of brandy from the flask on the walnut desk. A thoughtful man, not moved to hasty words or actions, he shook his head regretfully. "I talked with Father about it this morning, Wes. I'm sorry, but he doesn't want to take the chance with the company money."

Silently Weston rose and crossed the room to stare out the window. Lightning lit the sky, revealing tumbling clouds and trees bent reluctantly under the heavy hand of the wind. His shoulders slumped. He pocketed his hands and fought down a smothering sense of dejection. He had so wanted his family's support—not so much financially, but emotionally. Looking out into the darkness, he asked quietly, "And you, Aaron? How do you feel about taking the risk?"

"It's not up to me," Aaron said. "It's Father's money."

"But how do you feel?" Weston turned and pinned him with a direct stare.

Aaron sighed, sat down on the edge of the desk, and chose his words carefully. "We're not rich. You know that. But we're quite comfortable thanks to Father's good business sense. Where once he might have taken the gamble, he no longer feels he can. But . . . if it were my company, my money . . ." Aaron smiled slowly. "I think I would take the chance with you, Wes."

Weston grinned, finding absolution in those words. For him, that was enough. "Thanks, Aaron." The words were spoken softly, the sentiment completely heartfelt.

They left each other shortly after that, each retiring up the wide walnut staircase for the evening.

A flash of lightning illuminated Weston's room, and a reverberating clap of thunder echoed throughout the stillness of the sturdy house.

He sat on the edge of his bed and thought of Aaron, the brother he loved. The brother who believed in him, who trusted him.

The brother who would marry Beth.

Weston dropped his head into his hands.

Thou shalt not covet thy neighbor's wife.

Let alone thy brother's intended, he thought with self-recrimination.

But she was mine, his heart argued.

Was. Not anymore, logic reminded him.

But if he'd stayed—

He hadn't.

He cursed silently, lifted his head, stared into the inky blackness, and promised himself he would do nothing to dishonor his family or hurt his brother.

But later, before he drifted off to sleep, he found himself remembering just how good that blueberry pie had tasted.

Elizabeth lay awake, tired but restless, sleep eluding her.

She stared at the primitive shadows dancing on the wall, spurred on by the fierce winds of the sudden summer storm.

She sighed and tried to clear her mind of all thoughts and memories, but on and on it raced, while an image of Weston rose before her—handsome, laughing Weston gazing down at Gabrielle.

Her friend. One of her best.

Jealousy sluiced through her. She was appalled by its intensity.

Her eyes slammed shut.

You still love him, her mind taunted.

No, no. She didn't.

Then why was she lying here thinking about him instead of his brother?

I don't know. I don't know.

She flopped onto her back. *Go to sleep, Elizabeth. Don't think about him. It's dishonorable. Think about Aaron.*

But when she thought of Aaron, years and years of hollow emptiness stretched before her, and she felt a bleakness that chilled her. She tried to picture their children, but couldn't. Somehow the fact that she couldn't envision their faces made her feel all the more bereaved.

"Beth? Are you awake?" Abigail's soft voice came to her from across the room.

"Yes," Elizabeth said, turning onto her side to face her sister. "I thought you were asleep."

"No. Not yet."

"Not tired?"

"Yes . . . and no. But I can't sleep."

Elizabeth sighed and pushed her thick braid off her shoulder. "I know. Me, too."

They remained silent for several moments, listening as the wind grew violent outside. Branches from a nearby oak tree scraped against the side of the house like sharp talons, while cool rain swept in through the window, lifting the curtains outward like ghostly arms.

Elizabeth rose, her long white gown billowing out

behind her. She crossed the room and closed the window, then hurried back to burrow under the covers of her bed.

"Sometimes I love the rain," Abigail said thoughtfully.

"Yes. Me, too."

"Beth?"

"Mm-hm?"

"Is it wrong, do you think . . . to have feelings for a man who is in love with someone other than yourself?"

The question caught Elizabeth off-guard. She rose up onto her elbow, cradled her head in her hand, and remained quiet for a very long moment as she thought about her answer. At length she said, "What do you mean exactly, when you say . . . have feelings?"

Silence. A deep sigh.

Her eyes widened. "Do you mean to tell me you're in love with someone, Abigail?" The thought was sobering. Her little sister in love? And with someone who didn't return her affections? A fierce protective instinct rose within her. The bloody fool! How could anyone not love Abigail? Beautiful, gentle Abigail. Elizabeth was shaken by how much the idea angered yet at the same time saddened her.

Abigail flopped onto her back. "I knew you'd ask me that."

"Well, hell, Abigail!" Elizabeth said in exasperation, sitting up in bed and hugging her knees. "You asked me the question first. What do you expect me to say when you ask me something like that?"

"I expect you to tell me if you think it's a sin to love someone who's in love with someone else, that's what I expect," Abigail snapped, her voice uncharacteristically sharp.

Surprised at the shortness of her sister's statement, Elizabeth snapped her jaws shut. "Well . . . Gosh, I'm sorry, Ab," she eventually said. "Really I am."

Abigail digested her apology in silence. After a few moments, she asked, "Well . . . do you?"

"Do I what?"

"Think it's a sin?"

Elizabeth snorted. "No. Of course not."

"Even if the person you love loves someone you know?"

Elizabeth shook her head. "No . . . I don't think it's a sin. Sometimes . . . well . . . Sometimes you just can't help the way you feel."

"I suppose you're right."

"I know I'm right."

The pair grew silent. The sanctity of the dark room, blended with the soothing patter of the rain, inspired confidences that were sometimes hard to share in the light of day.

"Beth?"

"Hm?"

"Did you ever . . . you know?"

"Did I ever what?"

"You know . . . did you ever . . . with a man?"

"Abigail!"

"Well, have you?"

Though shocked at the brazenness of her sister's question, it never occurred to Elizabeth to lie. "Well . . . sort of, I guess."

"With Aaron?"

Elizabeth sighed softly and rested her chin on her knees, remembering. For a moment she felt the warmth of a memory infuse her. "No, not with Aaron."

"Weston?"

"Yes." Her voice was but a whisper. "It was Weston. Only Weston."

"Was it the time we found you on the island?"

Memories. "Yes. Then and before."

"What was it like?"

Elizabeth's eyes drifted shut. Her stomach tightened, and her breasts grew taut, her voice wistful. "Oh, Ab . . . it was scary, wonderful, nice . . . All of those things and more."

Abigail digested the information slowly. "Did you feel . . . well, sinful afterward?"

"No," Elizabeth said in frank honesty. "No, I didn't. Maybe I should have. Mrs. Caufield thinks any young lady who allows a young man to touch her in such a manner is wicked. But . . . it didn't feel that way at all. It seemed right with Weston somehow."

"Did you ever tell Aaron?"

"No!" Elizabeth was shocked. "Really, Abigail! No! Of course not!"

They grew silent; the seconds kept time with the slowing rain.

Then, in a still, small voice, Abigail asked, "Beth . . . does Aaron make you feel that way?"

Elizabeth wished Abigail hadn't asked her that question; for in contemplating it, Elizabeth was forced to acknowledge the answer. "No," she said after a long pause. "He doesn't."

"Well . . . maybe you should tell him."

"Oh, Ab . . . I can't. I just can't."

"I wish Mama were here so she could help us with these things," Abigail whispered.

Elizabeth remained silent. Mama couldn't have helped them with these things.

"Beth?"

"Hm?"

"Thanks."

"For what?"

"For understanding and for telling me about . . ."

Elizabeth plumped her pillow and lay down, cradling her head in her hands. "Sure."

With that Abigail turned onto her side. Within minutes she was breathing evenly.

But Elizabeth was not to find rest so easily. She lay awake long into the pink early morning hours, wondering just who it was her little sister loved.

On Friday morning of the following week, Weston made his way down lower Yonge Street with David Latham at his side.

Though not quite as fashionable as King Street, Yonge had a vibrant life of its own, boasting the Great Western Railway Station and the city's principal public wharf at the south end, along with a multitude of wholesale and retail establishments spreading out along Front Street and the streets running north.

"Bradford wants in," David said conversationally.

"Good." Weston smiled, remembering Bradford Stevens. "I saw him yesterday, but we were only able to talk for a few minutes." Weston chuckled. "He hasn't changed much."

As a boy, Bradford had been a tall, lanky redhead with a slightly eccentric personality and a quick, hot temper, interlaced with an equally short memory. As far as Weston knew, Bradford had never held a grudge against anyone for more than a total of five whole minutes. When they were ten, Weston had teased him about being a "carrot top." Bradford's face had grown as red as his hair, and he'd rushed Weston like a raging bull.

Weston, though shorter, was stockier and stronger and had walloped him, giving him a bloody nose. But the next day, Bradford had acted as if the incident had never occurred, and had offered Weston one of his mother's prized molasses cookies.

"He knows a lot about design," David remarked, trying to match Weston's longer stride. "His uncle is an engineer for the Union Dry Dock Company in Buffalo, New York. He's been teaching Brad some of the newer building designs. You know, he always did have a way with drawing and building things.

"Anyway," David continued, "he returned a couple of months ago, after spending nearly a year in Buffalo with his uncle."

"But can he design steamers?" Weston questioned, lifting a skeptical brow.

David smiled, and his voice rang with confidence. "He can design anything, Wes. Trust me."

"Then he's in," Weston stated flatly; the subject was closed.

Up ahead loomed their destination: Tully's Bank of Montreal. It dominated the intersection of Front and Yonge streets. The last time Weston had seen it, it had seemed hopelessly old-fashioned in comparison to the neighboring Customs House and the other commercial buildings in the city. But now it was a palatial structure.

Remarking on the change, David told him that they'd begun to rebuild it only this year and still weren't quite finished.

Yet it stood before them proudly, an opulent cut-stone building with a high roof, prominent dormers, and an almost obsessive layering of classical detail, the form of the building decisively influenced by some of the more renowned London clubs and mansions.

"Do you really think St. Clair will loan us the money?" David asked, doubt coloring his voice.

Weston shrugged, his stride slowing slightly. "I don't know. He's a fair man—not to mention a wise businessman. He will if we can convince him it's worth the risk. Besides," he said in all honesty, "I don't know any other bankers offhand, do you?"

David sighed heavily and stared down at his polished shoes. He was dressed in his usual formal attire, while Weston flaunted convention by wearing trousers, an open-necked shirt with the sleeves rolled up, and red suspenders.

"No," David answered after giving the question considerable thought. "I guess I don't. But . . ."

"But what?" Weston grinned. "You still scared of taking a little gamble, David?"

Affronted, David drew himself up to his full height. "Certainly not!"

Their steps slowed as they approached the bank. Robert Simpson came out of one of the large heavy doors. He was an impressive man who had established a small dry goods store near Queen and Yonge streets in 1872. His store had grown so well that he'd moved to a larger building southward a few years ago and inaugurated a horse-and-wagon delivery service, one of the city's first. "Munroe! Latham!" he boomed, his smile friendly as he passed them.

The two younger men nodded their greetings, while Weston's mind clicked. He raised an eyebrow and inclined his head in Simpson's direction, and David nodded and said, "I'll talk to him."

Weston slapped David on his back. "You worry too much, David. Relax and enjoy the ride. It's going to be an exciting one!"

Ten minutes later they were seated in expensive leather chairs inside Russell St. Clair's office. He sat across from them, a small man, dwarfed by his desk, with a bushy mustache and shrewd, though not unkind, eyes.

"Gentlemen," he said and leaned back, interlacing his fingers and creating a steeple with his thumbs. "What can I do for you?"

And so they told him. Or, rather, Weston did.

He wove his intentions into a story so full of enthusiasm, so ripe with expected success, so innovative and fresh, that the usually cautious St. Clair had to fight the urge to be swept away by the sheer fervency of the younger man's dream.

"Steamers," St. Clair said thoughtfully and tapped his pencil on the polished surface on his desk. "Hmmm . . ."

CHAPTER
6

"I don't believe it!" Gabrielle scoffed. She pushed her pert nose into the air and reached across the table for another warm scone.

"It's true," Elizabeth insisted calmly.

"Hmph!" Gabrielle snorted and smeared a generous amount of butter onto her biscuit, then abruptly changed the subject. "Abigail, your scones are wonderful."

"Thank you." Abigail inclined her head graciously, then seated herself at the table with the other two women. Across the table, Elizabeth's mischievous eyes met hers.

"She's simply not his type!" Gabrielle declared between bites, refusing to accept her friend's disclosure. "David would never ask Enid Evans to the summer ball! Especially not this one! This is the big one! The last of the season. Everyone who's anyone will be there. Queen Victoria herself would attend if she were here!"

"Well," Elizabeth said, raising one eyebrow, "I doubt the Queen will make it, and if I remember correctly, you no longer wanted David. You did say he wasn't your type," she reminded her friend none too gently.

"He's *not* my type! But I'm quite certain he couldn't find Enid the least bit attractive after m—" Gabrielle halted, leaving the sentence hanging, while glancing from one sister to the other. "Oh, my," she said, a stray sense of sensitivity dawning. She sighed exaggeratedly. "Ohhhh, I suppose that does sound terribly vain of me, doesn't it?"

"Just a bit," Elizabeth answered honestly, while Abigail rose to refill the platter with more of her fresh scones. "Not all of us are your equal in beauty, Gaby."

"Well," Gabrielle said as her expression grew petulant, her voice defensive, "it's not as though I can help it! Sometimes, I almost wish I could be intelligent like you, Elizabeth, and that the children in the church loved me and looked up to me as they do you. You can play their games and outrun any of them as though you were still twelve. As for me . . . I run like a duck." Gabrielle's eyes filled with an abundance of plump tears. "I've always run like a duck. And Abigail." She turned in the other girl's direction. "There isn't anyone our age who can cook and bake and sew the way you can. Not to mention organize church socials, head fund-raisers for the needy, and sing like a bird."

Elizabeth's heart softened a little toward her blond friend. "You have your talents, too, Gaby."

"Well . . . ," she replied sulkily, though somewhat placated. "I suppose."

"Enid does, also," Abigail said over her shoulder. "She's very kind and has a wonderful sense of humor. She's a very lovely person."

"And I'm sure David enjoys her company very much. So who are we to judge? 'Beauty is in the eye of the beholder,' " Elizabeth stated more gently.

With a quicksilver blink of her lashes, Gabrielle's tears vanished. She dropped her half-eaten biscuit onto her plate with a negligent plop and threw her hands up in disgust. "Oh pleeeeeze, you two. All you have to do is look at her and—"

"And what?" Tristan McRaney asked, entering the kitchen. In one hand he carried his well-worn Bible, in the other his favorite black bowler.

"Oh, nothing," Gabrielle answered, chastened by the thought of the reverend having heard their conversation.

"Hello, Gabrielle," he said, inclining his head in her direction. "Don't you look lovely today!" Tristan McRaney might have been a man of the cloth, but if he'd learned one thing in all his forty-eight years, it was how to say the right thing to the right person. Especially when it came to an attractive woman with an ego the size of Gabrielle St. Clair's.

Gabrielle beamed, her discomfort immediately forgotten. "Why, thank you, Reverend."

He crossed the room to place a kiss upon Abigail's brow, then did the same to Elizabeth's.

He'd known he'd find them in this room, their domain. But then, he had to admit, every room in the house was their domain except for his study. Not that he minded. It was the least he could offer his daughters: the decorated comfort of their own home. It was a decidedly feminine kitchen with sunshine cascading through the delicate lace curtains, lighting a path along the freshly polished floor. The walls were covered by flowered wallpaper; the counters with an array of what he thought to be useless female bric-a-brac.

"I'll be late for supper, girls. Visitation today, you know. And I may go out to the Lakeside Home if I have time. I haven't been out there at all this summer. The children always enjoy visitors." He turned to Elizabeth. "You'll check on Mrs. Dansworth for me, won't you?"

"Of course, Papa."

"Take her some of the raspberry jam you and Abigail put up this season."

"I will."

"And Benjamin?"

"I'll go out to the island today, too."

"Take him something, also."

"I will, Papa."

"Take the ferry, not the dinghy," he warned, knowing full well her prowess with the small boat. Though the townspeople had thought it outrageously improper, Weston hadn't been Benjamin's only pupil. As an adolescent girl, Elizabeth had mastered the use of a dinghy quite well and, though forbidden to do so, had frequently used one to cross the lake for her nightly visits to the island.

"Yes, Papa," she answered, her expression one of meek obedience.

Not in the least deluded by her pretended docility, he fought the urge to smile.

He turned toward the door, then halted. "Don't you and Abigail have a picnic planned with the congregation's children this afternoon?"

Both girls chorused, "Yes, Papa. We do."

"Ah, well." He sighed. "I suppose you have everything in hand."

"Yes, Papa. We do." All three women giggled.

Pleased, his gray eyes twinkled. "Then I'll be off. Good day, ladies." With that he affected a deep bow, topped his head with his hat, and left them, his chuckles lingering behind as he disappeared down the porch steps.

"You know," Gabrielle said thoughtfully, looking after him, placing her index finger against the fullness of her bottom lip, "your father is a very handsome man for his age."

"Gabrielle!" both girls exclaimed, their eyes wide.

"Welllll, I'm only making an observation."

"Well, observe in another direction!" Elizabeth snapped, peeved. She rose from the table and swiped Gabrielle's teacup out from under her nose so fast she almost sloshed the small amount of tea that was left in the cup right out onto Gabrielle St. Clair's perfectly starched lap.

"I have been!"

"So I've heard." Elizabeth's voice echoed sarcasm. She busied herself with making more tea, her movements brisk and agitated.

Six weeks had passed since the sculling match. Now, in mid-July, the summer days were melting away all too quickly. Elizabeth had made it a point to avoid Weston. So far she'd been quite successful. He, in turn, had not sought her out.

Of course he had no need to.

Aaron had mentioned that Weston had been seeing Gabrielle on occasion. And several of Elizabeth's friends had mentioned seeing the pair riding in Queen's Park.

"Well, I do have some information I'll wager neither of you has heard," Gabrielle said conspiratorially, widening her green eyes and tipping her head to the side.

Elizabeth tried to appear uninterested. Abigail remained quiet, studying the crumbs on the surface of the lovely lace tablecloth.

About three seconds passed before Elizabeth's curiosity won out. Setting the teapot down with a significant thump, she spun around, propped her hands on her hips, and snapped, "All right! What the bloody hell is it?"

Satisfied as a milk-fed calf, Gabrielle smiled. "Well," she began dramatically and turned in her chair to lean toward Elizabeth. "A certain young man, who at this time wishes to remain nameless, along with two of his young partners, who shall also remain nameless, have begun designing ships. Steamers, actually. Right here in Toronto."

Elizabeth crossed her arms over her bodice, her hazel eyes sparking irritation. "So?"

"Soooooo . . . should their venture prove successful, these young men could become very rich young men."

"So?" Elizabeth repeated, wishing Gaby would get to the point.

"So," Gabrielle stated, "I think Weston Munroe would make me as excellent a choice for a husband as Aaron does for you, don't you?"

Abigail's head came up. "I thought he was to remain nameless, Gaby," she chided softly.

"Well . . . I'm sure he won't mind if I tell only you and Elizabeth. After all, you are practically family to the Munroes."

Weston. Elizabeth's heart sunk to her toes like an anchor. Gabrielle continued to chatter on, but Elizabeth no longer discerned her words.

Weston as Gaby's husband.

Weston building ships.

Weston confiding in Gaby the dreams he once would have shared with her.

The revelation cut a slash across Elizabeth's heart. She dropped her arms to her side. "I wasn't sure he would stay," she said quietly to no one in particular. "Even Aaron wasn't sure."

"Oh, he's staying all right," Gabrielle declared with smug assurance. "Weston told me—" She covered her mouth with her hand to stop her words, then giggled. "Oh, there I go again." She rose from her seat and brushed the crumbs from her light-blue skirt. She didn't feel it necessary to inform her friends of the fact that she had learned this information through the closed door of her father's study. Nor did she feel it necessary for them to know that though she and Weston had shared a few deep kisses, along with a few intimate caresses which she had tactically allowed, no mention of marriage had yet been uttered.

"I suppose I should be on my way," she announced brightly. "Mr. Simpson ordered me a bolt of yellow satin along with the most gorgeous imported lace for my ball gown. They should be in by now." Her eyes widened, and she giggled again. "You should see what he's displaying! Mother and her friends are completely outraged." Gabrielle cleared her throat. "Corsets and other certain unmentionable underthings. Right out where everyone can view them. Can you imagine?" Without warning, she veered off on another topic. "I'm to meet Mother at Mrs. Grogan's for a fitting, so I'd best be off." She reached for her reticule and breezed across the floor, her crimped golden curls bouncing. "By the way," she said and whirled, "what are the two of you wearing to the ball?"

"I hadn't thought of it," Elizabeth answered softly, her thoughts distracted.

"Well, you'd best think of it! We only have about five weeks left. You don't want to go looking anything like you did the day of the picnic. Really, Elizabeth! I don't want to be embarrassed to talk with you!"

"I'm making us something special," Abigail put in with quiet confidence, her thoughts as distracted as her sister's.

"Oh, that's simply grand!" Gabrielle exclaimed on her way out the door. "Simply grand! You sew almost as wonderfully as Mrs. Grogan does! I'm sure your dresses will be quite lovely!"

"I'm sure," Elizabeth muttered in abject misery, completely unaware of what it was she was agreeing with.

Elizabeth strolled along the grassy bank, her basket full of Benjamin's favorite tidbits, her thoughts far removed from the warm summer day.

She'd fulfilled her father's request, having spent an hour and a half visiting with the elderly Mrs. Dansworth, then she and Abigail had picnicked with the children as they'd promised. Now it was her turn. She was off to visit Benjamin.

She wore a simple gingham dress sprinkled with tiny flowers, nipped at the waist, and covered with a starched white apron. The dress boasted no bustle, nor did she carry a parasol. With her many errands to run, she found it easier to disregard fashion in the face of comfort. Even without all the trappings, however, she was quite warm. But the gentle lake breeze was cooling, offering a measure of relief from the uncomfortable thickness of the afternoon humidity. Instead of fighting with her hair, she'd pulled it back with a ribbon, securing it at her nape, but willful curls had escaped and now whispered around her face. She brushed a tendril aside and turned her gaze toward the water. Blue water. Bluer sky. They met and fused into one lovely canvas, dotted with white sails and whiter clouds.

Farther out, men fished from the decks of their ships

for trout, grayling, muskellunge, and bass. The sails of their vessels billowed outward as though filled with the gusty breath of some great giant.

She turned her gaze inland. Summer was now well advanced, and spring's abundance of wildflowers had vanished, leaving behind the seedlings for another year's grand display. Farther inland, a multitude of fully leafed aspens, maples, and cottonwoods rustled, while the willow trees swayed gently, forgetting to weep this fine day.

Above her head, seagulls dipped low and complained raucously of her presence. "Oh, go scream over someone else's head!" she called out irritably to a particularly obnoxious fellow. "I belong here, too!"

"Yes," said a male voice from behind. "Ye always did."

Startled, she whirled abruptly, her hand flying to her breast, then upward to shade her eyes.

She tipped her chin up and met the bluest eyes she'd ever known.

"Hello, Beth," Weston said with a lazy grin.

"Weston," she whispered, feeling trapped and panicked. "I didn't hear you—"

He tipped his chin skyward. "Ye were talking to the bird."

For a few moments she didn't respond. She felt herself blushing profusely as the absurdity of the statement hit her, then she dropped her gaze and laughed self-consciously.

Weston chuckled, also, continuing to study her in quiet amusement. He shifted his weight and hung his thumbs in the waistband of his trousers.

Her gaze rose to his; her cheeks grew even pinker. "Yes. I suppose I was."

They stared at each other for several uncomfortable moments, until at length she felt a need to fill the empty silence. "I'm sorry I hit you with the pie, Wes."

He shrugged. His dimples deepened. "It was a damn good pie."

"It was Abigail's . . ."

"I figured. Ye never could cook."

She nodded agreement and, for the first time since his return, felt no animosity toward him. "No, I never could."

They grew tensely silent once again, each unsure of how to proceed, each desiring a truce of some sort, neither knowing how to offer it. She sighed, grasped the handle of her basket in front of her with both hands, and looked out toward the water.

Weston let his eyes take their fill.

Though he wasn't about to tell her, he'd purposely sought her out today. For reasons he couldn't completely formulate in his mind, he wanted to see her, to tell her about the dream he, David, and Bradford had. For reasons he couldn't entirely understand, he wanted her opinion, hungered for her approval.

The breeze blew tendrils of her hair across her lips. He fought the urge to reach out and loosen them. Touching her lips would be fatal. That he knew. Instead he used the freedom of the moment to study her. He liked her dressed as she was. No frills or fancy extras, and he was willing to bet she wore no corset or petticoat beneath her dress. She never had before; he doubted she did now. Involuntarily his stomach tightened as he remembered the texture of her skin, the smoothness of her belly, the silkiness of her . . .

She turned.

His eyes, revealing nothing, whisked innocently up to her face.

"I'm going to visit Benjamin . . ." Her voice was hesitant, suddenly afraid to finish the sentence. "Would you want to come along?"

He remembered the many times they'd visited the old man together and quietly replied, "Yes, I would. Very much."

He reached out and took the basket from her hands. His fingers brushed hers, sending a jolt of awareness throughout her body.

Briefly she reconsidered her invitation. Without the protective cloak of her anger, she found her attraction to him almost painful. As usual, he was dressed more like a dock worker than the son of one of Toronto's most respected businessmen. But Weston had never liked pretentious clothing or pretentious people, and Elizabeth had always admired him for that. She was glad he hadn't changed in that way.

She cast aside her apprehensions, reminding herself he was interested in Gabrielle now, not her. The reminder brought not only a brief flash of sadness, but also a healthy measure of relief. There was nothing to feel guilty about, to worry about, to be angry about any longer.

Their new relationship sensitively precarious, they walked together in uneasy silence, until finally Elizabeth said, "You're building ships."

"Yes." He didn't seem surprised that she knew.

"Steamers, is it?"

"Yes. We've begun design already. We're working out of a warehouse near the wharf."

"You and David?"

"And Brad."

"I see." She looked up at him, smiled, and in all sincerity said, "Good luck, Wes. I wish you success."

Her words freed something within him; his heart soared. "Thanks, Lizzy," he replied warmly. "It means a lot to me that ye'd say that."

They walked on for a little while longer, careful, oh so careful, not to brush against each other. Around them birds sang and squirrels scrambled and played, while water lapped against the shore, and two hearts beat out a silent, comfortable rhythm.

Then, to Weston's surprise, Elizabeth quietly ordered, "Tell me about Scotland."

Surprised, his eyebrows rose. "Ye really want me to?"

She cocked her head, her earlier resentment a retired memory, and honestly replied, "Very much."

Weston smiled down into her eyes, nodded, and began. "Ye'd love it, Lizzy. The heather is especially beautiful, the hills and glens lovely beyond anything ye've ever seen. And the castles," he said, his deep voice growing animated with remembrance. "Ah, God, the castles are much as they were centuries ago, and the people . . ."

As she listened, she relaxed, becoming entranced by the vortex of colorful pictures his words created. She watched his face, listened to his voice, marked the familiar way he tipped his head, the way he laughed, the way his eyes lit with excitement, the length of his stride, and pondered over the unfamiliar heavier shadow of beard along his jaw, the lighting of a cigar—he hadn't smoked before—his adult height and width.

So many familiarities, so many changes.

He told her about Scotland, London, France, Italy, and all the other places he'd seen, and a few of the people he'd known, along with several of the things he'd done and learned. Somehow, with his blue eyes dancing, he wove verbal magic, and the years they'd been apart slipped away. By the time they reached the lighthouse, much of their earlier tension had abated.

They found the door to the towering structure ajar as though in anticipation of a visitor.

"Benjamin!" Elizabeth called out, pushing the door open wider. The door squeaked its resentment. She took the basket from Weston's hand.

Inside, the lighthouse seemed dim and shadowed compared to the outdoor brilliance of the afternoon sun that slashed golden stripes across the open doorway. The main room was sparsely furnished, but meticulously clean and neat. And though the dull hardwood floor lacked luster, it was swept clean of all dirt and dust. In the center of the room sat a well-worn oak table, surrounded by equally well-worn spindle-backed chairs. A large black cookstove, on which a kettle steamed, flanked one wall. Opposite that wall sat an old cane rocker, a pair of weathered boots, and a small table, the top covered by a stack of books. The only ornamentation in the room was the wall behind the rocker, which was decorated with a vast array of colorful fishing equipment—from poles to openly draped nets and instruments used to hook and clean the catch.

But it was the unfamiliar, especially large piece of furniture sitting near the staircase that caught Elizabeth's immediate attention. Weston crossed his arms over his chest and leaned a shoulder against the open doorway, while she placed the basket upon the table, then walked to the stairs. Craning her neck upward, she hollered, "Benjamin! Are you up there?"

"Lizzy, is that ye?"

"Of course it's me!"

"I'll be right down! Just give me a minute!"

She turned to Weston and gestured toward the bookcase. "I wonder where that came from."

Weston shrugged lazily.

"It's beautiful," she whispered, running a hand reverently over one of the gleaming shelves. It was a huge, elegant piece, at least six feet wide and reaching nearly to the ceiling of the room. The craftsmanship was excellent. She lifted her gaze to Weston's. "He's always needed one." All who knew him were well aware that besides fishing and sculling, books were Benjamin's greatest love.

His heavy steps sounded on the stairs.

"Lizzy, darlin'!" The old man greeted her warmly from the last step. "It's about time ye come out and see this old man!"

She chuckled and walked up against his chest, as she'd done hundreds of times before, accepting a great bear hug from his still remarkably strong arms.

"Wes!" Benjamin boomed, surprised. He crossed the room to give the young man the same treatment. "So it's ye who brought this neglectful young woman t'see me."

Weston shook his head and smiled. A scrape against the door announced the arrival and admittance of the other permanent resident of the Gibraltar Lighthouse. "Actually," Weston said in response to Benjamin's statement, "she brought *me*." He went down on one knee, ruffled the head of the large dog fondly, and good-naturedly accepted the overly amorous, sloppy greeting of his old playmate. "Hello, Eli, old friend."

"Ahhh . . ." Benjamin nodded his understanding. "So that's how it is." He ambled across the floor to the table, his movements slow and ponderous. Where once he'd been as spry as any man in Canada, possibly one of the strongest, though still quite healthy, the past few years had found him reluctantly succumbing to the inevitable aches and pains of the elderly. "What d'ye bring me, Lizzy?"

Elizabeth joined him at the table and began pulling the items from the basket. "Jam, scones, cookies, among a few other of your favorites."

"That sweet little sister of yers has been baking again," Benjamin remarked.

Elizabeth smiled. "Yes, she has."

Benjamin hobbled over to the stove. "I'll make us some tea to go along with these treasures."

Weston joined Elizabeth at the table. They pulled out chairs and lowered themselves into them, careful not to touch each other.

"How do ye like my bookcase, Lizzy?" Benjamin asked over his shoulder.

"It's extraordinary," Elizabeth answered.

"It was a wonderful gift. A fine gift, indeed." He turned to the couple, his eyes settling on Weston. His voice grew hoarse with emotion. "I thank ye again, lad."

Elizabeth's eyes locked on Weston. "You, Wes?" she asked, stunned. "You gave the bookcase to Benjamin?"

Weston looked uncomfortable in the face of Benjamin's gratitude and Elizabeth's surprise. "I brought it home with me," he admitted, embarrassed. "I found it in England."

No more was said, and the trio had tea together. Then Benjamin entertained them with his famous Iroquoian stories—a few, the young couple suspected, grossly fabricated. And once, while the old man talked on, Weston's leg lightly brushed against Elizabeth's skirt. She looked up sharply, fully expecting to find his eyes lit with secret amusement. But he didn't seem to be aware of the contact, and she chided herself for remaining so suspicious.

But when at last soft evening shadows began to fall across the open doorway, Elizabeth rose and Weston followed.

Reluctantly they took their leave of their old friend.

They walked toward the ferry docks in companionable silence, Elizabeth still ruminating over Weston's thoughtfulness, until at length she said, "That was very kind of you, Wes." She looked up at him, her expression unguarded and sincere. It was a selfless gesture, one she would have expected from Aaron. But it had not come from Aaron, it had come from Wes . . . the boy who'd had his knuckles rapped daily, the boy who'd turned a jar of spiders loose in his classroom, the boy whose name was whispered more than any other behind the fans of Mrs. Caufield's friends.

The boy who was now a man. A thoughtful man.

More changes to ponder, Elizabeth thought. But when she spoke, all she said was, "It must have been very expensive."

"Almost a year's wages." He hooked his thumbs into his waistband and studied the glowing orb of the sun, setting slowly over the shining lake waters.

"Wages?" Her eyebrows rose.

He looked down into her eyes and smiled. "Yes, wages, Beth. What did ye think I did to fill my belly all those years? I worked the ships I traveled."

"Doing what?" she asked.

"Doing whatever they taught me to do."

She digested his disclosure in reflective silence. "The bookcase means a lot to Benjamin."

His words surprised her even more when he quietly replied, "Benjamin means a lot to me."

Their steps halted at the landing. "I'll take ye across," he stated.

She shook her head. "There's no need. I can—"

"Beth, I'll take ye," he insisted, and took her arm.

She looked up at him and thought about the afternoon they had just spent together. She said, "All right, Wes."

Not long after the young couple left, another visitor approached the lighthouse.

The expected one.

The one for whom the door had been left ajar.

Dressed in her usual black attire, her once radiant hair well-hidden beneath her veil, she'd missed the pair by only a few minutes, while on the west end of the island, at the Lakeside Home for Children, the Reverend Tristan McRaney visited with the lonely little ones—cheering them, praying for them, loving them, then leaving them, before the wings of night could fall.

CHAPTER
7

Weston saw Elizabeth to her porch steps.

At first she'd resisted his continuing company, insisting she could take a cab from the wharf. But Weston wouldn't hear of it. Instead, they walked side by side the somewhat lengthy distance to the little whitewashed house at the south end of Queen Street. And while shades of violet fell across the land and daylight faded into shadows, so did their conversation.

Though there were many things left to say, many things left to ask, both knew there was no proper way to say them.

When they finally reached the McRaney home, she turned to him, raised eloquent eyes, and found no words to speak other than "It was a lovely afternoon, Wes."

Somewhere in the night, a dog barked and a lonely whistle sounded, and they both felt the tug of their restrained emotions.

"Yes," he agreed quietly, "it was."

"Well . . ." Self-consciously, she gestured toward the door. "I suppose I should go in."

He nodded, tucked his hands into the back waistband

of his trousers, and rocked back onto his heels. "And I should go."

"Well . . ." she said again and half-turned, taking a step toward the well-lit steps. "Good night, Wes."

Reluctant to let her go, he followed. "Beth, wait."

She turned, hopeful, fearful. "Yes?" she whispered.

"I . . ." he began and lifted a hand in her direction. "I, ah . . ." He shook his head helplessly and swallowed. "About ye and Aaron—" Unable to complete the sentence, he dropped his hand limply to his side.

He stared at her in solemn silence. The urge to touch her grew strong. His eyes fell from her eyes to her mouth. A beautiful mouth. Not small and pouty like Gabrielle's, but full and soft and giving. Was it still giving? To his brother?

He felt a flash of shame, mixed with an intense desire to know every detail of every moment that had ever transpired between them. But as he stared down into her expectant upturned face, he found he couldn't ask her about those things.

He had no right, after all.

Wanting to stay, knowing he should leave, he searched his mind for words to alleviate the intensity of the moment, but when nothing materialized, he shook his head and only said, "I wish ye both the best."

The words choked him. They tasted bitter upon his tongue, and a heaviness settled deep into the pit of his stomach.

But she could not know that, for he smiled, made it a lopsided teaser, tipped an invisible hat, then turned on his heel and strode off into the night, while she looked after him, confused and disappointed and aching for the words she wished he'd said.

*   *   *

The warehouse was dark and damp, the lighting poor. Mice scurried. Mosquitoes buzzed and bit. But the three men who bent over the large workbench didn't notice the poor lighting, the winged or furry inhabitants, or the dismal condition of the building they'd let. Stretched out before them was a large piece of paper, and sketched upon it was the hope of their futures, the embodiment of their dreams. Those things in themselves were illuminating enough to chase away any and all other vexing inconveniences.

"Length?" Weston asked brusquely, leaning over the drawing.

Bradford absently scratched his tousled red hair and answered in quiet patience. "Two hundred twenty feet."

"Breadth?"

Weston fired the questions like gunshots, and without hesitation Bradford answered. Though at times his genius mind had been known to slip away to some unknown vicinity, such was not the case when he was designing a vessel.

Weston looked up, furrowed his brow, and said, "Not as long as the *Algoma*."

"It'll be more practical than the *Algoma*," David put in.

"And what's this over here?" Weston pointed.

Bradford followed the direction of Weston's hand. "The stairway. It'll be mahogany and will lead from the grand saloon to the upper deck."

"Whew!" Excited, Weston shoved the fingers of both hands through his hair and grinned. He clapped Bradford on his back. "It's great, Brad! Really great! How many staterooms?"

"Twenty-seven," David answered for Bradford.

"Couldn't we have more?" Weston questioned.

Bradford straightened, flushed, and raised an indignant brow. "No," he said slowly, "these will be larger than most and done in white and oiled cherry. They'll have full-sized brass bedsteads, rich carpeting, and will be airy, with plenty of lighting." Considering his answer more than sufficient and the subject closed, he bent his tall frame over the drawing once again, pointed, and continued, "Here is the dining room, over here the library—"

"The library?" Weston questioned, raising a skeptical eyebrow. "What the hell do we need a library for? And," he added with a hoot, "how do ye imagine we're going to afford such a luxury?"

Bradford pinned him with a direct stare from intelligent golden eyes. "That is David's and your problem. I'm the designer, your architect, not the financier."

Bowing to the truth of Bradford's statement, Weston accepted his words with nothing more than a good-natured shrug.

"The library," Bradford answered in response to Weston's previous question, "is for guests who might enjoy an intellectual diversion of sorts."

"Ahhh . . ." Weston nodded his approval, taking the intended jab with grace and a grin, and realizing the wisdom of Brad's planning. "I see."

David turned to Weston. "What about the engine?"

"I've already talked to the engineer at Toronto Dry Dock Company," Weston said.

"Will they build it?" David asked.

Weston shrugged. "Why wouldn't they?"

"Because we're a new company," David pointed out, his brow drawn tight. "Because we haven't proven ourselves yet. And I don't need to remind you that we're not exactly rich men."

"But they don't know that. And our principal stock-holders are rich men."

"You know," David said thoughtfully, "I'm still surprised that Mr. St. Clair threw in his lot with us even though he couldn't make us a bank loan. I never thought he'd put up his own capital. And with the other investors we've gathered . . . it'll still be tight financially. But if we're careful and nothing unforeseen arises, we'll build this ship. We'll build others, too." But ever cautious, he added, "Still, we do have plenty of competition, you know. Right here in Toronto."

A wicked grin creased Weston's cheek. Leaning toward his friend, he whispered, "So are ye scared of a little competition, David?"

David's jaw tensed and bulged. Off the roof he went again. "Certainly not! But every time I've seen my father lately, he's groaning and has his hand pressed to his chest, threatening a fatal heart attack if I should lose our money. My mother runs around ever ready with her smelling salts in hand. And my sister refuses to speak with me. It's not the competition I'm afraid of. It's my own flesh and blood."

Weston threw back his head and roared.

Bradford chuckled softly.

David frowned.

But after a few seconds, Weston felt a twinge of sympathy for his anxious friend and told him, "Don't worry, David. The lakes are big enough for plenty of steamers. Our objective is to build some of the best. And if they are, which they will be, the competition won't matter. Our work and integrity will stand on their own merit."

David nodded. "I suppose you're right."

"I know I'm right."

"So what are we going to name her?"

Weston shrugged, but Bradford, suddenly alert, shifted his gaze to his friends and said, "I would like to name her, if the two of you don't mind."

David exchanged surprised looks with Weston. It seemed odd for Bradford to take an interest in the name of the vessel. Usually his interest didn't expand beyond the architectural and internal aspect of a project. "It's fine with me," David stated.

"Sure, Brad," Weston said. "Just make sure it's a good one."

Curious, David leaned close. "So what are you going to name her?"

Bradford's eyes glazed over, and he returned his attention to his paper. "I haven't decided that yet. I'll let you know when I do."

"Abigail," Elizabeth whispered, crossing the room to stand before her bed. "They're the loveliest dresses I've ever seen." Although Elizabeth had never been one to become twittery over a piece of clothing, Abigail's exquisite designs took her breath away. She reached out and fingered the pale sea-foam-green confection, then the deep, rose-hued silk, as though they would melt away under her touch. "Oh, Ab," she said, genuinely touched by her sister's dearness. "Oh, Ab . . ."

The past five weeks had passed in a tumultuous daze for Elizabeth. Stalling Aaron had become an exhausting task as daily he grew more impatient for her answer, his kisses more ardent. Equally exhausting were her efforts to avoid Weston. Not because she was angry with him, but rather because she was not any longer. But her sister, organized sweetheart that she was, remembered what Elizabeth had forgotten: They both needed dresses for the ball. "Oh, Ab," she repeated, awed. "Whenever did you find time to make them?"

Abigail shrugged. Her cheeks were flushed with pleasure at Elizabeth's appreciative reaction. "I worked on them while you were on visitations and away with the children. I wanted to surprise you."

"And you did. Oh, my, you certainly did." Elizabeth turned and wrapped her arms around her sister's waist. "You'll put Gaby's Mrs. Grogan to shame, I'm sure."

"Well, I certainly hope so," Abigail said lightly. She smiled and whisked the green silk off the bed, then pressed it to Elizabeth's slender form and turned her toward the full-length mirror. Hands on her rounded hips, Abigail perused Elizabeth thoughtfully. "Hmmm, needs to be a taken in at the waist a little, I should think." She reached out and tugged at the already low neckline. "And lowered a little more at the neckline—"

One arm around the waistline of the dress, Elizabeth grabbed for the neckline. "Abigail!"

"Now, Elizabeth, we're not children any longer. We can lower the necklines of our dresses for an occasion such as this."

"But I have no reason to want to lower it. I have nothing to show."

"With the correct undergarments you shall."

"But what will Papa think?"

"He'll think we've grown up."

"But what will his congregation think?"

Abigail chuckled. "The same thing they thought last year when Papa decided that being Methodists didn't mean we couldn't attend balls and such. They'll think we're quite wicked. But they love Papa, so they'll get over it. Just as they did last year. Besides," she added, lifting her brows, "since when do you worry about what people think?"

"I don't know," Elizabeth answered miserably, hanging her head, remembering how horrified she'd been by her own actions toward Weston at the picnic. "It's been happening more and more lately."

"Well, never mind." Abigail dismissed the subject. "Now . . . about this waistline. I used last year's gown for a pattern, but you must have lost a bit of weight since then." She peeled the dress away from Elizabeth, tossed it onto the bed, and spun toward the dresser to retrieve her tin of straight pins. "Take everything off, Beth," she ordered. "I need to measure you."

"Now?" Elizabeth laughed, catching a measure of her sister's intoxicating excitement.

"If you're going to wear that dress tomorrow evening, we need to alter it now."

"But what about yours?"

"Mine fits fine. You'll see."

And so Abigail began—a nip here, a tuck there, another lengthy perusal, and finally a satisfied sigh.

"Perfect," Abigail announced. "Absolutely perfect."

Elizabeth gazed at her reflection in the mirror. She saw a perfect fit, in a perfect dress, with a not-so-perfect person encased within it. Hair too full and undisciplined, mouth too wide, eyelashes too short and stubby, eyebrows much too dark and dramatic. "The dress is lovely," she agreed, then whirled and raised anxious eyes to her sister. "Thanks to you. But me, Ab. I'm an awful mess." She held her arms out at her sides. "What will we do with me?" She lifted a hand to her hair. "This hair . . ."

"You needn't worry about you, darling, and I promise your hair will be lovely tomorrow. I went in to visit Mr. Simpson's store this afternoon and found some hairpins that are longer and heavier than any I've seen before. They'll be just what we need for your thick hair."

"You went into Mr. Simpson's store?" Elizabeth tipped forward and asked in amazement.

"Yes." Abigail gathered the remainder of her sewing project from the bed.

Elizabeth narrowed her eyes and leaned toward her sister. "You didn't really?"

"Indeed I did." Abigail raised her brows and answered matter-of-factly.

"Does Papa know?"

Abigail's gray eyes twinkled with merriment. "Indeed he doesn't."

"Well?" Elizabeth laughed, growing impatient for details. "Did you see the unmentionables Gaby told us about?"

"Oh, yes, most certainly."

"Well . . . what did you think? Did you find the display offensive?"

"No, actually, I thought it quite fascinating. You really ought to go and see for yourself."

Surprised, Elizabeth smiled, then sat down on the edge of her bed and chuckled.

Laying the dress aside, Abigail followed suit, then reclined onto her side, propping up her head with her hand. "You want to know what was even more fascinating?" she asked conspiratorially.

"What?" Elizabeth relaxed onto her back and turned her head in Abigail's direction.

"I saw Mrs. Caufield there, too."

"No!" Elizabeth's eyes widened in genuine surprise.

"Yes!" Abigail assured her. "I know it was her. I'd recognize that fan anywhere."

Elizabeth broke into hearty laughter, so hard that tears filled her eyes. When at last she calmed, she rolled onto her side, propped her head into her palm, and studied Abigail in quiet amusement. "Abigail, sometimes you really amaze me."

Abigail smiled indulgently. "Sometimes I amaze myself."

Weston rose from the table and turned to Mrs. St. Clair. "Thank ye for dinner, ma'am." He bowed slightly and bestowed his most disarming grin on her.

Not unaffected, she inclined her head graciously and smiled. "It's always a pleasure to have you, Weston." Like her daughter, she was a small, voluptuous woman, with glossy golden hair, always perfectly in place. Her mode of dress was fashionable and expensive, befitting the wife of one of Toronto's most prestigious bankers.

Weston extended his hand to Mr. St. Clair. "It was good to see ye again, sir."

Mr. St. Clair nodded, accepting Weston's hand. "Same here, Weston. We enjoy having you as much as Gabrielle does."

"Oh, Papa." Gabrielle blushed and rose to whisk her form around the large oval table, toward Weston. Reaching him, she took his elbow possessively and announced, "I'll see Weston out."

Outside, the air was sweet, the night sounds musical. They stood on the front porch, silently listening for a moment, then Gabrielle sighed, raised her eyes to Weston, smiled coquettishly, and said, "The ball is tomorrow evening."

Weston grinned down at her, knowing exactly where

the conversation was headed. "Yes, I know."

"Will I see you there?" She tipped her head becomingly, and waited for the invitation she was sure would come—the invitation that should have come weeks ago.

"I suppose," he answered.

"Aaron's taking Elizabeth," she stated, almost belligerently. "And David is taking Enid." She snorted and lifted her nose. "If you can believe that one . . ." Gabrielle St. Clair inwardly seethed every time she thought about David Latham. She would rather have had a face full of boils than ever let anyone know that David had actually thrown her over, claiming she had no depth of character. Imagine that!

"I can," Weston put in sincerely, in answer to her statement. "Enid is a wonderful girl."

Gabrielle wanted to grind her teeth in frustration. Did she have to hit him with a brick to get him to ask her to the ball? "And Reverend McRaney is escorting Abigail . . ."

"And ye," Weston interrupted with a knowing smile, reaching for her hand, "are waiting for an invitation from me?"

Surprised at his temerity, Gabrielle's mouth dropped open. She looked up at him, uncharacteristically speechless for several moments, then her cheeks grew beet red, and she stomped her foot bad-naturedly. "Well, I never, Weston Munroe! Why don't you just make me beg?" She plunked her hands on her full hips and strode down the porch steps toward a large pine standing regally in the front lawn.

Chuckling, he followed her. But she continued walking away from him, her shoulders swishing, and didn't stop until she had placed herself in front of the pine, where those inside the massive brick house could not see what transpired between the pair.

"Gaby, I'm sorry," Weston said to her stiff back, laughter still in his voice.

She spun and lifted large, tear-filled eyes. "Well, it's not as though we haven't been seeing quite a lot of each other, Weston."

"Yes," he agreed, "we have."

Then she almost forgot about her anger as he reached out and pulled her into his arms and kissed her intimately. She melted against him and responded with her tongue and mouth in a way that left no question that she'd had more than a little experience at this particular pastime.

It aroused him. She was a tempting piece. And Weston had no doubt that she was well aware of that fact. After several heated moments, he lifted his head and told her, "I was planning to ask ye. I just hadn't gotten around to it yet."

"Well," she huffed, refusing to relinquish her anger so easily, "it certainly took you long enough."

"I do things in my own time, Gabrielle," he said softly, rubbing the back of his fingers across her cheek, then down the length of her throat. But something about his tone conveyed a very subtle warning, and she knew she'd be wise not to assume too much where this man was concerned. He could not be manipulated quite as easily as David, or any of her other previous beaus.

He lowered his head and kissed her again, with slow deliberateness, and wondered just how far he dare take this thing. A man would be well advised to proceed with caution where this woman was concerned.

But he was young and wanting, and she was willing, so his hand strayed from her neck to her waist, then rode her corseted rib cage to her breast. She pressed herself into his large palm and sighed her compliance into his mouth, then pulled back, leaving him hungry for more, but vaguely amused as well.

"I'd better go in," she said, allowing her long lashes to drop discreetly and rest upon her cheeks.

"Yes," he agreed, but pulled her toward him once again. He kissed her again, this time deeper, wetter, but in the midst of it he found himself remembering a girl whose mouth was wider, fuller, less practiced, and whose innocent passion had sent him soaring over the edge in a way the kisses he'd shared with Gaby never had.

The next evening arrived swiftly.

The air coming in through the bedroom window was balmy, filled with the heady fragrance of late-summer perfume. The red sun dipped low, the last remnants of daylight fading, but the sky stubbornly remained blue. Yet the silver moon and stars already waited, pinned high above, anxious for their moments of unified glory.

Elizabeth stood before the mirror, corseted in her pretty new petticoat, staring at her reflection. Her waist was minuscule, her small breasts pushed high. She had curves! Hell's bells! Could you believe it, she had curves! Not the full curves of Gabrielle's voluptuous form, or the soft curves of Abigail's shorter, rounder figure, but curves nonetheless. Amazing! Elizabeth found the transformation of her body nothing short of miraculous.

Behind her stood Abigail. Their eyes met in the mirror, Elizabeth's anxious, her sister's quiet and comforting.

This would be their second summer ball. Last year's ball had set the stage for Elizabeth and Aaron's courtship. This year would set the stage for their future.

But she did not think of Aaron on this night.

Abigail, her cheeks bright with excitement, was already dressed, her lovely hair coifed to perfection. Her rose silk gown clung becomingly to her soft, rounded form, gently accentuating her femininity.

"Abigail," Elizabeth said sincerely, turning to her, "you're quite beautiful, you know."

Abigail smiled. Touched, she whispered, "Thank you, Beth."

Then, thinking of the night ahead, of dances to come, of sun-bleached hair and lake-blue eyes, Elizabeth's voice softly begged what her heart secretly ached for: "Make me beautiful, too."

CHAPTER
8

Elizabeth stared at her reflection for several disbelieving seconds: rose-colored lips, pink cheeks, glossy upswept hair, a lightly powdered chest, all above a slender hourglass figure that was elegantly encased in the palest of green-silk dresses. The gentle transformation Abigail had wrought made her feel special and enchanted, and for once almost beautiful. "Oh, my . . . Oh, my . . . ," she whispered over and over.

From behind, Abigail chuckled softly.

Their eyes met in the mirror. Abigail stepped close to lay her cheek against Elizabeth's, careful not to disrupt one iota of her handiwork.

"Oh, Abigail," Elizabeth whispered. She touched light fingertips to her face and peered into the mirror to get a closer look. "You're a miracle worker, do you know that?"

"Oh, nonsense." Abigail waved a hand, brushing the compliment aside, and crossed the room to her bed.

Straightening, Elizabeth looked down at her chest and frowned. She pressed both hands to her breasts, flattening

113

them. "I feel like I'm going to pop right out of this dress. If I bend over like this," she said and tipped forward at the waist, "it could be most embarrassing." Yet the dress held her firmly, though the corset pushed her up and out, baring much more flesh than she'd ever deemed possible on one as small as she.

"I don't think you need to worry about it," Abigail responded dryly behind a mischievous smile. "There's really not all that much to pop out."

Elizabeth straightened and whipped around. She tipped her head to the side and quipped, "Well, thank you very much for reminding me, Abigail."

Although Abigail seemed unaffected by her sharp statement, Elizabeth was immediately repentant; for it was neither Abigail nor her good-natured remark that had made her so tense. Under normal circumstances, Elizabeth would have shared in the humor of the state-ment. But this night was not normal. Though she felt more attractive than she ever had before, she also felt increasingly vulnerable. Her expression softened, and she lifted remorseful eyes to Abigail. "I'm sorry. Really I am." She squeezed her lids together, pressed both palms to her trembling stomach, and silently wondered, *What will he think when he sees me?* Then she immediately scolded herself with *What does it matter what he thinks, you silly twit.*

He will be with Gabrielle. The thought pricked sharp-ly.

And she would be with Aaron. Ah, but that's the one that got her every time.

Aaron: her future husband. Aaron: his brother.

"Ready?" Abigail asked, understanding only too well her sister's anxiety. From the bed she retrieved a light crocheted shawl for each of them.

"I suppose," Elizabeth answered, then crossed the room, her skirts swooshing musically with her movements, "I don't think I have much choice, do I?"

"No." Abigail smiled. "You don't. I didn't spend all this time working on you for nothing." She held out a shawl, then, as an afterthought, she halted, her expression almost plaintive. "Beth . . ."

"Mm-hm?"

"Would you do something for me?"

"Of course," Elizabeth answered immediately.

"Don't hit anyone with anything tonight if you can avoid it . . . all right?"

Elizabeth's eyes grew round as harvest moons, her expression one of genuine innocence. "Why, Abigail, I wouldn't even dream of it."

Their moods much lighter, they descended the stairs.

In the parlor, Aaron waited patiently with Reverend McRaney. Dressed impeccably in black evening clothes and a snowy-white shirt, top hat in hand, he turned to greet the two women as they entered the room. But all words died upon his lips. Astonished, he let out an audible whoosh, as he looked from one sister to the other.

The rapt attention brought a flush to both women's cheeks. But whereas Elizabeth met Aaron's eyes with her usual direct stare, Abigail's discomfort was noticeable. She dropped her gaze discreetly.

Tristan chuckled softly, proud of his lovely daughters, but especially pleased with Elizabeth's graceful transformation. For once she was indeed the picture of a well-bred lady, from the top of her head to the bottom of her toes. He wondered with stoic amusement how long it would last. "Well," he said, clapping the younger man on the shoulder, "shall we take our ladies to the ball and show them off?"

Aaron nodded, cleared his throat, and found his voice. "Most definitely."

And so, as twilight fell, the four rode through the dusk-laden city toward Front Street West and the elegant Queen's Hotel.

Horses' hooves clicked rhythmically upon the cedar-blocked streets. The streets were full and teeming with carriages, carrying a diverse amalgamation of people— Toronto's gentry, prominent officials, middle-class residents, young fashionables—almost all headed for the same destination as the McRaney entourage.

In time, Tristan halted the carriage among a sea of other arrivals in front of the regal hotel. It was a grand structure with its silvery spray of running fountains, elaborate gardens, and carefully tended gravel walks.

After stepping down from their vehicle, Elizabeth halted and turned. For a moment she stood transfixed, watching with fascination the carriages arriving before the hotel in quick succession, depositing their lovely freight at the entrance door. Her gaze swept them all, carriages and faces. But not finding the one she sought, she turned, stifled the welling disappointment, and allowed Aaron to escort her through the entrance door.

The ballroom was brilliantly lit, a room brimming with opulence and taste. On the walls mirrors reflected many a pretty face radiant with hope for the evening ahead. Above, handsome chandeliers, draped with long festoons of verdant wreaths, hung in graceful sweeps, while the scent of countless flowers mingled with that of the finest perfumes.

At the very front of the room a raised platform held a superb piano, a harp, and several other instruments that would provide the music for many a lover's waltz before the evening ended. While the guests filed in, the string quartet readied themselves and tuned their instruments to perfection.

An intoxicating merriment reigned supreme, as everyone arrived—almost everyone. Mrs. Caufield and her ladies were not present, for they did not believe in the frivolity of such "carnal" events. But Mrs. Munroe was present, along with young Daniel; Franklin Fuller and his parents and younger sisters; David and a remarkably pretty Enid in lavender satin; Mr. and Mrs. St. Clair; Bradford Stevens and his twin sister, who was every bit as tall and lanky, freckled and carrot-topped as he; the mayor and his wife; Rose and Michael Boswick; and Gabrielle and Weston . . .

Weston.

Elizabeth felt her pulse halt.

Ah, but here was a different Weston. No worker or seaman's clothing this night. He looked elegant and handsome in tailored black evening wear, his shirt as snowy white as his brother's, his shoes polished and smart, his hair still a bit long and carefree, but attractively neat, and bleached as golden as ever.

Elizabeth's heart launched into motion and beat out a tremulous warning; her palms grew damp.

Don't look at him, she told herself, pinching her eyes shut for a moment. If she didn't look at him, everything would be all right.

But her warning was to no avail.

She could look at no other. Beside her, Aaron squeezed her elbow affectionately.

She opened her eyes and met Weston's across the room.

Never had she been more aware of him. Never had

she been more aware of his brother at her side.

Gabrielle stood beside Weston, exquisite in her expensive yellow silk, her bearing regal. She waved gaily, grabbed Weston's elbow, and pulled him toward the other couple. Reaching them, she gushed, "Oh, Elizabeth, there you are! I wasn't sure you'd arrived yet! The streets were so crowded! For heaven's sake, you'd think the Queen was going to make it after all! I thought we'd never get here! I simply can't stand to be the last one to arrive. I—" She halted mid-sentence, her mouth agape, while she scanned her friend with careful scrutiny, her eyes widening in surprise. "Well, gracious, Elizabeth! Whatever have you done to yourself? You look . . . so . . . so . . ."

Her words hung in the air like a swarm of annoying gnats.

Elizabeth felt her cheeks flame. She dropped her gaze self-consciously. Pick, pick, pick, the thumb worked the cuticle. She wanted to melt. Feeling terribly conspicuous, she wished herself oceans away from this ball, from these people, from Weston Munroe.

"Beautiful," Weston put in softly, finishing Gabrielle's sentence. Then louder, his voice deep with stark sincerity, "You look beautiful, Elizabeth."

"Indeed she does," Aaron proudly agreed.

Elizabeth's gaze snapped to Weston's, fully expecting to see an open challenge written there.

But what she saw was much worse, much more dangerous.

Sincerity! Damn him!

He'd never called her beautiful. Pretty, yes. But beautiful! Well, hell! He'd never called her Elizabeth, for that matter. Always Beth, Lizzy—a thousand other childish names, anything, anything, but Elizabeth.

So why now? she wondered, fighting a conglomeration of turbulent emotions.

His use of her given name brought an intense awareness of their adulthood. While searching his eyes, the knowledge of their maturity deepened the crimson flush on her cheeks.

Behind her, Abigail blessedly lifted the tension by laughing lightly and adding to Weston's statement. "Yes, our Elizabeth is very beautiful tonight. But then, she always is." Gracefully she abandoned the subject and turned to her father. "I see someone we need to speak to, Papa." She took his arm and led him away, giving the others the opportunity to move on should they desire.

Elizabeth did so desire. Oh, did she ever.

But apparently Aaron felt no such compulsion. Instead he said, "Weston, I've been so busy lately I haven't had a chance to ask you how things are going with your project."

Weston shrugged negligently. "Everything's fine. Brad's a genius. Without him, I'm afraid David and I would be lost. We've begun construction. Ye'll have to come down and take a look. We've accomplished much in a very short time."

"I'll do that," Aaron promised. Then to Gabrielle he said, "And you, Gabrielle. You look most lovely tonight."

The petulant expression on Gabrielle's face lifted somewhat, and she allowed her heavy lashes to droop prettily, placated that someone had finally acknowledged her beauty, even if it wasn't the man she intended to marry. "Why, thank you for noticing, Aaron. You always were the perfect gentleman."

Her jibe was deliberate and obvious, but Weston found himself more amused than irritated. Gabrielle was obvious in everything she did. He'd known that from the beginning.

From the platform the orchestra began a waltz. Couples drifted toward the center of the room. Others visited, while a group of prominent older men gathered together and stepped outside to smoke cigars. Aaron slipped his arm around Elizabeth's waist and asked, "Shall we?"

Her throat still tight, she tore her eyes from Weston and nodded her acquiescence, deeply grateful for the reprieve. At least now she wouldn't have to look at him. At least now she would have some time to gather her composure.

Beautiful . . . He'd called her beautiful. Damn him to bloody hell!

An hour later, Reverend McRaney passed his youngest daughter into the hands of a perspiring Franklin Fuller and retired to a quieter place along a wall. Though certain officials and members of his congregation did not approve of his participation in the dancing, participate he did. He'd always loved to dance, but there was a time long ago, when he'd first entered the ministry, that he'd shunned such simple pleasures. In doing so, he'd deprived his young wife of many of life's innocent joys, and somehow he'd lost sight of a part of himself as well. Now, older and wiser, he was determined this would not happen to his daughters. If he'd learned anything over the years, it was that tolerance was much closer to godliness than cleanliness would ever be. And maybe most importantly, he'd learned it wasn't how saintly a man had been while living his life, but rather how well he loved and was loved in return.

So despite a few disapproving glances, he tapped his toe in rhythm to the music, sipped a cup of punch, and remembered with nostalgic tenderness the young, gay girl who'd stolen his heart many years ago at a ball very much like this one.

A good two hours passed before Elizabeth felt herself begin to relax. Though she'd never been much of a dancer, she danced with Aaron, her father, Franklin, Bradford, David, and several others.

But not Weston.

Gabrielle hadn't released him from her clutches for so much as a single moment.

But a little while later, during a particularly lovely piece of music, while Elizabeth was dancing with young Daniel, Abigail swept by in Weston's arms. Perfectly attuned to each other's movements, both were wonderful dancers. Elizabeth felt a rush of pride in watching them. When they passed, Weston grinned, while Abigail winked and smiled, obviously enjoying herself.

Elizabeth searched the room for Gabrielle and, finding her, stifled a chuckle. She was cornered by Franklin and another young man, and was making no effort to hide her irritation and boredom.

"I don't think Gabrielle is very pleased to lose your brother," Elizabeth said to Daniel.

"Aw, she's a pill," Daniel complained, grimacing, his eyes level with hers.

"She's quite lovely," Elizabeth remarked honestly.

"Yeah, so. She's also a bore," Daniel returned, unimpressed. Then he widened his eyes, batted his own long blond lashes, and mimicked, "Oh, gracious, my hair is such a frightful mess! I simply can't stand windy weather! It just destroys everything! It blows my brains right out through my ears!"

Elizabeth's lips twitched as she fought back a smile. "She's really not that bad, Daniel."

He leaned close and whispered, "You're a helluva lot more fun than she is, Beth."

Elizabeth tipped her head back and allowed the laughter to come. "Well, thank you, Daniel. You are a true poet with your compliments."

The second time around, Abigail pulled her partner to a stop. "Daniel," she exclaimed brightly, "I've been waiting all evening to dance with you!"

"You have?" Daniel's cheeks grew sunset red.

"Indeed I have!" Abigail replied, spinning away from Weston and out onto the floor with a befuddled but flattered Daniel.

And so they stood face-to-face, in the midst of swirling dancers, two hearts beating with uncertainty. They could walk off the floor or dance with each other. Which would it be? Which would be the least conspicuous? Which would be the least painful?

He held out his arms. She went into them stiffly.

"It's good to see ye, Lizzy," he said with a grin, hoping to lighten the mood.

She didn't answer. What could she say when what she wanted to say could not be said properly?

His hand on the small of her back, he felt her tenseness, her hesitancy, and understood only too well, for inside, his own stomach was quivering. It had been so long since he'd touched her. So very long. He'd held her only briefly the night on the island, the night she'd run away from him. Since then, he'd held her only in the secret recesses of his heart, in the forbidden corners of his memory.

Their movements were stiff and slow, lacking the grace and fluidity of the other waltzers.

But neither noticed.

Their silence seemed exclusive—exclusive of the

music, of the laughter, of the presence of all others.

But eventually even the silence seemed empty, and both felt a need to fill it.

"I—" she began.

"How—" he said at the same time.

Her eyes lifted to his.

Silence again, then very softly he said, "I meant what I said, Lizzy. Ye do look beautiful."

Her gaze danced away to a place over his shoulder, while she tried to concentrate on the movement of her feet.

One, two, three. One, two, three. All she needed was to end up on her backside. Ignoring his statement, she remarked, "You said things are going well with your ship?"

Okay, he thought, stung that she wouldn't acknowledge his compliment. Fine! If she wanted to play this game, they'd play it to the hilt!

"Quite," he bit out, his jaw tight.

"Good."

They danced on, the silence thick, the tension palpable.

"Well," she said at last, only too aware of the warm width of his hand across the small of her back. "I'm glad for you."

"Yes, well, if everything goes as we hope it will, I'll have something to leave my sons one day."

Her eyes lifted and lingered on his face. His sons? His and Gabrielle's? The thought was piercing. She struggled to keep her voice impersonal. "But you'll have a part of your father's company, also."

He shook his head and smiled crookedly. "I'll have my own company. And I'll make my own way. Aaron's the oldest. He's the one who's kept things going since

Father's illness. The company should belong to him and his sons. Daniel's, too."

Skirts swished by, music enveloped them; an obviously plagued David passed by with Gabrielle, while Enid waited patiently against the wall. But all ceased to exist for Weston and Elizabeth, as they gazed at each other with thundering hearts, and remembered . . .

They should be our sons. Yours and mine. His hand tightened on hers.

It's too late, Wes. Her heart constricted. *It can never be.*

Panicked, she pulled away and frantically searched the room for Aaron. Aaron, her anchor.

"Elizabeth, wait," Weston said, reaching for her.

But she pivoted away from him and said, "Aaron's waiting. I have to go."

In defeat, Weston acknowledged that truth. He stared at the straight, stiff line of her back, instantly sorry for having upset her, for he'd had no intention of doing so tonight and wasn't quite sure how he'd managed it. Yet he had.

Dejected, he smothered his disappointment and searched the room for Gabrielle. But she was still dancing with David. So he scanned the room for Enid. He found her, standing against the wall, her patience wilting into self-conscious uncertainty. Feeling a surge of understanding and compassion for her, he crossed the room, offered her his hand, bestowed on her his most sparkling smile, and led her out onto the floor.

"It's quite warm in here," Aaron remarked a few moments later. He set his goblet down on a linen-covered table.

"Yes," Elizabeth agreed, feeling slightly claustrophobic. From Aaron's side, she watched Weston sweep a now confident and laughing Enid around the dance floor for the fourth time and realized there was much, so very much, she had not bargained for in judging this older Weston.

His kindnesses were much more disconcerting than his boyish thoughtlessness had ever been.

He wasn't a boy any longer.

A few moments later a harangued David decided to unload his burden and reclaim his partner. Gabrielle was back in Weston's arms. They were a sight to behold, for there wasn't a more handsome couple in all the Queen's. So when Aaron suggested they step outside to the gardens, Elizabeth readily agreed.

They escaped the crowded ballroom and followed the gravel walk toward the private garden east of the hotel. Crickets sang their choruses out into the night, while a legion of sparkling fireflies faithfully kept their vigils.

The fragrance of late-summer flowers hung sweetly in the evening air. Above, the moon was full and bright, a luminescent guardian.

A lover's moon, Elizabeth thought, gazing up at the glowing orb.

But for whom? she wondered.

They stopped beside the cast-iron fountain. She stared into the tinkling waters and breathed deeply of the fresh night air, wishing it were proper to loosen her corset.

"Better?" Aaron asked quietly.

"Oh, yes. Much better," she answered truthfully. "It's so close inside."

They stood silent for the space of several heartbeats, he anxious, she apprehensive.

Gazing down at her, he thought her lovely. Almost

as lovely and ladylike as her sister. "Elizabeth," he said at length, then took her by both arms and turned her to face him. In the moonlight, his face was handsome and earnest, his eyes ardent. "Elizabeth," he repeated, "I want to marry you. I don't want to wait much longer. Please say yes."

She thought about his patience, his kind nature, the day he'd tried to save the bird for herself and Abigail. She thought about Weston, about Gabrielle in his arms, about the fact that the two were spending more and more time together.

And she thought about the constant danger of his nearness, and before she could change her mind and stop the words, she whispered, "All right, Aaron. All right, I'll marry you."

"Oh, Elizabeth," he muttered, his expression one of pleasure and surprise. "That's . . . that's wonderful." His hands moved up her arms to her shoulders, then around to her back. Through her dress, he lightly caressed her shoulder blades. Then he slowly pulled her closer.

She felt the heavy thudding of his heart and waited for her own to trip and respond as their stomachs touched. But it didn't. Yet when he lowered his head to hers, she didn't have the heart to turn her face away. His chest pressed into her breasts the same instant his lips grazed hers, and she allowed her eyes to drift shut. He opened his mouth and touched his warm, wet, tongue to her lips. She jerked at the unexpected intimacy, but he held her fast and urged her mouth to open to accept his offering.

"Please, Elizabeth," he uttered into her mouth, his voice hoarse, "please allow me this."

And so she did. Forgetting propriety, her young body as hungry as his, she thought of another and lost herself in the brief forbidden thrill of the moment.

His mouth opened wider, and his tongue tangled with hers. He groaned and shuddered and spread his hands upon her back; then one traveled to her waist and kneaded the tight flesh there for a slow moment before riding her rib cage up to her breast.

"Elizabeth," he whispered hoarsely, his hand closing over the small mound. The sound of his voice pierced her consciousness, reminding her of who she was with and what she was doing, and with the reminder came a flood of guilt and reason.

She drew back quickly and met his eyes, shame washing over her. "No, Aaron. Please. We mustn't do this. Not yet."

His face registered hurt, immediately followed by remorse, for he had not intended to take such liberties with her. "I'm sorry," he said, meaning it. "I'm truly sorry. I didn't mean to . . ."

Touched by his sincerity, she raised a palm to his cheek in a gesture as tender as any lover's caress. "Oh, Aaron. It's all right . . . Really it is."

He swallowed and embraced her, holding her close for several passionless seconds, then whispered into her hair. "I would never want to do anything to offend you, Elizabeth. I care for you far too much to ever do that."

She accepted his brotherly embrace, returning it with a heartfelt one of her own.

A moment later, they broke apart, carefully avoiding each other's eyes, both feeling awkward and ambiguous.

Then they turned toward the hotel, toward the welcoming strains of music, toward the sanctity of a bright ballroom, toward the safety of friends and family, away from the moon, the flowers, and the rampant confusion they both felt—neither one noticing the telltale scent of nearby cigar smoke that drifted on the soft night wind like a silent, unacknowledged sigh.

CHAPTER
9

Several hours later, Elizabeth lay awake.

She stared at the dark ceiling, listened to Abigail's steady breathing, and in her mind recalled the evening's developments over and over: Aaron's proposal, her acceptance, the boldness of his kiss, the words he'd spoken, and most importantly, those he hadn't . . .

"I want to marry you, Elizabeth," he'd said. "Please say yes." But as she searched her mind, she realized that in all the time she'd known him, he'd never said, "I love you, Elizabeth. I need you."

It seemed odd to think she'd overlooked this fact. Yet she had.

Were those words so important? she wondered.

Yes, she thought sadly. At least, they should be.

They'd both agreed to wait until tomorrow to tell their families about the engagement. She knew she should be happy now that the decision had been made. But all she felt was a vague, hollow resignation.

She sighed heavily and turned onto her side, cradling her cheek in her palm. She watched the shadows play across the wall and recreated every moment of the dance she'd shared with Weston: the earnest way he'd looked at her when he'd called her beautiful, the way he'd said her name, the way his hands felt, the exact color of his eyes, his exasperating, crooked smile, the way his dimples deepened . . .

Weston weaved his way down Queen Street. He was angry. And more than a little drunk.

After ungallantly depositing Gabrielle at her door, claiming fatigue, not bothering to claim a kiss, he'd gone in search of David, a tavern, and as Mrs. Caufield would call it, "the Devil's draught."

"Where are we going?" a partially unclad David had asked from his parents' door.

"To a tavern," Weston answered tersely.

"Which one?"

"I don't care."

"But why?" David lifted his hands in question. After all, they'd just returned from a ball.

"To get drunk," was Weston's short reply.

"Yes, I figured that much. But why?"

"Because I damn well feel like it, that's why!"

"Aw, hell, Wes," David said regretfully, "I don't feel like—"

"Fine!" Weston turned and jumped over all four porch steps to the ground. "I'll go alone."

"Aw, Wes . . ." David took a reluctant step after him. Sighing in defeat, he knew he'd best get dressed. It was late, and too many things could happen to a man alone at this hour. As in any city, there were desperate unsavory characters who ventured forth at night, hoping for an opportunity to waylay a lone, well-dressed gentleman. Especially one well into his cups. "All right," he said in resignation. "Just give me a minute."

Now, several hours later, David lay in his bed, bruised and wretchedly ill, wondering how he'd ever allowed himself to be manipulated into such a foolhardy escapade. They'd gone out to the Red Lion Tavern, which was located in the very center of the old village of Yorkville. Although the tavern was quite a ways out, it was a comfortable place for a man to drown his sorrows unobtrusively. It was crowded nightly with farmers who, over their glasses, discussed the future prospects of the country and the political questions of the day.

Seated in a dark corner, Weston became drunk as a lord, encouraging David's reluctant participation.

Once they'd both achieved a completely inebriated state, Weston made the mistake of teasing a big Scotsman about his overly bushy beard. Unfortunately, the Scotsman, who had fists as big as hams, had a much smaller sense of humor.

Under normal circumstances, Weston could have handled himself and the situation quite well.

These were not normal circumstances, however.

Like the loyal friend he was, David had hurried to Weston's aid, and though they both carried the evidence of the Scotsman's wrath, it was David who continued to suffer as his stomach irascibly objected to his actions.

Meanwhile, Weston found himself heading toward the source of his frustration, completely oblivious to the pain in his jaw, his swollen eye, and the soreness of his joints, his brain focused on only one thought.

He'd seen them!

He'd seen her kissing Aaron, caressing his cheek, allowing him liberties that had once belonged to Weston alone. And they were doing it right there in the gardens, right under his and everyone else's nose!

Damn her anyhow! She hadn't wanted to accept his compliment, but she was accepting a hell of a lot more than a compliment from his brother!

By God! He'd give her a piece of his mind if it was the last thing he did! Then, if it was Aaron she wanted, she could bloody well have him.

He didn't give a damn!

Forget her, Munroe! he told himself illogically, trying to focus on the direction in which his body was lunging.

He walked on, his thoughts as unsteady as his steps; for it had not occurred to him, either in his intoxicated state or in his previously sober state, that he was being unreasonable or that he was acting out of blatant jealousy.

Not that it would have mattered if it had.

Tap!

Elizabeth awoke suddenly, her eyes flying open.

She lay still, staring into the darkness, toward the open window. She waited a few moments, then, hearing nothing more, relaxed and allowed her eyes to drift shut once again.

Tap!

There it was again.

This time she sat up in bed. She glanced over at Abigail, who lay peacefully undisturbed.

Tap!

She threw off the covers, rose from the bed, and crossed the floor cautiously, her long white nightgown sweeping the floor behind her. Reaching the window, she bent forward and peered out the opening.

Another stone whizzed by her nose, hitting the pane above her, missing her head by only a few inches.

Startled, she drew back, but not before she saw the culprit.

He stood beneath the oak tree, gazing up at her belligerently, minus his evening jacket, shirtsleeves rolled up, one palm pressed to the trunk, one foot hooked over the opposite ankle.

"Welllll," he drawled thickly, not bothering to keep his voice low. "If it ishn't 'lizabeth, the beautiful."

"Weston," she snapped, hiding her surprise, "what are you doing down there?"

"Wouldja rather I come up there?" He cocked his head and leered up at her suggestively.

"Certainly not!" She prudishly clasped the high neckline of her nightgown in both fists.

He hiccuped loudly, pushed himself away from the tree, and wavered, then launched into his own rendition of a bawdy sailor song, lewd enough to make even Elizabeth's ears burn.

"Shhhh," she hissed, cringing at the thought of her father waking, "you're going to wake Papa and Abigail."

But he ignored her, howling all the louder, his eyes shut tight, his chin tipped upward toward the stars.

She released the neck of her gown and leaned over the edge of the windowsill to get a better look at him. Narrowing her eyes suspiciously, she grasped a sturdy branch from the large oak outside her window and braced herself so she wouldn't fall over the edge. "What the hell is wrong with you, Weston?"

He waved his arms and belched. "Nothin'. Jus' came fer a little visit."

She eyed him with growing suspicion for several seconds as realization sunk in. "Why, Weston Munroe, you're intoxicated!"

He tipped back his head and gazed up at her, frowning. "Certainly not," he stated, slapping a wide palm to his chest and almost toppling over with the effort.

"And you've been brawling!" she exclaimed, studying his half-closed eye and puffy jaw.

"The hell you say!" he retorted, affronted. "I'm not intoxi—" He hiccuped, weaved, and burped. "—cated, I'm downright dirty drunk! And you should see the Scotsman, he—"

"Oh, for heaven's sake, Weston," she said, her voice thick with disgust. "Are you all right?"

"Of course I'm—"

"Do you need a doctor?"

"No, I—"

"Then go home and sleep it off!"

"Don' wanna sleep. Wanna talk." He gestured her down. "Come on down, Lizzy Beth."

"Are you insane?" Her voice rose two octaves higher than normal. Her brows dropped low, and she gazed at him as though he were the most recent escapee from the Provincial Lunatic Asylum. "I most certainly will not! Papa could wake at any moment!" Reminded of that possibility, she waved him away and lowered her voice to a vehement whisper. "Go home, Weston!"

But instead he chuckled wickedly and broke into another song, this one lewder and louder than the other.

Mortified, she drew her head in to glance at Abigail. But all was silent and still within the bed across the room.

Elizabeth leaned back out the window. Her braid fell forward and began to loosen, her long hair escaping.

"Will you stop," she exclaimed shrewishly. "You sound like a wolf baying at the moon! You never could sing! Not even when you were stone sober!"

He halted mid-sentence, his face registering indignation. "Neither could ye if I 'member!" he shot back, stung by her remark.

"I know that! That's why I don't stand outside someone's window in the middle of the night howling like a banshee!"

He grew silent, his foggy mind considering the logic of her statement for several moments, while she reflected on the absurdity of their conversation, still uncertain as to why he had come to her home at such an ungodly hour.

"Weston," she said wearily, pushing a wayward strand of hair out of her eyes, "what is it you want?"

Good question. He scratched his chin, then winced at the tenderness there.

He tucked his hands into the waistband of his trousers and stared at the toes of his shoes silently, while he tried to remember. Then it hit him in a flood, and his anger returned, renewed and hot. He tore his hands loose and pointed a finger up at her. "You! I saw you!" he accused, his words amazingly sober.

Confused, she shook her head. "What are you talking about?"

"Tonight . . . with Aaron . . . in the garden at the Queen's. I saw you!" His words were as clear and cold as ice.

Her face grew warm. She was thankful for the darkness that hid the telltale color from him.

"I don't know what you're talking about," she snapped, fighting the prickles of guilt that rose at his accusing words.

"The bloody hell you don't!"

"I don't!" she lied.

He crossed his arms over his broad chest and glared up at her through his good eye. "How long did ye wait before ye let him have his way with ye, Lizzy?" he asked coldly, carefully masking the hurt that rose at the thought of the two of them together.

She stared down at him incredulously for several moments, trying to think of an intelligent response, but none came forth, nothing but an aggrieved denial. "He hasn't had his way with me," she whispered, wounded, her anger diminishing in the face of his low opinion of her morals.

"Hmph!" he snorted.

Stung, she felt her indignation return fourfold. She leaned out of her window so far that if she hadn't been supporting herself with the branch, she would have tumbled to the ground. "You listen to me, Weston Munroe!" Her voice was sharp and caustic. "You left me five years ago with a promise! A promise you didn't keep!"

"I—" he tried to interrupt.

"What I've done or haven't done while you were gone or since you've returned is none of your damned business! I don't owe you any proof of my chastity or any explanations about my behavior!" Then for good measure she tipped her head to the side and snidely added, "And need I remind you that when I was doing it with you, it was fine! 'It's all right, Lizzy! Enjoy it, Lizzy! There's nothin' wrong with it, Lizzy!' " she mimicked, then narrowed her eyes and jabbed a finger in his direction. "What the hell have you been doing for five years, Weston? Don't even try to tell me you haven't touched another woman. I know you better than that. And I'm quite certain whatever you've been doing with

Gabrielle St. Clair since you've returned couldn't even be discussed publicly without Mr. St. Clair launching into some very hasty wedding-preparations!"

She ended her tirade and glared down at him. How dare he have the audacity to accuse her! He, who stood there, his purple jaw hanging open, peering up at her, one eye swelled almost completely shut.

With an arrogant toss of her braid, she added, "I'm not going to discuss this any further with you, Weston. Now, go home!" She ducked inside the window and closed it with a solid bang, frigidly dismissing him, momentarily forgetting the other occupants of the household.

He stood silent as a shadow for several seconds, then, finally finding his voice, he yelled back, "Like hell I will!" His jaw bulging, he stared up at the closed pane of glass. Who the hell did she think she was letting loose on him like that and not giving him a chance to defend himself? Damn it all if she hadn't turned into a cold little piece. "Ye come down here right now, Beth!"

Silence.

"Now!" he ordered.

Silence.

He let loose with a long string of mumbled obscenities, then stared up at the limb above his head, gauging the distance he would have to jump to reach it.

Having made his decision, it took him three awkward attempts. But eventually he lay atop it, hugging it desperately, waiting for the liquor-induced nausea to pass before attempting to climb farther.

When finally he felt steady enough to go on, he decided to give her one more chance. "If you don't come down, I'm coming up!" he warned, hoping she would relent. He really didn't feel like climbing this tree tonight.

"Oh, good heavens," Elizabeth muttered, realizing that he meant what he said. She pressed her shoulder blades to the wall beside the window and peeked through the pane to see him clinging precariously to the tree limb closest to the ground.

"Here I come!" he announced and began to slowly inch his way upward.

"Lord have mercy," she moaned.

"You'd better go down and talk to him, Beth," Abigail whispered from beneath her covers.

Startled, Elizabeth jumped. "I thought you were asleep."

"Who could sleep through all that noise?" Abigail peeked out from beneath the quilt. She yawned widely and rose up on an elbow. "It's been a long time since he's climbed that tree, and he's likely to fall out and break his neck as drunk as he is."

In heavy resignation, Elizabeth leaned her head back against the wall. "Papa's probably awake by now, too."

"Probably not. His bedroom is on the other side of the house, and he's a much heavier sleeper than we are. But if Weston falls and starts hollering, he's liable to wake even Papa eventually."

"I know. You're right. I suppose I have to go down and talk to him."

"I suppose so," Abigail agreed. Then she dryly stated, "It would be difficult to explain his dead body beneath our window."

"Oh, Abigail. That's a morbid thought." From outside came a muffled curse and the quarrelsome rustle of leaves. "But a terribly satisfying one." Before the mental picture could become a reality, Elizabeth reached down, lifted the hem of her nightgown, separated front from back, and tied them into a large knot between her thighs. Then she lifted the window and climbed out into the dewy night air.

Once comfortably perched on a limb, her bare legs hanging beneath her, she looked down at the mussed blond head of her tormentor. "Get the bloody hell out of my tree, Wes, before you kill yourself! I'm coming down!"

He'd been so engrossed in keeping his balance, he hadn't noticed her appearance. Hearing her voice, he searched for her through a heavy cluster of leaves. Then, finding her, his eyes raked her naked limbs, and he grinned smugly. "I knew ye'd see it my way."

It seemed like forever before he managed to work his way down the few branches he'd climbed. Elizabeth watched him in disgust, certain he'd hurt himself, but at last he managed to drop unceremoniously to the ground. Her blood boiling, she began her agile descent.

When she reached the lowest limb, just as she was prepared to leap, he offered her his hand. But she slapped him aside, and dropped lightly to the ground before him. Uncomfortable in the face of his leering grin, she wasted no time in loosening her nightgown, allowing the hem to fall to her bare feet. Then she planted her stance firmly, crossed her arms over her chest, and demanded, "Why won't you go home and leave me alone?"

He stepped closer, his eyes remarkably focused as they examined her face. "Is that what ye really want, Lizzy?"

"Yes!" she snapped coldly. "I want you to go home. I want you to leave me alone. I want you out of my life!" But as he came closer, the light of the moon shone upon his beautiful battered face, and Elizabeth felt an unwanted rush of sympathy. "Oh, Wes," she scolded, fighting the urge to reach out and touch his swollen eye, "your face is a mess."

He shrugged, then grinned and chuckled. "Ye should see David."

Her brows drew tight in reproof. "You didn't take David out and get him beat up like this, too, did you?"

"Well," he answered in all innocence, "I didn't exactly plan it that way."

"Oh, Wes . . ." She sighed. "You're incorrigible."

They stood wrapped in a blanket of silence for a long moment, each forgetting the anger that had propelled them only minutes ago.

It was Weston who finally spoke, sounding almost sober now, as he eloquently searched her eyes. "Elizabeth . . . I'm sorry . . ."

She shook her head, her gaze darting away to a safe spot along the ground. Elizabeth again. This unfamiliar sincerity he'd adapted of late was a terrible thing. It was the one aspect of his personality she didn't know how to deal with.

"About what I said . . . about ye and Aaron. I had no right."

"No," she agreed softly, refusing to meet his eyes, "you didn't."

Several heartbeats passed. Their breathing seemed forced, and the moment became fraught with awareness.

The cool, gentle breeze coming off the lake sobered him further, and he studied her silently while he struggled with his conscience. She stood in nothing more than a nightgown. He'd seen her in less, but seeing her now, with her hair defiantly escaping the bonds of what was left of her braid, with all traces of the evening's garnishing gone, her face clean and clear and painstakingly young, had far more impact on his control than he'd ever imagined it could. Her shoulders were hunched forward, as though she were suddenly self-conscious with him, and he realized at that moment that he loved her, had always loved her.

But his brother loved her, also.

He thought about the unfairness of the situation, which he had to admit was his own fault. He was the one who had gone away. He'd been the one to break his promise. He thought about honor and duty and loyalty and Aaron. About his goodness, his faithfulness.

Despite their differences, he recognized that Aaron was the most trusting and trustworthy person he knew. Wes thought about the good times they'd had while growing up, the many times they'd stuck by each other.

He thought, *I'm sorry, Aaron,* as he closed the small distance between himself and Elizabeth, reached for her, and pulled her roughly into his arms with a fierce possessiveness.

"He's my brother . . . I love him . . . But when I saw ye with him," he whispered into her hair, "it did something to me. I—"

She held herself stiff within his embrace, trying to quell the tremors that moved through her body at his touch, searching her mind for the right words, only to say, "I care for him, too, Wes."

He held her tightly, moved by her trembling, desiring her as he had no other woman, while she hesitantly returned his embrace with growing need, felt the hallowed cadence of his heart against her own, and whispered his name over and over in her mind like a blessed benediction.

He smelled of rum and smoke, but it was the familiar scent of him, the scent that made her pulse leap and rush through her veins like a spring-fed brook, that offered her a deep sense of fulfillment. She'd missed it so.

His hand rode her back to her shoulder and then to her neck. He grasped a handful of her loosened hair and tipped her head back, not asking or waiting for her acquiescence.

Her eyes slipped shut, and she waited, aware of what she was doing, knowing it was wrong, knowing she needed it, at least this once.

His lips brushed hers lightly—so lightly, so reverently, she lifted her mouth to enhance the contact. But he withdrew slightly and left her wanting. She opened her eyes in question, to find him studying her, his blue eyes dark and intense. Then his head descended once again, and she felt the silky touch of his tongue on her bottom lip. He drew her lip in, tugged gently, then trailed slow circles over the remainder of her mouth.

She moaned softly, reached her hands upward, grasped his head in her hands to bring him flush, and accepted his greedy kiss with the healthy response of her own.

It was the same, yet wonderfully different. No longer the inexperienced, experimental kisses of their youth, this joining was fuller, deeper, richer, more lustful, more intense.

He released her hair, and his wide hands traveled her ribs, moved upward to her breasts, and, finding them, he held her gently in his palms, silently marveling at the differences that had been wrought in her body, the fullness that had developed in his absence.

His thumbs lightly caressed her taut nipples through the thin material of her gown, while he felt his own want for her grow and threaten to undo him.

She felt the heat of his touch and knew they should stop. But his touch was magical, a wondrous drug she'd ached for, hungered for, for so very long. And unlike the

kiss she'd shared with Aaron, this one created no need
to wait for her heart to trip and run, no need to think
of another. The image of the proper lady she wanted
to be vanished, and the uninhibited young woman she'd
always been surfaced.

Insatiably they sought and found, savoring each other
with breathless abandon.

His hands traveled down, over the soft dip of her
waist, over the gentle swell of her hips, around to her
buttocks, clasping her, pulling her in close to his pelvis,
allowing her to feel the extent of his need for her. Then
he grasped both sides of her nightgown in his fists and
inched it upward.

"Aw, Beth," he whispered against her mouth. "There
hasn't been a night I haven't thought of you, haven't
wanted you. Is it like this with him? Can he make
you—"

His words and the rush of night air upon her bare
thighs brought sanity. Aghast, she pulled back. *My God,*
she thought. *Aaron.* Aaron, her betrothed.

She drew back, and sensing the change in her, he
expelled a ragged breath, released her nightgown, and
watched it drift to the ground at her feet.

"Wes," she whispered softly, her hazel eyes anguished.
"What are we doing?"

"I think it's pretty obvious," he replied, his voice
quiet, puzzled at her sudden withdrawal.

"It's wrong. We can't. It's not just you and me anymore. There are other people involved. Aaron and Gabrielle—"

"Gaby's nothing to me, Beth."

Elizabeth swallowed thickly. "She's my friend. I've
known her all of my life. I care about her, and I think
she cares for you very much."

He shook his head in denial.

"And Aaron is something to both of us."

This he could not deny.

He reached for her, but she backed away. "I want ye, Elizabeth," he said, his bruised jaw working. "I . . . I love ye—"

She shook her head vehemently and reached out with her fingers to cover his lips and stop the words she'd once longed to hear. He'd never said such words to her before. To hear him say them now sent a pain, sharp and sweet, to the very center of her being. "Don't," she whispered. "Please don't, Wes. Not now."

"Why not?" he asked, his expression pained. "I know I'm not like Aaron. It'll be a long time before I'm financially stable. And I'm not proper. I never was. Ye know that. I don't dress elegantly. And I'll never be a romantic man who woos ye with perfume and poetry and says all the right things," he said earnestly, drawing closer, "but the most romantic thing I can think of is holding ye close every night for the rest of my life."

Elizabeth drew her breath in sharply, her bottom lip quivering as tears threatened. For several seconds she struggled to say the words she knew must be said, and finally they obediently came in a very quiet, very resigned, voice. "It's too late."

He held out his hands to her and shook his head, his brow knitted tightly. "It doesn't have to be. I'll make him understand. Ye haven't accepted him yet—"

"Yes," she interrupted sadly, lowering her eyes. "I have."

CHAPTER
10

Those two words brought a deep silence.

Weston's arms dropped to his side, and he stood before her, wordless, for what seemed like an eternity. And when at last she could stand it no longer, her eyes lifted to his.

"When?" he asked at last, his voice low.

"Tonight . . . Tonight in the garden."

She watched the emotions play across his face: first surprise, followed by frustration, and lastly, stoic acceptance. She thought about her mother, the years of suffering her father had endured, and wrestled with emotions that were far too complicated for her to define.

Whom had she betrayed? Weston or Aaron or both?

She longed to reach out to him, to explain somehow. But how could she explain what she couldn't fully understand? All she knew was that she was pledged to Aaron, and, by honor, bound to him, no matter what her feelings were toward Wes.

What had been between her and Weston could be no longer.

They both knew it.

By unspoken agreement they did not touch. Weston finally spoke, his voice tight and restrained. "You'd better go on up. It'll be dawn soon."

The night wind ruffled his hair, and a lock fell across his forehead. She fought the urge to reach out and brush it back. Instead she nodded the agreement her burning throat could not verbalize, then reached down and tied her nightgown the way she had when she'd made her descent.

He averted his gaze respectfully, laced his fingers together, and stepped close, offering her the means by which to reach the branch above their heads.

She hesitated only a moment before placing one bare foot into his rough palm and one hand upon his sturdy shoulder—wanting with all her heart to fling both arms around his neck and tell him that she loved him, would always love him.

He hefted her easily, and she reached for the limb, grasping it, as though it alone were the source that could save her. Then she swung her body up into the tree.

He looked up after her. "Go on," he said, hooking his hands on his hips. "I'll wait until you're inside."

Tears stung; her chest hurt. She shook her head. "You don't have to—"

"Go on, Beth," he insisted, looking away, wishing she'd hurry. "Just go on."

She began to climb as though the hounds of hell were after her. But when she reached her window, she turned, looked down at him, and choked out, "I'm sorry, Wes. I—"

He refused to look at her. "Me, too, Lizzy," he said softly, turning away, anxious to go before the light of day could reveal the depth of his pain. "Me, too."

It took a while, but eventually Elizabeth cried herself to sleep.

But as feathers of pink dawn stretched illuminating fingers into their room, another lonely figure lay awake, huddled deep beneath her covers, blinking away the hot tears that threatened to reveal her secret.

It was time to go back to the city.

Summer had faded into a golden memory, and the final weeks of September marked the end of the children's sojourn at the Lakeside Home.

Mary Grace had said her good-bye to Benjamin several days ago, for it would be June of the next year before she would return to resume her weekly visits.

She would miss the old man terribly.

He, her favorite fragrance, a few other personal items, and her Sunday evening vigils were the only links she'd kept with her past.

All were unequivocally precious to her, and she held them close to her heart.

As she and Mrs. O'Rourke helped the children into the long line of carriages in front of the island ferry docks, she found herself looking forward to resuming her weekly routines.

"It'll be good to get home and get settled," she said to the older woman, while she tucked a blanket around the thin, useless legs of a little girl. "There, Victoria." She patted the child's frail hand. "How's that, darling?"

Victoria smiled, grateful for the concern that came from the kindly woman, when no such kindness came from the family who would not care for her.

"Aye," Mrs. O'Rourke agreed. "There's a chill wind comin'. I can feel it in my bones already. The island's too cold for this old woman in the winter. Take me back to the city, where the buildings can shield me and the lake winds aren't quite so fierce."

Mary Grace nodded and smiled. But she grew still and her smile faded as she looked off into the distance, silently acknowledging the muted evidence of summer's end. "The seasons pass quickly, don't they?" she remarked wistfully.

Mrs. O'Rourke halted her movements and lifted wise, understanding eyes to the younger woman. "Indeed they do, child. Indeed they do."

Gabrielle St. Clair preened before the mirror for the sixth time that morning.

A product of her parents' adoration, she was an only child on whom they lavished all their love, along with anything else her heart desired.

She turned sideways and admired her lovely new outfit. It was a deep forest green, a hue that brought out the color of her eyes. She tugged at the snug-fitting jacket with the embroidered scalloped neckline, and smoothed the front of the fashionably tied-back bustled skirt, then sucked her stomach in, watched the high swell of her breasts, patted her midsection, and noted that she'd better leave off eating so many of Mama's pastries. Her waistline was the first part of her anatomy to show signs of overindulgence.

But nevertheless she was indeed beautiful, and it never hurt to be reminded of that fact. The problem was she was so beautiful that she sometimes worried about what was going to happen when the time came—and she was no fool; she knew it would—that her beauty diminished. It had happened to Mama, but she had been lucky enough to be married to Papa, who loved her regardless of her outward appearance.

Would she be so lucky with Weston?

That she didn't know.

What she did know was that she wanted him. She wanted to live with him in the grandest house in the richest section of Toronto, among the city's most elite gentry. She wanted to shop in only the finest stores on King Street and Victoria Row. She wanted to dine in only the most elaborate establishments, where luxury and taste were available only to Toronto's golden.

He wanted those things, too.

He just didn't know it yet.

Which was why she had coerced her father into taking her with him this morning. She knew he visited Weston weekly to report to the other stockholders on the progress of their investments. So what better opportunity to put herself right under Weston's nose and remind him of what he could have for the asking!

He'd been unusually distant lately. For several weeks, in fact. Ever since the night of the ball, she'd felt his interest waning. Oh, when they were alone, she could still arouse him, but she was beginning to feel that even that was something he could take or leave without any significant sentiment either way.

It stung her to make that admission, even to herself.

She'd thought about laying a trap for him by allowing him the final intimacy. Then he would have to marry her. But knowing Weston, she wasn't sure "have to" belonged in his vocabulary. So she couldn't bring herself to take the risk. After all, she was a young lady with certain moral values. And if by some unlikely chance he was not the man who would become her husband, she wanted to save herself for the man who would.

She deserted her reflection, crossed the room to her bureau, and snatched up a hat that was the exact shade of green as her clothing.

"Come along, Gabrielle!" her father called from below. "I've only a short time this morning, then I must get back to the bank."

"You needn't chaperone me, Papa," she said, pulling on her dainty gloves while hurrying down the mahogany staircase. "Weston can see me home."

"I doubt Weston will want to take the time. He works right along with his men. He won't be wanting to stop and clean up in the middle of his day just so he can escort you home safely."

Well, we'll see about that, she thought as they made their way out of the house and down the steps to the carriage.

In the cool autumn air, they rode through the awakening city and on to Front Street, to follow the line of the shore along the harbor front.

They passed a young woman who wore an odd garment, much like a pair of trousers, but instead of reaching to her feet, the garment ended just below her knees. Swerving around them, she peddled a strange, awkward-looking contraption that had a seat and two wheels on either end of a steel frame.

"Hmmm," Mr. St. Clair remarked with interest. "Curious-looking invention, isn't it?"

Gabrielle snorted disdainfully.

"I believe she was riding a bicycle," he observed.

"That will never last," Gabrielle said dryly.

"Oh, I don't know. We live in a world of progress, daughter. So many new inventions. Edison's phonograph and electric lights and . . . Who would have thought our city would have electric lights?" He waved an arm. "But it does. Ninety-one to be exact." He shook his head. "Imagine that. Ninety-one electric lights. Someday," he said thoughtfully, "gas lighting will be obsolete. As for these bicycles . . . I've heard they're quite popular in the eastern sector of the United States."

Gabrielle raised haughty brows. "Well, I can't imagine any woman wanting to make a spectacle of herself in such a manner. The only female I know who might dare such a vulgar thing would be Elizabeth!"

Mr. St. Clair nodded. "Ah, yes, Elizabeth."

"Riding those . . . those things and wearing trousers. Before you know it, women like her will be wearing gentlemen's clothing as though it were the most natural thing in the world."

Usually a man of vision, Mr. St. Clair chuckled, lit his pipe, and slowly savored the flavor. "Now that," he said derisively, "I truly can't imagine."

They found the wharves and docks along Toronto's shoreline teeming with life.

September brought a deluge of ships carrying imports into the city; at the same time, the anticipation of the coming winter sent exporting schooners out while Lake Ontario's waters were still friendly and the winter wind had yet to blow its icy breath across the lake.

Still, Toronto's harbor was less icebound than any other Canadian harbor on the lake. Only during deep winter was the ice heavy enough to keep a ship from sailing.

And though the railway had begun to take over the waterfront during the 1870s, and was beginning to change the outline of the harbor with extensive landfill, lake shipping remained as busy as before, symbolizing trade and commercial prosperity, essential to the growth and survival of Canada's exuberant child: Toronto.

Gabrielle and Mr. St. Clair found Weston outside a large building, supervising the arrival of some of the materials he'd been awaiting. Shirtsleeves rolled up over muscular forearms, he worked as hard as any man he employed, expecting no less from himself than from them.

Seeing their approach, he wiped an arm across his sweaty brow and waved. "Mr. St. Clair, Gaby, hello!"

Mr. St. Clair stopped the carriage, climbed down, and moved around the vehicle to offer his daughter a hand, while Weston took a ragged cloth from his back pocket, cleaned his hands as best he could, then turned to his men and said, "Rest for a while, men. I'll be back in a few minutes."

"Weston," Mr. St. Clair said with a smile, extending his hand, "how are things going?"

"Fine, sir. Just fine."

Gabrielle wasted no time with such an unimportant question. She sidled up to Weston, affected a pout, and remarked, "I thought you'd be joining us for dinner last evening."

Weston shrugged carelessly and grinned. "We worked late last night. Brad and I had some things to go over."

"Well, let's see what you've done." Mr. St. Clair strategically changed the subject and moved toward the building. "I don't have much time this morning." He glanced at Gabrielle to make sure she understood his meaning. He loved his daughter dearly, but he was well aware that she was a spoiled, sometimes self-centered, individual. He laid the blame at no one's door but his own. Unable to have more than one child, he and his wife had indulged her far more than was wise. And they both knew she would need a strong, patient man for a husband. He held no illusion that Weston Munroe was that man, even though he knew she believed differently. No, Weston did not have the quiet tolerance that his Gaby would need. But Gaby would have to learn that for herself.

"As ye can see," Weston said, leading them into the large warehouse, "many of the interior materials have arrived. Thanks to David, his father has supplied us with most of our lumber so we needn't worry about quality."

He took them through a tour of the building. The lighting throughout was poor, but the place was clean and organized, with a distinct air of busyness and purpose. A vast number of workers milled about, quietly intent on their various projects, all content to be employed by these three fair-minded young men.

"The engine won't be here for some time yet. We expect it mid-spring at the latest. Bradford"—he waved toward the tall man, who, with his brow furrowed, stood immersed in deep concentration over his sketches—"estimates we'll be ready for service by late summer of next year."

From across the warehouse David spotted the trio and waved a greeting. Then he deliberately resumed his conversation with one of the carpenters.

"What are you going to name it?" Mr. St. Clair asked conversationally.

Weston shrugged and propped his hands on his hips. "I'm not sure. Ye'd have to ask Brad. He requested the honor."

They joined Bradford at his worktable. He didn't seem to notice their arrival, and continued to make quick marks with his pencil on the drawing before him.

But never one to be ignored by anyone, Gabrielle peered over his shoulder to see what could hold his intention so raptly while she stood so near. "Gracious,

Brad. Whatever are you drawing?"

He didn't answer. Minutes ticked by while Weston folded his arms across his chest and watched in silent amusement. He had come to recognize her antics well.

"Bradford!" she exclaimed with growing impatience. "You're being quite rude!"

Slowly he lifted his eyes from his drawing and turned to her. It took him a moment, but finally his golden eyes lost their faraway look and focused. "I'm sorry, Gabrielle. I was working," he said calmly.

Insulted, she stomped her dainty foot, her green eyes flashing. How dare he ignore her in such a bold manner! Her eyes coldly raked his tall form, from the top of his bright hair, down his lanky frame to his dusty boots, then back up again. The only other man who'd ever been able to treat her that way and get away with it was Weston, and there were times she truly hated him for it.

Bradford continued to study her, his eyes probing, though compassionate and kind. His gaze flicked over her figure once with hasty disinterest, then returned to her face immediately. "I am sorry, Gabrielle. When I'm working, I tend to become very involved in what I'm doing. Please don't take it personally."

She returned his clear gaze for a brief moment, but soon grew uncomfortable beneath the intensity of it. As the moments passed, she found herself uncharacteristically speechless.

There was something unusual about Bradford. He could see into her. She was sure of it. Right into the very depths of her soul. She had the strangest sensation that somehow he knew things about her no one else did.

And she didn't like it at all.

How was it she'd never noticed this quality about him before? Then she realized.

Though they had grown up together in the same city, had attended the same school, in all the years she'd known him, she'd never, not even once, spoken directly to him.

She'd never thought him worthy of that much of her attention.

The realization brought a stinging sense of shame and confusion. Coloring, she turned her head, dismissing him, rudely ignoring his kind apology. She could have handled his interest and appreciation of her finer assets. Even rudeness from him would have been more acceptable, since that was something she understood.

But kindness from a man she'd always thoughtlessly ignored?

What an unforgivable affront.

The rest of the visit was taken up with Bradford and Weston's explanations of the complexities of the project to Mr. St. Clair.

Still upset by the inner revelation Bradford had exposed, Gabrielle had to remind herself of the reason she'd come for this visit.

"It's hard to imagine," Bradford said, hooking his pencil behind his ear and leading them outside to a great iron skeleton set up on a series of heavy timbers stationed on a flat piece of land along the shore, "what goes into the construction of one ship. When we're finished, I'm estimating we could use over a thousand tons of steel, as well as over a hundred tons of iron, in the construction of the hull, the two largest castings, not counting engine castings, and the two cylinders that could weigh as much as fifteen tons each. We'll also need about eighty tons of rivets. And in the cabins, decks, and other woodwork, I estimate fifty thousand cubic feet of timber, along with several tons of nails, fifteen tons of paint, and probably thirty barrels of oil to finish the hull alone. As for the boilers . . ."

On and on he talked, his voice quiet and confident, while Gabrielle tried to refuel her anger toward him.

But somehow, as they examined the monster that would soon become a ship, she found herself releasing her earlier irritation, overlooking the fact that no one had noticed her beautiful outfit, momentarily losing sight of her plan to trap Weston into seeing her home, and finding to her amazement that she almost enjoyed listening to Bradford's esoteric explanation of the shipbuilding process.

October brought a blaze of color: flaming maples, the rich gold of western aspens and cottonwoods, cast against the eternal beauty of the emerald-green Canadian pine forests.

The air was fragrant. Beyond the city, the lake lay blue, the sunlight dancing like sparkling fairy dust upon its satin surface. Far, far out, white sails billowed.

The faint perfume of decaying leaves hung in the air like a promise, reminding all that this brief Indian summer day would soon give way to winter's chill.

Elizabeth walked along the bank, gazing at the shore, with Aaron at her side. He held her hand loosely in his own.

She wore a proper high-necked dress, her skirts tied severely back, the color of the material so dark a blue it was almost the hue of a midnight sky.

A light wind caressed their faces, bringing with it the pungent scent of pine needles, while above them seabirds loudly protested their presence.

Aaron had discarded his overcoat this day and was dressed casually in gray trousers and white shirt. He halted his steps along the bank and lowered himself to the ground, gently pulling Elizabeth down into the grass beside him.

He rested his arm across one bent knee and drew a slow circle in the center of her palm with his thumb. "Elizabeth, it's been almost six weeks since you said you'd marry me. It's time we set a date, don't you think?"

Though her dress was restricting, she knelt on her knees before him, met his pale gaze, and nodded, knowing it was foolish to have thought she could delay him indefinitely.

"Would late winter be all right with you?" he asked quietly.

He was so kind, always so considerate. Her heart flooded with affection and compassion for him. "Winter is so cold, Aaron. I think late spring would be much better," she offered, desperately hoping for those few extra months of freedom. "Winter is always so busy with Christmas and the New Year's visits. And Abigail and I organize the Christmas program and celebration for the children, you know, and then there's the caroling and . . ." On and on she rambled, hoping to deter him by offering what she hoped were viable excuses.

Disappointment marked his face, and he studied her silently for several seconds as though he would somehow discern her true motives. Then, unexpectedly, he tugged her hand, pulling her close. His arms went around her, as his mustache brushed her lips. His mouth found hers, and he kissed her hard, surprising her with his intensity. His tongue parted the seam of her lips and demanded entrance.

She allowed it, thinking only of the differences between the two brothers, knowing in time she would have to allow this brother more, much more than mere kisses.

When at last he drew away, he cupped her chin between his thumb and forefinger, looked deep into her eyes, and asked, "Is there any other reason you would want to wait, Elizabeth?"

She averted her eyes. "Oh, Aaron . . . I only want us to be sure . . ."

"I'm sure," he interrupted, his expression registering his hurt. "I've always been sure. You and I . . . we care for each other. We want the same things . . ."

But do we? she thought. *Do we really?*

His voice grew softer. "Or is it that you're afraid?"

She lifted her eyes to his, and knit her brow. "Afraid of what?"

"Of what happens between a man and a woman?"

Her cheeks grew warm, but she did not lower her gaze. "No, Aaron," she answered truthfully. "I'm not afraid." She simply couldn't quite visualize the act with him, an act she had easily visualized a thousand times with his brother.

He smiled, relieved. He did not want her to fear what was right and natural. "Then late spring it is."

"Late spring it is," she repeated softly, wishing the words could bring an ecstatic joy instead of a calm acceptance of what felt like an impending lifetime sentence.

He kissed her again, this time with gentleness.

She tried to quiet the little voice that taunted, *He's not Weston. He never will be.*

She knew that.

He'll never hang beneath your window and howl at the moon.

She knew that, too.

You don't love him.

But she cared for him.

Would that be enough?

She pinched her eyes shut, tentatively returned Aaron's kiss, and with sad finality, thought, *This will have to be enough.*

CHAPTER
1 1

Gabrielle burst into the kitchen like a wintry cyclone, bringing with her a blast of icy air and the first feeble sputterings of early November snow. "Elizabeth! Abigail! Have you heard?" she asked breathlessly.

Both women turned away from the bread dough they were kneading and fixed their attention upon the girl who stood shivering in the open doorway, her dainty nose cranberry red.

"For heaven's sake, Gabrielle," Elizabeth said calmly, untying her apron, "close the door before we all freeze to death."

Abigail wiped the flour from her hands and crossed the room to close the door. She took the excited young woman's muff and wrap and hung them on a peg. "Come and sit down. We'll make some tea, and you can tell us what it is you're talking about."

But Gabrielle couldn't wait for tea. She launched into an almost senseless summary before her bustled bottom even hit the edge of the chair. "It's absolutely horrible!" she exclaimed, the tone of her voice bordering on hysteria. "A tragedy. So devastating. Weston and Papa said it happened when she left Owen Sound on her usual run on the fifth. Two days later she ran into a terrible blizzard on Lake Superior. Somehow she became lost in the blowing snow and struck Greenstone Rock on Isle Royale and broke in two just forward of the engine room. The forward end foundered in deep water and—"

Concern creased Elizabeth's brow. "Slow down, Gaby. What are you talking about?"

Gabrielle's hands fluttered in exasperation. She rolled her eyes dramatically. "The *Algoma*! She went down! They believe as many as thirty-eight lives may have been lost!"

The two sisters lowered themselves into chairs, while the room echoed a stunned silence. Finally Abigail managed to whisper, "How awful. How truly, truly awful."

Gabrielle nodded, and her eyes filled with genuine tears, alarming both girls. Gabrielle rarely displayed such artless emotion. Her voice grew shaky as she wrung her hands. "Franklin Fuller was aboard." A sob broke from her chest. She lowered her chin to her chest. "They haven't found him yet."

"Oh . . . ," whispered Elizabeth, stunned, remembering the shy young man. She dropped her forehead into her hands. "Oh, my . . . Oh, my . . . How terrible for his family. Poor Franklin." She knew this sadness firsthand. She'd felt it, lived it, experienced it. The waiting was excruciating, and for her it had never ended. They'd never found Mama's body. While she sat contemplating the tragedy, its sadness enhanced by her own poignant memories, she realized how fortunate they were that Weston had not met the same fate. All those years spent at sea, and yet he'd come home safely.

"I should have been kinder to him." Gabrielle's full

bottom lip quivered. "But I was so cold. I'm sure I made him feel as though he didn't matter at all. And he was new to our crowd. I could have made him feel more comfortable, like he belonged." She swallowed and sniffed noisily. "If they find him alive, I'll be ever so much nicer to him—"

Abigail patted Gabrielle's hand consolingly. "There now, Gaby. You mustn't take on so."

"I may not have wanted him for a beau. But I liked him . . ." Her eyes flicked from Elizabeth to Abigail, desperately hoping they would offer her words of exoneration. "Really I did."

Elizabeth understood her need. "Of course you did."

"And I wouldn't wish anyone dead."

"We know that, Gaby."

They consoled their friend as best they could, plying her with tea and eventually a piece of apple cake, and several hours later, they bundled her warmly and sent her off into the leaden afternoon before twilight fell.

Elizabeth looked thoughtfully at her sister. Abigail's eyes mirrored her own sorrow and bewilderment. "I've never seen her react in such a fashion."

Elizabeth turned back to the rising bread dough. "Sometimes it's harder to grow up when you're already grown."

"Hmmm," Abigail murmured reflectively, joining her at the table. She dusted her hands with flour, then rubbed her palms together. "I never thought of it that way, but I suppose you're right." She fell silent, immersing herself in her work. "I hope they find Franklin."

"Me, too." Elizabeth placed a plump loaf into a greased pan.

"It's awful not ever knowing for sure."

"Yes . . . it is . . ."

"Well," Abigail said with a deep sigh, "the Fullers could use some fresh bread, don't you think?"

"I think they would appreciate it very much," Elizabeth answered, her eyes lifting to her sister's. "I know we did."

For several days afterward, the city mourned the lives lost in the wreckage of the *Algoma*. The news reverberated throughout the cities along the shores of the Great Lakes, bringing sadness and a shared mourning among those who understood—as only sister cities could—the loss of one of your own.

Gabrielle had been correct. There were thirty-eight deaths in all.

But Franklin Fuller was not one of them.

By some divine intervention, he survived to tell his story, and when he returned home to Toronto, he became one of the city's most sought-out personages, who no longer needed to worry about shyness or loneliness.

True to her word, Gabrielle treated him with a newfound respect and kindness that surprised everyone except Abigail and Elizabeth.

Franklin's survival served as a healing balm and helped to lift the gloom that had fallen over the city at the news of the tragedy. And the colder weather and the advent of the Christmas season brought an abundance of indoor as well as outdoor gatherings.

Life went on.

When finally it snowed significantly, Elizabeth sought out the congregation's children. Of all the unmarried ladies her age, they loved Elizabeth best. Together they built snowmen, often ending their excursions with unrestrained snowball battles, which Elizabeth won easily.

"Not fair," little Johnny Marsh would cry. "You always

could throw better than anybody else. Even better than my big brother, Tom."

She would laugh and allow him a small victory, while bittersweet memories of the one who had taught her such feats surfaced.

The children, as well as Elizabeth and Abigail's circle of friends, checked the ponds and the harbor weekly, anxious to see if the ice had frozen thick enough for skating, knowing it would most likely be weeks before they'd be able to do it safely.

One evening in late November, amid all the seasonal activities, Sarah Munroe held an engagement party for Aaron and Elizabeth.

This was the inevitable event Elizabeth had been dreading.

She'd not seen Weston but for a brief passing since the night of the ball. She heard he'd been busy. She also heard he was still spending time with Gabrielle, though she didn't know how much. Discussing Weston with Gabrielle was something she carefully avoided.

Yet, despite her misgivings about the night ahead, she knew they could not avoid each other interminably. After all, they would be part of the same family. They would share the same name.

This daunting thought brought a jumble of turbulent emotions.

She dressed carefully that evening in a dress she was sure would meet with Aaron's approval. It was a high-necked gown of jade and cream, with a fitted bodice above a softly gathered skirt. Abigail, blessed Abigail, had become most adept at arranging her hair, and tonight, once again, it was decorously tamed.

All of their friends and family had been invited to the gathering. The Munroe house was quite elegant and plenty spacious enough to accommodate such a crowd.

When the McRaneys arrived, Sarah Munroe embraced Elizabeth warmly, welcoming her to the family. From across the room, seated in his wheelchair, Aaron's father feebly nodded his agreement. But it was sadly apparent to all that his health was failing fast. In his prime, he'd been a large, blond, handsome man of considerable height. But since his stroke, he'd shriveled into a mere ghost of the man he'd once been.

After depositing her coat, scarf, and muff, Elizabeth left her father and sister at the door and crossed the room, taking a seat on a small settee beside the sickly man. Her father had often said that Everitt Munroe in his younger days had been an aggressive, sometimes brash, young man. Very much like Weston . . .

For Everitt Munroe had a dream, also.

He was the second son of a pair of hardworking Irish immigrants. His father bought a piece of land north of the St. Lawrence Valley and successfully farmed it well enough to clothe and feed his four sons. But Everitt wanted more than to farm his father's land. As a young man, he'd hauled the produce to town, selling it to the highest buyer he could find along the wharf. Then he'd spend the remainder of the day watching the ships come in and go out, and he'd dream of someday owning a shipping company of his own.

By the time he was twenty-seven years old, his dream had become a reality. A year later, he married his childhood sweetheart, Sarah.

Elizabeth had always been especially fond of him. Though he'd been a stern father to his sons, he'd been a comrade of sorts to her. "How are you feeling, Mr. Munroe?" she asked.

He blinked and attempted a smile. The right side of his

face complied, but the left remained completely expres-
sionless. Yet his eyes, every bit as blue as Weston's,
were clear and sharp, revealing the keen mind that lay
imprisoned within the slowly deteriorating shell.

She leaned close and asked, "Do you remember the
time you caught me throwing apples at Mrs. Caufield's
house?"

Again, another half smile.

"I never thanked you for not telling on me."

His hand crept up the arm of his chair and slowly
turned over, offering her his wide palm.

She placed her hand in his. The once strong fingers
closed tentatively around her own, squeezing lightly,
while his eyes sparked amusement.

"And the time I managed to get my skirts caught in
that big oak tree in the churchyard? You helped me to
get loose without tearing them." She leaned closer and
kissed his lined cheek. "You saved me from an awful
thrashing that day, I'm sure." Her voice grew soft. "I've
never forgotten."

His eyes sunk shut, and he laid his head back to rest,
but not before she saw the telltale glint of dampness.

She sat with him in companionable silence for several
minutes and sensed he would not be long in this world;
she wondered which son would suffer the most at his
departure—Aaron, the steady, obedient one; Daniel, the
youngest; or Weston, the adventurer, who was so much
like this man.

Aaron eventually claimed her attention. "I'm sorry,
Father," he said regretfully, with a smile. "But I'm afraid
I'm going to steal her away for a little while." Then to
Elizabeth, "I have an aunt who's visiting from New York
City I want you to meet."

So she met Aaron's aunt, his uncle, and a multitude

of cousins she didn't know existed, then they greeted the rest of the arriving guests.

Gabrielle arrived late. She was her usual giddy self, chattering on about any flippant idea that flew into her head. But a few moments later, when Bradford and Weston entered the room, she grew unusually silent and uncharacteristically restrained. Though she was dressed in her usual expensive finery, the dress she wore this night was a bit more conservative and refined than her usual attire.

Not long afterward, dinner was announced.

Weston had been conspicuously absent for most of the evening. He knew it was best that way. Best for him, Beth, and his brother. He'd managed to keep himself immersed in work during the past two months, but the cold weather had begun to slow things down a bit. He found himself growing restless with his thoughts and memories.

If there was one thing he didn't need, it was free time to think.

When they were all seated around the large table, Aaron rose. Smiling, he swept the faces of all present with his gaze, all the faces of the people closest to his heart. "I want to thank all of you for coming. Of course, all of you know you're invited to the wedding, which will be held the last Sunday in June." He nodded his head in Reverend McRaney's direction. "I'm hoping the reverend will agree to officiate for us." He turned and focused on Weston. "And while my brother is here and I can pin him down, I want to ask him to be my best man."

Weston's smile froze for a flicker of an instant, but he recovered quickly, before anyone noticed.

But Elizabeth had noticed, and her heart turned over.

Oh, Lord, she thought despairingly. As though this wasn't hard enough as it is.

Weston rose. He picked up his glass and did the only thing he could. He bowed to Aaron and said, "I'd be honored." Then he held up his glass in a toast. "To my brother and his future bride."

Concurring murmurs sounded throughout the room, but Elizabeth's mind closed them out. Over his glass, Weston's eyes met hers. What she read there drove a spike to the very center of her being, and she wondered how she would ever manage to get through this night as his brother's fiancée, let alone the rest of her life as his brother's wife.

After dinner, Weston disappeared. The small orchestra began a series of waltzes. With forced gaiety, Elizabeth danced the first with Aaron, then several more with David, one with a rather clumsy Bradford, and two with her father. Finally claiming fatigue, her face hurting from constant smiling, she managed to retire to an abandoned corner to watch the festivities.

Aaron was dancing with Abigail. Elizabeth couldn't help but notice how lovely her sister looked tonight in her lavender silk. Her eyes were bright, her cheeks flushed and rosy. It was good to see her enjoying herself once again. She'd seemed withdrawn lately. Elizabeth had attributed it to the news of the *Algoma,* for Abigail was a sensitive soul, always one to suffer for the tragedies of others.

Which was only one of the reasons Elizabeth loved her. Not only was she outwardly beautiful, but Abigail McRaney was inwardly one of the most beautiful people she knew.

Someday, Elizabeth thought, Abigail would make a very fine wife to a very lucky man.

When Elizabeth was certain her exit would go unnoticed, she located her cloak and slipped out the back door. She stood alone in the cold, black night, staring up at the lucid November moon, wishing she could make sense out of her emotions. *Oh, Mama,* she thought, her heart heavy. *Why did you have to go? I need you so. I need you here with me, as you were before* . . .

The sky was awash with the heavy dusting of countless sparkling stars. The wind shuddered and shook the clacking tree limbs. Drawing in a long draft of chilly air, she shivered and gathered her coat closer, then walked a short distance away from the house. She stopped beneath the arbor, and through the twilit gloom she gazed at Sarah Munroe's rose garden. The bushes reached barren arms upward, the blooms now gone, having long ago dropped away.

"So ye really intend to go through with it?" His voice came from behind and filled the empty night air.

Startled, she pivoted, her heart hammering. She stared at the outline of his familiar broad shoulders, knowing without question to whom the voice belonged. "Yes." She forced the word out of a tight throat. "Yes," she said again, stronger this time.

He stood without protection of an overcoat, feet spread wide, hands in his pockets. He stepped closer, searching her face through the moonlit darkness.

He was tall, several inches taller than Aaron. Why was it, she thought sadly, that every time she was with one or the other brother she played this silly comparison game?

She tipped her head back to meet his stare, knowing she must stand her ground, certain it would be a mistake to vacillate about her decision.

"Ye're happy, then," he asked in a low voice.

Oh, that damn sincerity again. She swallowed, nodded, and lied, "Very."

A blast of cold air buffeted them, blowing his hair back from his forehead. She tried to read his expression, but found she could not.

"I wondered," he said. "I wanted to be sure."

"You can be." Her voice sounded strange to her own ears. She lowered her gaze to the windswept ground.

"Ye know I love ye." The wind caught his soft-spoken words and flung them in her face.

She lifted melancholy eyes to him. "And we love him," she said. "We both love him."

He nodded while he fought the urge to reach for her. His heart felt swollen. He damned himself a thousand times for ever having left her, knowing nothing in the world—nothing he could attain, nothing he could build or accomplish—was worth this pain—or worth the loss of the one woman he loved more than his life. He wished he'd been man enough to realize that five years ago.

Footsteps sounded, and a moment later Aaron's voice came to them. "Elizabeth! Wes! Are you out there?"

Her eyes pleaded for understanding. "Yes, Aaron!" she called out. "We're here in the garden!"

He joined them, his shoulders hunched forward, his chin tucked down into his heavy coat. "What are you two doing out here? It's freezing!" They turned to him, away from each other, while his eyes searched their faces for a moment, and he wrestled with an uncomfortable prick of uneasiness.

Then Weston grinned lazily, put his arm around Elizabeth's shoulders, squeezed hard, and alleviated his brother's uncertainty by saying, "Just giving Lizzy some advice on how to deal with my stuffy older brother, that's all." He released Elizabeth and extended his hand toward Aaron. "I wish ye all the happiness in the world, Aaron." He squeezed Aaron's hand hard. Then he turned on his heel and, with long determined strides, walked back toward the house.

CHAPTER
1 2

A few days later, on a cold Wednesday morning, Elizabeth took the electric railway from Yonge Street to King, then on to Church and Front.

Toronto was the first city in Canada to boast this new mode of travel. When first introduced to the city, it was expected by some to be a failure. But despite previous doubts, it had become an ultimate success, used by many, providing an exhilarating ride, and especially appreciated by the city's more adventurous citizens.

Elizabeth sat on a hard seat in back of the car, her hands wrapped into her furry mit, while she mentally reviewed her shopping list. The car rocked rhythmically, clacking noisily over the rails, blending in with the other early-morning sounds of an awakening city.

Vendors lifted their blinds and dressed their windows, preparing for holiday sales.

Hawkers, stationed on street corners, dressed in their heaviest winter garb, called out to passersby, urging them to purchase their wares, which ranged from clothing and imported jewelry to hot potatoes—perfect for cold hands, baked in coals—right where they'd set up their outdoor shops.

Gaiety reigned as the city prepared for the Christmas season.

Elizabeth and Abigail had made many of their gifts, but there were certain items Elizabeth hoped to find at some of the local shops: a novel of some sort for Benjamin, and some tobacco, too, would be nice, for she knew how much he enjoyed his evening pipe.

Find them she did, and the very next day she readied herself for departure once again, her basket laden with treasures.

"I should be home by early evening," she said to Abigail. "But if I'm late, don't worry. You know how it is with Benjamin. He's so hard to leave at times."

Abigail pulled back a corner of the lace curtain to peek out the window.

Though the weather was cool, this was an unusually mild November day. The sun was bright and clear, almost crystalline, the sky so perfect a porcelain blue it could have been painted by an artist's gifted hand.

"Just be careful," Abigail warned. "You know how unexpectedly the weather can change this time of year."

"I'll be fine," Elizabeth assured her, covering her head with a warm woolen scarf. "I've crossed the lake many times alone."

"Not at the end of November you haven't! Why do you think the ferry shuts down for the winter season? You should have gone several weeks ago, when Captain Avery could have taken you across," she admonished.

"The weather is mild today, Ab. Please don't worry."

"Papa won't like it."

"Papa won't know. I'll probably be back before he is."

"I don't like it, either."

"Oh, Abigail," Elizabeth said patiently, pulling her coat tight, "you worry too much."

But Abigail was right.

Though the sun was warm and kind, the wind was not. And true to Abigail's words, before Elizabeth could make it across the lake, the wind picked up intensity and the waves grew choppy. Whitecaps frothed, and steely, leaden clouds moved in from the north and gathered swiftly.

Elizabeth's arms soon grew tired from rowing, and her cheeks and lips became chapped. Her heart hammered in her chest. The crossing seemed to take forever. In calmer conditions, she could have easily reached the island shore in less than an hour. For a while, with water sloshing into her boat, she questioned her own sanity at attempting this visit. But stubborn as always, she persisted, refusing to turn back.

Eventually, though exhausted, cold, and shaken, she reached the opposite shore safely.

She secured the dinghy and wasted no time in heading out toward her destination, for the afternoon was fast growing dark with the approaching storm.

The island, usually bustling with people and activity, seemed deserted today. The trees were bare of leaves, the lake and beach windy, gray, and bleak. Even the birds were wisely absent, having abandoned the beach to find a windless shelter.

A fine, pelting snow began, and the wind hurled the stinging particles into her face like hundreds of icy needles. She tucked her chin down into her coat and hurried toward the lighthouse, her clothing papered against her by the howling gale, her skirts quickly growing cold and sodden.

A vicious gust of wind hit her, stealing her breath away. She lifted her head and halted a moment to get her bearings. Up ahead she spotted the outline of the lighthouse. From its windows came a welcome glow of golden lights. A warm rush of relief swept over her. She would have been in a fine fix if Benjamin had not been home.

She leaned into the wind and within minutes reached the lighthouse. She didn't hesitate to knock, but immediately tried the door.

Only to find it bolted.

Unusual. Benjamin seldom bolted his door.

Bemused, she called out his name, but the building northwester caught her words and bore them away. So she banged her foot against the door and tried the latch again.

A few agonizing moments passed.

Glancing at the window, she again knew relief. A bobbing shadow moved toward the door.

Expectantly, she danced from foot to foot, anxious for admittance, until finally she heard the latch lift.

The door swung open. A strong gust of wind blew her in with a whirlwind of snow flurries. "Benjamin, I—"

But before she could complete her sentence or gain her bearings, a deafening roar to her left nearly stopped her heart.

She dropped her basket. The contents spilled out around her. She pivoted, lurched backward, and pinned her shoulders against the open door. Her eyes grew round, and a muted scream tore from her throat, while she looked up at the poker poised high above her head, ready to descend should she give any indication that the action was necessary.

The instinct for survival rose. From out of the past came Weston's protective teachings. She dipped low, whirled, and brought her elbow sharply into the groin of her attacker.

"Omph!" The air left his lungs in a whoosh as he doubled over, dropping the poker. He moaned, fought for breath, then let loose with the longest, loudest, string of profanities she'd ever heard, while she wasted no time in scrambling for the poker.

But sensing her destination, he stretched out his boot, hooked her ankle, and sent her tumbling.

A moment later they lay entangled in a twisted sea of sodden skirts.

"Beth!" Weston exclaimed, one hand still cupped protectively over his groin. He released himself and reached for her, grabbing her shoulders in two painfully strong hands. He shook her so hard her eyeballs rattled. "Beth! My God! I could have killed ye!" His alarm was evident as he searched her face.

Elizabeth's surprise was instantly replaced by haughty indignation. "Kill me!" she squeaked. "Kill me! Why it's you who's injured, you bloody fool!"

His expression grim, his voice grew louder. "I thought I told ye never to hit a man that low unless you mean to disable him!"

"I did mean to disable him!"

"Well, ye almost did!" he roared. "I'll probably never have children!"

She threw him a disgusted glare. "Don't you think you're overreacting a bit?"

His brows shot clear to his hairline. "The hell ye say!"

"Well, how was I to know it was you?"

"Who did ye think it was?" he went on in an injured tone.

She leaned toward him and quipped, "I didn't know. That's why I hit you there! If it makes you feel any better," she added, "I'm sorry."

He rose to his feet slowly. He hunched over slightly, digesting her words for several tense minutes. Though she tried to conceal it, a violent shiver ran through her. Sighing, he grabbed the front of her coat in his fists and unceremoniously hauled her to her feet. He kicked the door shut behind her and dropped the latch into place.

Her teeth clattered together furiously, but whether from cold or shock she didn't know. At this point it didn't matter.

"Aw, Jesus, Lizzy. C'mon," he said, worry replacing his irritation. Her lips were blue, her face white. "Come over to the stove and get warm. Ye're nearly frozen."

He didn't give her a chance to protest, but pulled her toward the welcome fire, peeled her coat and scarf away, then set her down in Benjamin's rickety rocker.

Her nose was running, her hair flat and shapeless. Her eyes felt as though they would be forever frozen open. She shivered again, blinked several times, and tried to make sense out of the situation.

He reached into his hip pocket and produced a handkerchief, stuffed it into her hands, and waited patiently while she blew her nose.

"There," he said, kneeling down before her on one knee, chafing her icy hands briskly. "That's better."

"W-where's Benjamin?"

"I found a note. He went out to the Iroquoian reservation to take the children the toys he'd carved."

"When's he coming back?"

"Probably not for a couple of days. He won't travel through this storm."

She sniffed loudly and asked, "What are you doing here?"

He grinned and nodded toward her upturned basket. "The same thing ye are, I imagine. I came to visit the old man before Christmas. I brought him a bottle of good rum to keep him warm on nights such as this."

She blinked again, her eyes still stiff with cold. Confused, she asked, "What the hell were you doing with that poker?"

"I came out a week ago. Benjamin said he'd seen some rough-looking characters on the island a while back. Thought they might be smugglers. He thought someone might have tried to break in one day, but Eli scared him off."

"Where is Eli?"

"He must be with Benjamin."

Her hands began to tingle beneath the steady friction he applied, and soon blessed heat infused her palms and fingers. After a few more moments, he released them.

"Ye better get those wet things off before a chill sets in." He reached for her foot, unlaced her shoe, pulled it off, then did the same with the other shoe. He set them both to the side, beyond the braided carpet he knelt on. "Stockings, too," he ordered, flipping her skirts up to her knees. He reached high up under her skirt, freed a stocking, and peeled it from her leg.

Along with thawing came sanity.

As he reached for the other stocking, she slapped his hands away, her brows meeting crossly. "Get your bloody hands off me!" she snapped shrewishly.

He halted his movements and sat back on his haunches, hung his hands between his knees, and studied her with quiet amusement. She was a comical sight with her nose swollen and red, her eyes wide with indignant anger. He found himself hard-pressed not to laugh. "So ye'd rather catch yer death." He shook his head in amazement. "Ye know I've seen ye in less, darlin'."

Her cheeks flamed, and her hazel eyes sparked fire. "Ohhh," she ground out caustically. "Are you going to remind me of that for the rest of my life?"

He shrugged and grinned. "Probably."

"You're despicable!"

"I've been called worse."

"Oh, I'll just bet you have." She rose and ungraciously turned her back to him. Grudgingly she reached up under her soggy skirts and peeled off the wet stocking, almost slapped him in the face with it, then tossed it over the chair. She might be angry, but she was no fool. She had no desire to catch her death. "There," she snapped, turning. "Happy now?"

"Not quite." He inclined his head. "Skirts, too."

Her eyes bulged, almost leaving her skull. She hooked her hands on her hips and tipped forward, outraged. "In a pig's eye!" she exclaimed, using the words she'd used as a child.

He sighed heavily. "Ye can take them off yerself, or I can do it for ye. What'll it be, Lizzy?"

"But," she sputtered, "I have nothing to wear!"

He stood slowly, widened his stance, folded his arms across his red flannel shirt, and quietly faced her down. "Ye can wear one of Benjamin's nightshirts. At least it'll be warm and dry." Then he logically added, "It's no time to be prudish, Lizzy."

A quarter of an hour later, she sat huddled in the over-sized garment, her heels hooked on the edge of the chair, her knees pulled tight to her chest, feet tucked under the warm material. She tried with growing impatience to work a comb through her matted hair.

Weston prepared tea and searched the cupboards for food, while she skewered his back with her eyes, wishing she could drive a harpoon directly through the middle of the broad expanse, unreasonably blaming him for the wicked storm that buffeted the island and kept them stranded.

"Papa and Abigail will be so worried," she bit out angrily.

"Yes, they probably will."

"I can't imagine what everyone will think."

"I can." He turned to her, an infuriating grin crinkling his face.

Finding no amusement in his response, she resolutely closed her eyes, dropped her head to her knees, and softly moaned, "Oh, God . . . Oh, God . . ."

Weston opened the stove lid and with exaggerated patience stuffed a log into the opening. His grin had faded at her words. "It's not his fault either, Lizzy, so ye may as well let off trying to find someone to blame."

"But poor Aaron . . ."

He stared at her dejected form perched on the chair— a caged bird desperate for flight—and felt a surge of protectiveness well up from within. Very quietly he said, "Aaron'll believe whatever we tell him." He closed the stove lid, crossed the room, and held a cup of steaming tea out to her.

She looked up. The comb dropped to the floor.

Outside the wind cried out a lonely plea.

Inside, two hearts followed suit.

"And ye needn't be afraid of me. If that's what's got ye so upset." His eyes were dark and earnest. "After all the years we've known one another, ye ought to know I'd never force ye to do anything that was against yer will."

Beleaguered, she fought the urge to cry. Of course she knew. She'd always known. But how could she tell him it was not him she feared?

She didn't trust herself.

He turned away, only to return a few minutes later with a platter of cheese, some dried beef, and biscuits. "It's the best I could do," he said apologetically and pulled a chair up beside her. "Here." He offered her his meager findings. "Ye'd better eat something."

She did, and found it tasted remarkably good, filling the gnawing vacancy in her stomach, but offering little solace for the empty yearning of her heart. Afterward he rose and refilled their teacups, then returned to her once again.

Together they sat side by side, sipping their tea, while time ticked by. Animosity slipped away, and familiarity calmed them somewhat.

"Remember the morning Papa and the search party found us out here?" she asked softly, giving up resistance to the burgeoning memories.

He nodded, chuckled quietly, and asked, "How could I forget? Yer father was ready to kill me with his bare hands. Probably would have if Benjamin hadn't been there to save my hide."

"We never should have lain down in the dinghy that night."

He turned, studied her profile in the flickering lamplight, and sipped his tea. "No, we probably shouldn't have."

She raised her eyes to his. A ghost of a smile flickered. "I never thought you'd fall asleep."

He returned her smile with a lazy one of his own. "I never thought I would either." Silence, then, "Especially with ye lying beside me."

She blushed and lowered her gaze to her hands. Both palms were wrapped tightly around her cup, drawing warmth and comfort from the contents. "They watched me for months afterward, you know." Her voice was soft with recollection. She glanced back up at him. "For a long time after you went away, they watched to see if I was pregnant."

He examined her smileless eyes, sorry for the loneliness and humiliation he'd caused her, unable to put his swelling emotions into words eloquent enough to convey his sincerity. "I'm sorry, Lizzy. I'm so, so sorry . . ."

She looked away, toward the window, toward the cold, barren darkness. "Aaron and Abigail were the only ones who believed me. Benjamin, too. Papa wanted to, I know. But," she said with a shrug, "he wasn't quite sure. After all," she added with an uncertain smile, "they did find us wrapped up together, naked as the day we were born." She sighed and grew silent, then turned her attention to the stove and the little visible patch of the fire that sputtered and hissed within. "But Aaron . . . ," she whispered at length, "he was so gallant, so protective. He wouldn't allow anyone to slander my name. Because of him people accepted me once again." She expelled a small huff of breath. "You know, he once told me that even if it were true, even if I were pregnant, he would still want to marry me." She turned to Weston and lifted misty eyes. "Can you imagine that?"

"Yes," came the soft reply. "Anyone in his right mind would want to marry ye, Lizzy." Weston dropped his gaze to his hands and selfishly wished he, not his brother, had said those chivalrous words to her.

"The worst part of it all," she said so quietly that he had to strain to hear her above the howling wind, "was that I wanted it to be true, Wes. Even though I knew it couldn't possibly be, I still wished I'd gotten pregnant."

Her soft-spoken admission moved him deeply. His eyelids slid closed and trembled. He swallowed the lump that collected in his throat and knew a deep, deep regret.

They sat for several more seconds, each lost in reflective silence.

Then, wordlessly, he rose, reached across her lap, took the cup she grasped so tightly, and set it with his own on the table. Offering no apologies or explanations, he went down on one knee before her and drew her into the protective circle of his arms.

Her knees pressed into his middle, her mouth against his shoulder. She sighed and shuddered but didn't struggle. He smoothed her hair back from her brow, stroked it, and kissed her crown.

For several moments he rested his chin on top of her head, while his heart struggled with his conscience, and he thought, *My Lizzy Beth. How can I give you up to someone else, even if that someone is my brother? Even when that someone deserves you much more than I do?*

His emotions warring, he silently begged, *Forgive me, Aaron. Please forgive me.*

He pulled back slightly to search her eyes. But her lids were pressed tightly together, as though in keeping them shut she could shut out the reality of what was happening within their hearts.

With his forefinger he tipped her chin upward. "Open yer eyes, Beth," he commanded gently. "Look at me."

Her lids opened slowly, and she swallowed thickly. "Oh, Wes," she whispered, her eyes tortured, her voice shaky. "What are we going to do?"

An eloquent silence was his only answer.

He took her arms and gently pulled her down onto her knees before him. "If this is wrong for ye," he said carefully, clearly, his eyes fixed intently upon her face, "then stop me now."

When she didn't answer, his wide hands moved up to her neck. He encircled the graceful column and laid his thumbs over the pulsing hollow of her throat. Then, slowly, his head descended.

Her lips parted, her eyelids fluttered shut, and she fought for breath.

With infinite tenderness he kissed each eyelid, her cheek, throat, jaw, then finally, very slowly, his mouth touched her lips.

Her palms sought his chest and rested against the soft flannel of his shirt. She felt the tensing of his muscles, the beat of his heart, the warmth of his flesh, the gentle, narcotic touch of his lips upon hers, and found herself starved for the sustenance he offered. Her hands formed fists around his suspenders and held fast.

His tongue drew circles upon her lips, then came searching, slowly at first, then boldly, impatiently, exactly as she remembered.

She answered his quest, learning about him all over again. Taste, touch, smell. All wonderfully him, all wonderfully familiar. But older, better, finer.

His hands released her neck and skimmed downward over her curves, investigating her dips and hollows. Some he remembered, some he did not. He bracketed her hips, pulled her close, and allowed her to feel the fullness of his tumescence.

"Wes, oh, Wes," came the hungry plea, as prudence fled and desire surfaced. She released his suspenders and touched him—his neck, jaw, chest, arms—and found him harder, larger, and knew the boy she remembered had faded away into memory, and a man, a wonderful man, had now taken his place.

He drew her down onto her back and braced himself on elbows over her. His thumbs caressed her jaw, while his head hovered above hers, his eyes begging permission. With a caress as light as butterfly wings, she touched his cheeks and granted him permission.

"Ye're not scared?" His voice was gruff.

Her clear hazel eyes met his squarely. "No."

"I don't want you to be sorry . . ."

Tears formed, and her voice quavered as she honestly answered, "I think I would be sorrier if we never did this."

His head dipped downward, found her breasts, her nipples, and wet them through the material of the nightshirt.

Their caresses grew impulsive and abandoned, greedy and needful, hot and wild.

He rose up on his knees, gripped the nightshirt in his fists and eased it upward. She did not halt his movements, but lifted her body to accommodate him. In a second, she lay naked before him as she had so many years ago.

"Ahhh, Beth." The words escaped his throat in a reverent whisper. He reached his hands out to touch her naked breasts. "Ye're so much more beautiful than I remember. Ye really have grown up."

A self-conscious smile flitted across her lips, then disappeared. With adulthood came the sharp realization of how forbidden this fruit was. But when he straightened and hooked his thumbs in his suspenders, she knew she would never be complete until she'd tasted it with him. His suspenders hung in loops at his hips. He tugged his shirttail out of his trousers. Moments later, he knelt before her, shirt, suspenders, trousers, socks, and boots in a heap on the floor.

He was a magnificent sight—all gold and blond and beautiful. His years at sea had added a roughness to him, a hardness, a deepened maturity. The light from the fire played across his chest, turning the shafts of hair to a dusting of shimmering gold.

Her wide eyes drank him in. "Wes," she humbly corrected him, "you've always been the beautiful one."

To this he chuckled and lay down beside her. His arms drew her close. Their breath mingled as he touched his tongue to her bottom lip, wet it, and drew it in, while his hands cupped her breasts. They hardened and grew taut beneath his touch, throbbing with impatience and life. His hands rode her waist, as his tongue trailed a wet path down to her nipples.

She arched against him, whimpered a fervent plea, gripped his shoulders tightly, then drew his head back up to receive her welcoming kiss.

His head rose, and he stared down into her eyes as his hand played over the curve of her stomach, then lower, lower, and found her warm and wanting. The passing of time had not changed her. He knew her well, as no other ever had. His Lizzy Beth, all fire and passion.

He took her hand, guided it down over the golden mat of hair on his own body, and closed her fingers around his hardness. With a control he hadn't known he possessed, he tutored her in a way the boy hadn't been able to all those years ago.

Her touch was tentative at first, but gradually she gained confidence. He was hard and satiny and totally male, and as her hands adapted a rhythm, his breathing grew ragged. His lids slid closed, and when he groaned and eased away from her, she found joy in knowing that this time she would offer him completion.

"No more of that," he said gruffly. He rolled over and braced himself above her. "I want ye to know, Beth. I love ye. I always have."

Her eyes filled, and her throat worked wordlessly for a moment. Then finally the words broke loose, "I love you, too, Wes."

To him, her words were a blessed benediction.

"The first time . . . It might hurt a little."

"It's all right . . ."

He placed his flesh against her. "Ye tell me if it does."

She nodded and drew his head down. "I will."

But there was no need. His entrance was slow and splendid, kind and glorious.

She sighed and accepted him, her eyes sliding shut.

All barriers both physical and emotional melted away, years meant nothing, broken promises were forgiven.

Elizabeth and Weston became one.

Oh, Wes, so this is what it's all about, she thought, lifting herself to hold him deep, possessing him with body and soul, her love for him billowing to overflowing. All those years they'd toyed with lovemaking, been on the brink of it, she never would have guessed—this, this grand fullness, this man inside her body, was the final acclimation for which she'd hungered.

He moved within her patiently, his strokes slow and easy, waiting for her to join him in this rapturous journey. It didn't take long. As always, she followed his lead obediently, loving the feel of him, the thrumming of his heart against her breasts, his ragged breath puffing against her cheek, his tutored hands gripping her hips, his sunny hair tapping his forehead.

They rocked together in youthful, wanton abandon.

Then his movements became more intense, deeper, swifter. Her own heart picked up tempo to match, and she learned a newfound harmonizing, as, wonder upon wonder, an unexpected rush spilled over her a mere second before he arched, groaned, called out her name, and shuddered above her.

Imbued by his nearness, she lay sated.

He lay upon her silently, still buried within her, his possession complete. His forehead rested against her collarbone.

The fire hissed and sputtered. The night wind howled but could not chill them. Tomorrow could not touch them.

She held him close, pushed aside all the worries that would become reality in the light of day, and gleaned from the moment a lasting sense of blessed completion.

CHAPTER
13

In time, Weston's breathing steadied.

With infinite tenderness, he lifted his head and kissed the hollow of her throat. "I didn't hurt ye, did I?"

"No . . . not a bit," she answered softly.

He withdrew from her slowly, carefully, rolled to his side, and pulled her flush against him.

"Would ye tell me if I did?"

"No," she reiterated truthfully. "Probably not."

He chuckled, amused at her frankness. "Ye always were a tough one."

She kissed his neck and felt the sting of tears. The moment became fraught with tenderness—a tenderness she never would have expected from Weston the boy, but found an unexpected gift from Weston the man.

The fire grew low, and she shivered. He rose and left her, only to return a few moments later with a heavy quilt. He took another second to add another log to the stove, then returned to her side.

They lay wrapped beneath the quilt, in the hallowed safety of each other's arms. But before sleep could claim them, he kissed her, slow and deep. When finally he lifted his head, his blue eyes gazed into hers with a painful intensity. "Ye can't marry him, Beth," he said tenderly. "Not now."

She nodded. "I know."

"I'll speak to him. He's my brother. He'll understand." His eyes echoed his sincerity. This time there would be no regrets.

"No, Wes," came her reply. "I should be the one to tell him. It's only right."

"We could do it together, Lizzy." He looked down at their melded bodies. "We did this together."

She reached a hand to his cheek. "But this I must do alone. I owe him that much."

Weston gathered her close and knew a moment of premonitory disquiet. "All right," he said in acquiescence. "We'll do it your way."

During the night, the storm gradually abated.

Elizabeth woke to bright sunlight, streaming through the lighthouse windows, bouncing golden fingers off her eyes and face.

Warmth enveloped her, not from the sun but from human contact, splendidly redolent.

She lay still, gazing at him silently for several moments, allowing tranquility to infuse her. Then, very gently, she brushed a lock of hair back from his brow and leaned close to kiss his forehead.

She loved this man. She couldn't let him go.

He opened his eyes slowly, offered her his first sleepy good-morning grin, and tightened his arms around her.

A bittersweet tenderness made her heart feel swollen to bursting. She'd wondered about moments such as these, pictured them hundreds of times. But never with Aaron. Sadly, she realized, she had never pictured herself with Aaron.

"Damn," Weston said, his grin widening. "This was long overdue, Lizzy."

"Indeed," she agreed softly. "I've always wondered what it would be like."

He stroked the dip at the base of her back and laid one heavy leg up over her hip. "And was it like ye pictured?" His voice was husky with sleep and the reawakening of desire.

She felt a lump form in her throat. "Yes . . . And no. Better. So much better."

He drew her close and kissed her thoroughly, worked his magic once again with a mastery that only he knew how to employ. And for a brief nagging second, she felt a fleeting sense of transience, and the precious moment became fraught with apprehension. She clutched him passionately, wishing the moment could be frozen, wishing time would cease.

He pulled back and gazed at her and knew a deep satisfaction. He wanted a lifetime of mornings like this one. He wasn't even sure if a lifetime with this woman would be enough.

After a while, he sat up. He wanted more than anything to love her again, but knew it would not be wise. He pulled the quilt across his lap.

She sat up, also, as innocently indifferent to her nakedness as she'd been as a child. "Wes . . . ," she invited guilelessly, reaching a hand to him, almost breaking his reserve.

He swallowed, fighting temptation.

Why not? he argued with himself.

Because he didn't want to be a bastard this time, that's why not.

"We shouldn't, Lizzy," he said gently. Hurt clouded her expression. He took her arms and pulled her close. "I want to, believe me." He took her hand and placed it over his lap. "See?" He grinned playfully, then his expression grew serious, his blue eyes intent on her face. "But if last night didn't leave ye pregnant, there's no need to tempt fate now. When the time is right, we'll have our children. I don't want people to count back to this night and blame ye or label our child a bastard for what happened between us."

She didn't know what to say. Here was another unexpected consideration. How very much he had changed over the years.

"Lizzy," he said, "the storm's over. It'll be cold, but the water won't be frozen. I can get us across the harbor." He watched worry flit across her face and gently added, "We can't stay here forever."

"I know." Her voice echoed sadness at this truth. "But I wish we could."

"Don't be afraid. I'm with you this time."

She closed her eyes and lifted his hand. She pressed it to her cheek, held it there, and sought strength in its warmth and hardness as if once again she were fifteen and frightened, very young and so vulnerable to the gossip of her peers and acquaintances.

But he's with me this time, she repeated mentally.

His heart contracted with tenderness for her. All the time she'd hid behind her anger, she'd been hiding the truth of what his abandonment had done to her. Brave Lizzy Beth. She would not want him to know how difficult it had been.

But he knew. Gazing at her now, he knew.

Spotting the comb on the floor, he reached for it, then eased her up, took her by the shoulders, and gently turned her. He cradled her hips between his legs, her bottom against his groin, and with slow patience began to work the comb through her tangled hair.

She sighed, pushed doubt away, and became lost in pleasurable sensation as his large hands—rough, callused seamen's hands—soon had the heavy mass loose and hanging free.

With a smile in her voice, she said, "You used to pull my braids so maliciously."

He chuckled. "I remember." His gentle ministrations brought a warm, relaxing tingle to her scalp.

A companionable silence ensued.

She looked toward the window and watched dust motes float languidly in a shaft of cold December sunlight.

"Wes," she said hesitantly.

"Yes . . ."

"What we did last night . . ." She swallowed, then continued, damning the demon in her that wanted to know. "You've done it all before, haven't you?"

He halted his movements with the comb halfway down a lock of her hair. Then slowly he resumed his motions and honestly answered, "Yes. I have."

She had thought she was prepared for his answer, for the pain it would bring. "I thought so," she whispered, fighting hard to hide the hurt and sense of betrayal his words had elicited. "You're very good at it. But then you always were . . ."

He took her by the shoulders and turned her, bringing her across his lap. He looked down into her eyes and said, "The way it is with us, it never was like that with anyone else. I never wanted anyone but ye. Not really. And in my heart, it always was ye, Lizzy. Always."

She met his gaze squarely. His eyes never wavered. She knew he could have lied, could have denied that he had experience, but he hadn't. There was one more question she had to ask, though the image of them together brought forth a very real, very fervent, agony. "With Gabrielle?" came the reluctant question. "Have you done these things with her?"

Damn. Did she have to ask him that? "Some of them," he admitted and brushed his thumb across her bottom lip.

"Please don't lie to me," she said.

"I'm not lying," he replied. He hesitated a moment, then added, "What we did last night, me inside ye, I've not done that with her."

The fact that he'd touched Gabrielle in any way at all brought a piercing pain. But knowing he'd not shared this final intimacy with her brought a rush of relief so sweet Elizabeth almost cried.

An hour later they stood dressed and ready for departure. They'd put Benjamin's room back in order and placed his Christmas gifts upon his old, worn table, along with a note that said they'd both been there and remained throughout the storm. There was no need to lie. Benjamin would know they couldn't have crossed the harbor in such a storm.

Weston wrapped a heavy scarf around his neck, buttoned his coat, and pulled on his gloves. Elizabeth did the same.

He opened the door, but before allowing her to pass through, he tugged her coat tight around her neck, then pulled her into his arms and said into her hair, "It'll be all right, Beth."

The waves, though still choppy, were no longer steep. But the air was chilling, a cold reminder of yesterday's ravaging storm.

Long before they reached the shore, they could see
the frantic movement of the gathering crowd. A search
party was about to set out to find them once again.

Elizabeth squinted across the dark waters, her face
turned into the stiff lake breeze, and made out familiar forms: her father, Abigail, Gabrielle, Mr. St. Clair,
David, Bradford, even Franklin Fuller, Sarah Munroe—
so many others, some she didn't know, some she did,
and of course Aaron.

Her stomach churned, and the first wave of burgeoning guilt washed over her.

She looked toward Weston, and their eyes met.

I love you, they silently told each other.

Knowing what awaited them, the crossing seemed
interminable.

Weston labored on, his breath escaping in rhythmic
puffs, his powerful strokes never faltering. He was calm
and determined. This time she would not suffer humiliation because of him. He would down the first man who
dared question her virtue, even if that man were his
brother.

As they neared the shore, a series of reverberating
murmurs rippled through the anxious crowd, followed
by the first relieved cry: "There they are!"

"Praise the Lord!"

"Amen!"

Elizabeth's insides trembled. *Indeed,* she thought dryly. She forced a smile, waved, and silently prayed her
face would not betray her turbulent emotions.

Throughout the next lengthy, uncomfortable minutes,
Weston managed to secure the dinghy. He reached a
hand to help her out, his eyes speaking volumes, while
the crowd rushed forward to envelop them.

"Beth!" Abigail reached them first. She threw herself

against Elizabeth, grasping her tightly. "Oh, Beth," she choked out. "We were so frightened. The storm was so vicious. When you didn't return, I was so afraid . . . I had to tell Papa where you'd gone—"

"It's all right, Ab. And I'm all right. I'm fine," she reassured her trembling sister.

"Elizabeth."

Elizabeth turned to meet her father's worried eyes.

"You're all right, daughter?" He spoke with genuine love and concern, yet ever aware of Weston's presence beside her, she sensed there was much more to the question than was being voiced.

"Yes, Papa." She went into his outstretched arms and felt her throat clog with love for him, along with remorse for having caused him such worry. "I'm fine. Really I am."

"You're sure?" Over her head, he pinned his calm gray eyes on Weston.

"Yes, Papa. But if it hadn't been for Weston—"

Weston stepped forward. "We both picked yesterday to take Christmas gifts to Benjamin. The weather changed so quickly, we knew we'd never be able to make it back across. We stayed out at the lighthouse."

"And how is Benjamin?" came the reverend's quiet inquiry.

Weston thought of Elizabeth and minutely weighed the question before deliberately answering, "He's fine, sir."

"My God, Elizabeth! Weston!" Aaron interrupted the meaningful exchange. He pushed his way through the crowd and pulled Elizabeth into his arms, holding her so tightly her breath caught in her throat. "Elizabeth! We were worried sick!" He lifted his anxious eyes to his brother, relieved to see him standing there safe and strong. "We were almost certain Weston would find shelter. But you . . . Thank God Weston was out there with you. Thank God he was there to take care of you!" He swallowed thickly and tightened his embrace.

Weston looked on in silent agony, fighting a profound emotional battle: love for his brother, shame for the infallible trust his brother placed in him, possessive jealousy—for Aaron held in his arms the one person Weston loved above everything. He wanted to tear her from his grasp, hold her to himself. But he could not. All he could do was look on and try to quell the terrible loneliness the sight before him evoked.

Elizabeth felt torn. Her heart was wrenched by confusion. With Aaron's arms around her, she tentatively returned his embrace and lifted haunted eyes to Weston. He stood proudly, his stance wide and sure, the sparkling December sun glinting diamonds off his hair. But there was a somber hopelessness in his eyes. For a long moment she couldn't tear her gaze away and relived once again the beauty of his touch, while her heart reached out and begged for understanding.

Gabrielle burst upon them in a flurry of skirts, with an endless log of questions.

"Gracious, you two! Whatever have you been doing for all of these hours? This whole town was ready to set out and search until we found you!" She turned toward Elizabeth. With a note of accusation in her voice, she stated, "Surely you know better than to cross the harbor in December, Elizabeth!" Then she looked from one to the other, babbling on and on in what seemed unintelligible syllables until neither Elizabeth nor Weston heard or cared.

Sarah Munroe wrapped her arms around her son. "Your father will be so relieved, darling. We were worried about you when David said you'd not returned when he expected." To Elizabeth, she said, "Are you all right, dear?"

Elizabeth nodded. "Oh, yes, Mrs. Munroe. I'm fine."

David joined them. "Glad to see you, Wes." Then, with a grin, he added, "Can't imagine how bloody boring life would be without you around to get me into trouble."

With David came Bradford, who surprised them all by quietly voicing his relief at their safety, then taking Gabrielle's elbow and leading her a small distance away. At first she resisted, throwing him a haughty, defiant glare. But something about his steady gaze and the gentle pressure of his hand on her arm stilled her indignant complaint.

Slowly the crowd dissipated; the excitement was over.

With Aaron's arm around Elizabeth's shoulder, they made their way toward the carriages.

But Mrs. Caufield and her friends remained.

They stood in a small cluster, clutching their Bibles, watching with unconcealed interest as the young people passed. Sensing their gazes upon her, Elizabeth lifted her eyes to meet Mrs. Caufield's. The old woman's gaze tried her, convicted her, damned her, then moved on to a place behind her.

Elizabeth knew, without turning, that the woman's eyes had locked on Weston and damned him, too.

The following days were tense and emotionally charged.

But for Elizabeth the nights were the worst.

They were long and lonely, full of restless dreams. She dreamed of Weston. Sometimes they were together at the lighthouse again. The howling wind swirled outside. But they were safe, wrapped in each other's arms, and their joining was hauntingly beautiful.

Then, other times, she dreamt he stood before her, shrouded in a thick fog, arms outstretched, his eyes full of love, and he would say, "Come, Lizzy Beth, come to me." But a violent wind would come and envelop him, spiriting him away, while she cried out his name and reached aching arms toward his fading image.

She would awake frustrated and guilt ridden, needy and empty, longing for his arms to comfort her.

The days brought a strained sanity and a measure of peace. She found solace in readying the house and church for Christmas. She and Abigail found a tree to grace their parlor, as decorating pine trees to celebrate Christmastide was fast gaining acceptance in Canada as a symbol of the holiday season.

Refusing to allow him rest until he did their bidding, the young women persuaded Tristan to chop down such a tree for them and attach it to a stand. They wrapped the pine in lace and ribbons and fastened to its fragrant branches small candles they would light on Christmas Eve.

The reverend asked no further questions of Elizabeth, and for that she was grateful. She had no desire to lie to him and was not sure that she could bring herself to do so.

She knew that gossip about herself and Weston had been reignited, but she also knew that no one, not even Mrs. Caufield, would dare challenge her father about such a private matter without significant proof of wrongdoing.

Aaron came to see her daily. She knew she could not put off breaking their engagement. She found his continued attentions stifling. But he was so kind, so considerate, so dear, she could not find it within herself to disappoint him in such a way, especially with the holiday season so close.

Abigail was quiet, but loving and supportive. She knew about Elizabeth's nightmares, for she was the one who woke her from them. Ever prudent, she asked for no explanations, but there were times—quiet times when they were alone—that her gentle eyes rested upon Elizabeth with a legion of unspoken questions.

The storm that had stranded Elizabeth and Weston on the island brought a lasting stretch of frigid arctic air. The heavy snows came. Winter forests were transformed into groves of crystal, each branch bending gracefully under its brilliant burden.

Toronto was merry. The ponds and harbor would be frozen for skating in time for Christmas. Sleds appeared, bobsleds, too. The city's cab service brought out sleighs that could make their way through heavy snowdrifts, though they were sometimes aided—as on the McCaul Street grade—by male passengers, who frequently had to get out and push if any progress was to be made. Such help was rewarded by grateful drivers, who, on these routes at least, had no objections to stopping in front of someone's house instead of the next corner.

On one such wintry day, a week before Christmas, Gabrielle helped Elizabeth deliver packages to some of the area's needy. "You are going caroling this evening, aren't you?" Gabrielle inquired.

"I suppose," Elizabeth answered, but there was no enthusiasm in her voice.

"And what about the skating party next week?"

"Aaron wants to go."

"And you don't?" Gabrielle asked, her eyes wide.

"It's not that I don't want to go. It's simply that there's so much to do with Christmas so close. Right now, Abigail is at the church helping the children prepare for their Christmas program while we do this—"

"Oh, pooh, Elizabeth McRaney," Gabrielle said and waved a hand airily. "That's just an excuse, and you know it. You've been hibernating like a bear ever since the night you and Weston were stuck out on the island."

Elizabeth felt her cheeks grow hot. "That's not true," she lied.

"Yes, it is." Gabrielle's tone was mildly accusing.

Elizabeth stopped. The snow fell softly around them, nesting in the tree branches, making the world seem pure and perfect, white and sacred. She turned beleaguered eyes to her friend.

The shorter woman met her gaze guilelessly, then lowered her eyes to examine her nails carefully. "If you're worried that I'm jealous, you needn't be—"

"I'm not, I—"

A snowflake fell on Gabrielle's pert nose. She brushed it away, then lifted sparkling green eyes. "I think I'm in love, Elizabeth." Her voice was soft with wonder.

Elizabeth's heart plummeted. "I see," came the whispered reply.

"No . . . You really don't. This time it's so different. It's . . ." She shook her head and dropped her gaze. "I never expected it to happen. Especially not with him." Her head lifted. "Love's a funny thing, isn't it?"

"Yes, it is."

Gabrielle's expression grew somber. "How can it feel so wonderful when it hurts so much?"

This mystifying paradox was one Elizabeth had also pondered. But she had no explanation for it. "I don't know, Gaby. I truly don't."

"I haven't told him yet. I haven't had the opportunity." Gabrielle rolled her eyes and sighed deeply. "It's not something I can just blurt out, you know."

Elizabeth nodded, swallowing a conflicting sense of grief and betrayal, mixed with the genuine affection she felt for her friend. As she stared at Gabrielle, she knew the sudden, sad loss of girlish innocence. They were no longer children, but grown women facing life as it sometimes was—uncertain and unpredictable, hurtful and beautiful, all things wonderful, all things sad.

Gabrielle gave a short self-deprecating laugh. "I'm not even sure how he feels about me."

"I see," Elizabeth reiterated quietly.

"That's never happened to me before," she admitted. "Not like this. I usually know where I stand with a man. Even if it's not to my liking."

They grew reflectively silent and resumed walking. Before long, they arrived at Queen's Park. No matter what the season, it was a beautiful place to visit. It was laid out for the grandest possible effect, with a wide central carriageway and boulevards and walkways on either side, shaded by double rows of chestnuts that bloomed wonderful pink blossoms in the summer. The chestnuts were prized possessions, as they were specially imported from the United States. The gardens were tailored with distinction and the fountains were elaborate, one designed with four tiers from which water gracefully cascaded.

But now the fountains were quiet, resting in peaceful winter slumber.

The two women strolled along the walkway. Before them, two black squirrels danced merrily around each other, then parted company, one of them turning his attention to the nearly frozen white carpet. He dug frantically for a misplaced nut but found nothing. Finally giving up, he scampered off in search of other entertainment. Above them, sheltered in the snow-laden arms of a particularly large maple, a brown squirrel chattered noisily, objecting cantankerously to their presence.

"Do you ever wonder about all the lovers who've had rendezvous here?" Gabrielle asked quietly, as though speaking louder would awaken their ghosts.

Elizabeth turned and studied her, wishing her answer could be different. "Yes . . . I have."

Weston stood alone on the wharf. Lost in deep thought, he stared out into the distance. A light snow fell, forming a frosty crust over the nearly frozen waters. He sighed heavily and withdrew his hand from his pocket. He held a small black box in his fist. He gazed down at it a few long minutes before slowly opening it.

Inside was a brooch. It was gold and very delicate. Around the edges it was encrusted with several small translucent pearls. In the very center sat a large, clear emerald.

He'd bought it for Elizabeth years ago.

He'd found it in a small shop in Scotland and knew the moment he saw it that it would look lovely with her auburn hair and green-flecked eyes.

He picked it up and turned it over, reading the inscription, remembering when he'd had it engraved. Three and a half years ago. A long time. Who would have thought he'd come home to find her with Aaron?

Staring down at the stone, he wondered if she would like it. Then he wondered if he'd ever be able to give it to her.

He'd not seen her since the morning they returned from the island. He wanted to give her time to talk to Aaron.

But lately a demon had been whispering in his ear, and he'd begun to wonder if she would, if she could, if maybe she loved Aaron more than she thought she had.

Gently he set the brooch back into its velvet cocoon. *How long, Beth? How long will ye wait to tell him?*

The snowflakes grew larger, lacier, and collected like a crocheted blanket across his wide shoulders.

With a dejected sigh, he turned away and headed up Yonge Street. There was to be caroling tonight, and he had promised to take Gabrielle.

CHAPTER
14

Mary Grace sat at the long wooden table.

The table was placed in the center of a room not nearly large enough for the many small beds that lined its walls.

The children who were well enough to leave their beds gathered around her, while those who could not watched with wonder as the large Christmas pine beside the table was adorned before their inquisitive eyes.

Mary Grace carefully cut out a pair of less than perfect paper wings and, with a smile, presented them to the little boy who had drawn them. "There, Joseph, your angel will be the finest ever with such lovely wings. He will look wonderful on our tree."

The little boy blushed and fidgeted, then intently attached the shapeless wings to the less than perfect angel.

Mrs. O'Rourke chuckled softly and bent over the shoulder of a small girl. "Here, darlin'. Let me help you with those." She patiently instructed the child how to string the cranberries.

"Will Saint Nicklaus visit us?" the little girl asked, glancing up from her task.

"But, of course," Mrs. O'Rourke answered merrily. "He visits all good children. And he knows all of you are especially good."

"Indeed," Mary Grace agreed softly, staring at the bent head of the young boy. She reached out and brushed a lock of dark red hair back from his brow. "You have a very special name, Joseph."

"I do?" His head came up.

"Yes, you do."

"Why?" His five-year-old eyes grew wide with interest.

"You've heard the Christmas story, haven't you?"

Joseph's head bobbed enthusiastically.

"Well," Mary Grace went on, "Joseph was the name of Jesus' earthly father. Do you remember?"

"Yes," the little boy whispered, but he really wasn't sure he did.

Mary Grace added, "He was a very fine man, chosen by God for a most special and important task."

"Ohhhh . . ." His lips grew lax, his small hands still.

She cupped his chin in her hand and met his gaze squarely. "You're special, too, Joseph. All children are special."

"To God?" he asked.

"Yes. To God. And to me, and Mrs. O'Rourke, and Dr. Benning, and the Reverend McRaney. To many, many people."

He smiled, puffed his chest up a bit, then, with a child's innocent curiosity, asked, "Do you have any children, Mary Grace?"

For a few moments she didn't answer. She blinked and turned toward the window. Beyond the frosted panes, snow fell softly on an insulated, cottony world. "Yes . . . I do."

"Did you help them make angels?"

Memories hovered. "Oh, yes. Many times . . ."

"Where are they?"

"Oh . . ." Mary Grace smiled, still gazing at the window, no longer seeing the snow. "They're grown now."

"All of them?"

"All but one."

"Where is that one?"

Mary Grace turned sad eyes to the little boy. "He's with God."

"Ohhhh . . ."

"His name was Jacob, and he looked very much like you. Though not quite so grown-up." She reached a hand to his hair.

"Do you miss him?"

She smiled again. "Yes, darling. I miss them all."

Mrs. O'Rourke put a comforting hand on the younger woman's shoulder. "The reverend will be coming for his visit soon."

"Yes," Mary Grace said, rising. "I know."

From outside came the soft murmur of voices. The voices grew louder, more distinct, more unified. "Joy to the world, the Lord is come. Let earth . . . receive . . ." The voices sang out—some young, some old, some perfectly harmonious, others not so perfectly tuned.

"Come, children. Come listen to the carolers." Mrs. O'Rourke shepherded the children toward the window. She opened the window a crack to allow the voices to reach them where they stood, high on the second floor.

Mary Grace watched for a few moments, then quietly left the room, making her way up to her own. Once there, she, too, cracked a window and stood a little apart, but

near enough to be able to gaze down at the heads of the
carolers—especially the heads of two young women—
one whose voice was clear and perfect and rose above all
others in distinct harmonious clarity; the other who could
not sing in such an excellent manner but sang anyway,
and whose voice Mary Grace found every bit as lovely.

Together, the combined voices of those two women
were the finest Christmas gift Mary Grace could have
received.

Elizabeth looked up. "God rest ye merry gentlemen,
let nothing you . . ." While she sang, her attention was
drawn to the window on the third story of the building.
A woman stood back from the glass. It was impossible to make out her features, but there was something
about her, even from this distance, that was naggingly
familiar.

Elizabeth's attention was diverted a moment later when
Abigail called, "Oh, there's Papa!"

Both women waved, as did most of the group.

"Brisk evening for this, isn't it?" the reverend called
out cheerfully, his arms laden with a variety of small
treats for the children. With a nod, he disappeared into
the building, and the carolers moved on up the street.

The mood of the crowd was light and festive. David
teased Enid and drew her behind a tree, where he kissed
her soundly. Her giggling filled the still night air and
brought bright blushes to the cheeks of some of the other
young women.

Bradford was in attendance, much to the surprise of
most everyone. He'd never gone caroling with them
before. Usually intellectually withdrawn, he seemed to
be enjoying himself this night, and surprised his friends
with his wonderfully rich baritone, which blended particularly well with Abigail's splendid soprano.

Elizabeth tried to be gay. But the truth was she felt terribly awkward.

She was ever aware of Aaron at her shoulder and Weston and Gabrielle at her back.

She was simply no good at duplicity.

The confusing feelings she'd experienced over the past several months had grown sharper, more pronounced with each passing day. What was worse was the awful guilt. Gabrielle's intimate confession had only added to her bemusement.

To whom was she to be loyal?

Did Weston still want her? And if he did, how could they ever be happy at Gabrielle's and Aaron's expense?

And what would Papa say about all of this? The thought of disappointing him once again left her feeling utterly bereft.

Regardless, she realized that she had no choice but to tell Aaron that she could not marry him now. It would be dishonorable to do anything else. After all, she had lain with another—his own brother.

But how do I tell him?

The past few days had grown increasingly frustrating for Weston Munroe. He sang out the words of the Christmas song while his eyes sought out the face of the one he loved.

But she would not look at him.

She had not looked him full in the face since the day they'd returned from the island.

So what the bloody hell did that mean? And what was he supposed to do now?

Three weeks had passed, and he hadn't heard a word from her. Not a damned word. He knew she wasn't one to play with a man's emotions. Not Elizabeth. But that knowledge added little immediate comfort.

She lay with me, he reasoned. *She let me love her, loved me back, told me that she loved me.*

But whatever was going on in her head lately, he didn't know.

Right now, standing in a hushed, snowy world, lonely but not alone, his pulse beating erratically at the mere sight of her, he wished he could throttle her and be done with it.

Why did he let his body rule his head? But he knew that what he felt was more than physical heat, more than lust.

He truly loved her.

He turned his gaze to the woman at his side and tried to imagine her as his wife, as the mother of his children, tried to imagine feeling for her what he felt for Elizabeth.

He couldn't.

Yes, he thought as his eyes sought Elizabeth out, it was much more than lust.

He just didn't know what he should do about it.

The evening grew late, the air much colder. Church bells rang out into the night a majestic, chiming symphony. The carolers began to dissipate one by one as they sang before their respective houses.

They stopped before Franklin's house. His parents stuck their heads out the door and offered the chilled crowd chocolate and biscuits.

The group stomped the snow from their feet, then gathered in the drawing room, huddled in front of the fire, warming their hands, chattering on about the coming skating party.

Mr. Fuller drew Aaron aside to talk business. Weston,

David, and Bradford excused themselves. Gabrielle, Abigail, and Enid followed Mrs. Fuller to the kitchen.

Elizabeth was left alone. She stretched her hands out toward the flames, absorbed the warmth, and wondered about the woman she'd seen in the upper window of the Children's Hospital. What was it about her that seemed so familiar? Was it the way she stood? The way she held her head?

Lost in thought, she didn't hear Weston come up behind her. "Hello, Beth."

She spun as if blasted by a gusty wind. Her hazel eyes snapped up to his.

"We have to talk," he said solemnly, pocketing his hands.

"Not now. Not here," she said in a fervent whisper.

"Then when?"

Her eyes became frantic. "I . . . I don't know."

"Tomorrow," he said flatly. It was a statement, not a question.

What could she say? She needed time. Time to work this confusion through her mind. She searched for a way out. "No, not tomorrow."

"Tomorrow," he reiterated somberly.

"Weston, please . . . please . . ."

His brows drew together. "Please what? Please go away, Weston? I don't want you, Weston? I haven't told him, Weston? I don't plan to."

She threw him an impatient glance. "You're not being fair."

A long silence, then, "No, Elizabeth," he said purposefully, his blue eyes intent. "It's ye who's not being fair." He stared at her for several seconds as the others began to regroup, then he turned away and said low under his breath, "Think about it."

*   *   *

The reverend held a child on each knee. At his feet sat several others. They clutched their treasures in their hands as though the items they'd been given were too precious to release for even so much as a moment.

"Tell us the Christmas story! Tell us the Christmas story!" they cried in unison, their young voices excited.

He chuckled warmly, then smiled up at Mrs. O'Rourke.

"Yes, Reverend. Tell us the Christmas story," she said.

"All right, then," he began, adjusting a child upon his knee.

But one small boy was not ready for the Christmas story yet.

"Mary Grace says I'm special," little Joseph interrupted proudly.

"Ahhh," the reverend said with interest, turning his attention to the child. "She does, does she?"

"Yep." Joseph shook his head so hard his bangs beat his forehead. "Because my name's Joseph, like the baby Jesus' earthly father." Then he added, "She says all children are special."

"Well, this Mary Grace must be a very wise woman."

"She is," Mrs. O'Rourke put in quietly. "A very kind and loving woman, too."

The reverend gave a small laugh. "All these years, and we've never met," he reflected softly. "Funny how we keep missing one another this way."

"Did you know she used to have a little boy like me?" Joseph asked matter-of-factly. "But he died." The small boy's expression grew solemn. "It makes her sad. I can tell."

"Yes," Tristan McRaney answered, "I imagine it does. I once had a little boy myself."

"You did? What was his name?" Joseph asked.

"Oh, come now," Mrs. O'Rourke interrupted, "tell us the Christmas story, Reverend."

"Yes, yes, tell us, tell us!" heralded the other children.

So the reverend smiled and solemnly began, "And it came to pass, in those days, that there went out a decree from Caesar Augustus, that all the world should be taxed . . ."

Much later, the reverend covered one of the many sleeping children with a blanket.

"Thank you, Reverend," Mrs. O'Rourke said with deep sincerity. "The children get so few visitors. You've made them very happy."

"It's always my pleasure, Mrs. O'Rourke. I'll stop by Christmas Eve if all goes well."

"That would be lovely."

"Good night, then," he said, donning his hat and pulling on his gloves.

"Good night, Reverend."

He walked down the quiet hall, deserted but for a doctor who was finishing his rounds. Looking down the long corridor, he caught sight of a woman. But it was only a glimpse, and she disappeared almost instantly up the staircase to the third floor, in a flurry of dark skirts. When he reached the stairway, he hesitated before going down.

A very faint, very familiar perfume still lingered behind her.

The next evening found Elizabeth tense and irritable. When Aaron arrived with a horse-drawn sleigh to take her and Abigail to the harbor, Elizabeth was distant and withdrawn.

It had snowed all day but had ceased an hour before nightfall. Above, the moon and stars burned bright. A luminescent light cast delicate shadows across the ice. Tree branches hung pregnant and full with their white wintry burden.

Laughing skaters formed groups gathered around several small fires and warmed their hands. A golden glow lit their happy faces. Ladies wrapped snug in their heavy winter cloaks held their furry muffs and shivered in the cold night air, while their gentlemen partners found this an excellent excuse to gather them close.

Aaron helped Abigail attach the sturdy blades to her shoes, while Elizabeth waited.

"Thank you, Aaron," Abigail said with a shy smile.

"Always my pleasure." Aaron's eyes rested upon her a little longer than usual before moving on to help Elizabeth with her blades. "Save me a skate, will you, Abby?" he said over his shoulder.

Abigail blushed and answered, "Of course." Aaron was the only one who called her Abby. He'd called her that since she was a chubby little girl.

The task completed, Elizabeth and Aaron stepped out onto the ice. They made a couple of practice rounds, then linked hands and skated around the harbor with enviable grace. Though she was not much of a dancer, Elizabeth was quite a skilled skater.

The rest of the group arrived. Aaron and Elizabeth went in to greet them.

"How's the ship, Wes?" called Evan Sparks, a friendly young man whom Wes remembered well from his school days.

"Going fine!" Weston waved a greeting.

"Did you bring something to keep us warm?" David

called out, Enid's hand clasped tight in his.

Weston wiggled his brows. "What do ye think?"

Gabrielle was at his side. "After church tomorrow evening, everyone is invited to my house for games and dancing," she called out. "Then we'll light the candles on the tree."

Tomorrow was Christmas Eve, a blessed, holy night. Elizabeth wished she could feel more excited.

"I'll be back," Aaron said to her, capturing Abigail's hand for his promised skate. Franklin Fuller stepped forward and captured Gabrielle's. The crowd broke apart, and others swept out onto the glistening ice.

Elizabeth stood facing Weston. He pocketed his hands, studying her.

"Don't look at me like that," she accused.

"Like what?" His voice was soft and deep.

The magnetism between them became almost tangible. Any fool could have sensed it. More than anything in the world, she wanted to go into his arms. At the same time, she wished him miles away.

Abruptly she whirled and hobbled away on her blades.

"Elizabeth! Wait a minute!" Quickly removing his blades, he caught her easily. He took her arm and spun her around. "We are going to talk!" he bit out.

"No," she snapped. "We're not!"

"Why?" he asked, his fingers unintentionally digging into her arm. "What have I done? What's changed?"

She shook her head vehemently and tried to pull her arm away, her eyes frantic. "I don't want to talk about this right now!"

A small distance away, several couples watched their heated exchange.

Mortified, Elizabeth closed her eyes.

"Ye see we have our usual audience," he said low, dangerously. "Now, either ye can take a walk with me,

or I'll make a scene they'll never forget, and then I'll
find Aaron and tell him about what happened between
us at the lighthouse."

Her face registered bald surprise; her lips dropped
open. He watched her go white and felt a pang of guilt.

A very small pang.

It was a lie. He wouldn't do any such thing. But he
was a man in love, and he was desperate. And the
situation was beginning to call for desperate measures.

"You wouldn't do that," she whispered, stunned. "Not
to your own brother."

He raised an eyebrow. "Are ye sure about that,
Lizzy?"

She weighed his words while she tried to read his
indecipherable gaze.

"I don't believe you." She lifted her chin. "You're
trying to bully me. And I—"

"Am I?"

Silence. Several heartbeats passed. In the distance an
owl hooted.

"All right," she snapped at length. "All right."

"I'm glad to see ye still have some sense, Beth."

He took her arm. Her steps were awkward, her blades
sinking into the snowy ground. But his steps were slow
and patient as he led her away from the harbor to a large
grouping of tall pines.

He didn't waste a minute. He hauled her behind the
screen of trees and reached for her, scooping her into his
arms, lifting her off her feet.

She braced her palms against his chest, struggling.
"Put me down. Are you mad?"

"Maybe," he admitted. "I don't know. All I know is I
love ye, Lizzy." His gloved hand was rough as he jerked
her head down to his and slammed his mouth into hers,
impressing upon her all the desperation that had built up

and tortured him during the last several weeks. Finally he broke away and allowed her to catch her breath. "God, Lizzy," he said more gently. "I can't stand this anymore. Him seeing ye every night while I wait." He gave a short, bitter laugh. "I'm beginning to hate my own brother."

"No, Weston . . . no," she said, aggrieved.

"I can't help it," he said against her cool cheek. "I want it to be ye and me. I want to hold ye all night long, love ye all night long . . ."

His head dipped once again. Her hand came up to his cheek. His lips were cold, his breath warm upon her mouth, and with a heavy sigh of resignation she gave up the inner battle and allowed her heart free reign. She opened her mouth and met his kiss with an ardent, welcoming one of her own. Frenzied and wet, their tongues danced while their breath mingled and escaped in short visible puffs of air.

He lowered her feet to the ground, their mouths still locked. His gloved hands slipped beneath the folds of her cape to find her warm, uncorseted waist, then her breasts, the globes of her buttocks, her thighs—all the parts of her body that made her unique, made her his.

When finally they separated, their breathing was harsh.

"I want ye." His expression was earnest. "Right now, right here if I could."

"Me, too," she whispered.

"Oh, Lizzy," he said, tortured, frustrated. He leaned his forehead against hers.

"We have to get back. They'll miss us."

"Not yet . . . Just a few more minutes."

She closed her eyes, clutched him close, breathed him in, felt his hardness, his roughness, the gentleness of his hands upon her body.

He pulled her cloak apart, knelt, and laid his head

against her breasts. She held him to her as he drew hot, wet circles against her nipples through the material of her dress.

"Oh, Wes . . ." She slowly opened her eyes to gaze at his head, silver and glorious in the lucid winter moonlight.

A footstep sounded.

Before they could separate, a tall figure came around the grove, almost colliding with them.

"Oh," he said softly, surprised, his golden eyes confused. "I'm sorry . . . I—" He looked from one to the other, his confused expression quickly changing to one of quiet understanding.

Elizabeth leapt back, almost tumbling over with the effort. A small, mortified gasp escaped her throat as tears of humiliation rose. She covered her mouth with her hand.

Sensing her panic, Weston reached for her. "Easy, Beth. It's only Brad—"

But she jerked away, frantically pulling her clothing into place. She broke into an awkward run while Weston rose to his feet and looked after her, his heart aching.

"I'm sorry, Wes. Really I am," Bradford said sincerely. "I had no idea you were out here."

Weston plunged his hands into his heavy coat. "It's all right, Brad. Don't worry about it."

"So . . . it's you and Elizabeth." There was no accusation in his low voice.

Weston met his gaze. "It's always been me and Elizabeth."

"Yes," Brad said. "I thought so."

He left Bradford at the pines. Looking out at the frozen harbor, he hurried to find his blades, while he watched Elizabeth sweep out onto the ice.

CHAPTER
15

"Ye can't run away from this forever!" Weston yelled, drawing abreast of her. "Ye can't run away from me forever!"

Ignoring him, she raised a hand and impatiently dashed away the shiny droplets that hung like liquid diamonds from her chin.

"Elizabeth!" He reached out to grab her arm, but she jerked away.

"Leave me alone!"

Frustrated, he considered it for the space of about two whole seconds.

"We need to get closer to shore, Beth," he warned, noticing they had skated out farther than was wise. "The ice hasn't been tested out here yet."

"Then you go in!" she snapped.

"Not without ye," he said calmly.

She stopped. He did also.

She faced him, her eyes shooting darts. "Then you'll have a long, cold wait, because there is no way I'm going back there and facing those people." She jabbed a finger in the direction of the other skaters.

He sighed, looked up at the sky, and crossed his arms over his chest. After a couple of thoughtful seconds, his gaze found her again. "Brad's the only one who saw us . . ."

She threw up her hands, her expression angry. Yet her bottom lip quivered when she said, "And did he ever! My God, Weston, he certainly did see us—"

"What are ye running away from, Beth? Brad or me or yerself?" His words were soft, yet they hit her with the force of an icy slap.

"You know bloody well—"

"No, Elizabeth . . . I don't think that's it at all. Ye want to know what I really think?" His expression grew dark; his brows met above his eyes. He jutted his chin forward. "I think ye're scared. I think ye're scared and running away from yerself, Lizzy. Yerself and the memory of yer mother and the truth about both her and yer baby brother. As if by atoning for her sin, ye can make everything right. As if by marrying Aaron and making yer father happy, ye can take away his sadness." His expression grew weary. Frustrated, he shoved gloved fingers through his hair. "When are ye going to realize what happened wasn't yer fault? It wasn't yer fault yer mother left. When are ye going to quit punishing yerself for something ye had nothing to do with? When are ye going to realize ye couldn't've saved yer brother? Nobody could've . . . Not ye. Not yer mother. No—"

She hit him—hard, cutting off his words.

His face went white while the imprint of her hand blazed an angry, accusing red.

"Damn you to hell, Weston Munroe!" she said under her breath, her voice impassioned. "Don't you dare say that about my mother! How dare you? She loved us!

There was no sin to atone for! You know full well she was on her way to visit an aunt in New York when that ship went down!"

He drew a deep, calming breath before he could continue. His voice was gentle when he said, "Yes, Lizzy. She did love ye. And I remember her well. Better than ye do, I'll bet. She was a fine woman. As fine a woman as my own mother. But she left ye just the same, and most of the townspeople know it. Yer father knows it, too. Why don't ye ask him?" he challenged quietly. "Why have ye never asked him?"

"You're a filthy liar!" She swung and hit him again. He didn't even attempt to deflect the blow. His head snapped back from the impact.

Her eyes filled with hot tears. Blinded, she turned as she sobbed and skated away as fast as she could, her strokes long and determined.

"Aw, Jesus, Lizzy," Weston said wearily, shaking his head, his heart breaking for her. Then, seeing what direction she was headed, he yelled, "Elizabeth! Don't go out there—"

But it was too late. Even as he yelled the words, he heard the ice cracking.

The sound was ominously loud, filling the still night air like reverberating gunshots.

"Elizabeeeeth!"

She never had time to scream.

The ice collapsed beneath her, and the dark waters swallowed her.

It was cold. So very cold.

She raised her arms high above her head and clawed upward. She broke the surface and gasped for air. From somewhere, she heard voices screaming. And another voice, a beloved one. "Hold on, Beth!" it yelled. "Hold

on, darlin'!" She hooked her arms on either side of the
jagged ice, trying desperately to hang on, to keep her
head above water, but she heard more awful cracking,
and more ice broke away, sending her down, down, into
the depths of the cold black waters.

She opened her eyes, looked up, and saw shadows
moving above her. *I'm here!* she wanted to scream.
Here! She tried to come up for air once again but
couldn't find the opening in the ice. Her skirts wrapped
around her legs like giant tentacles of an octopus. Her
lungs felt ready to burst. Her heart throbbed painfully
in her ears. Panicked, she tried again. But as she threw
her arm upward, a hazy blackness gripped her. Reality
became distorted. In front of her eyes loomed a small
chubby hand. She reached for it.

Hold tight, Jacob. Hold tight to Lizzy's hand, she
thought, as consciousness left her. *I'll get you out.*

And then the darkness took her . . .

Weston lay on his belly on the ice. "Hold my feet,
David!" he commanded. "Don't let go!" He watched her
fight her way upward, thrust her hand toward him, and
with a valiant effort he leaned over the ice and down into
the frigid water, immersing himself to the waist. *C'mon,
Lizzy. C'mon, darlin',* he wordlessly pleaded.

And then he had her.

Gasping for air, he lifted himself up, his head and
clothing dripping. "I've got her!" he yelled. "Help me
pull her out! Watch yer footing!" He held tight to her
hand. She was limp and heavy. With a mighty groan, he
pulled her up, managed to get her head above water, and
hooked his hands under her armpits. "Over here, Brad!
Get behind David and help him pull my legs! That's it!
Now slow and easy."

Inch by inch they tugged him, stopping only when the

ice made a threatening sound, until finally they were able to pull the two to safety.

His expression worried and tense, Weston stood, scooped her into his arms, then skated toward shore. He carried her to the nearest fire and laid her down into the snow. Her eyes were closed; her lashes appeared stuck to her cheeks like small, dark, frozen crescents. Her lips were purple.

She was alarmingly still.

Weston's heart banged against the walls of his chest. He chafed her hands, loosened her cold, wet clothing, and muttered unintelligible words of encouragement, completely oblivious to the presence of the others.

"Oh, Elizabeth!" It was Gabrielle, cutting through the crowd, her voice revealing her hysteria.

"Get a doctor!" someone cried.

"Is she breathing?" someone else asked.

Soft weeping came from over Weston's shoulder.

Instinct took over, and he began to pump her stomach, his breath coming in short, desperate puffs, while inwardly he prayed, *Dear God, don't let her die! Please, don't let her die!*

After what seemed an eternity, she coughed.

He immediately flipped her over onto her stomach. She took several great gulps of air, coughed again, then vomited a rush of water.

Murmurs of relief rippled through the anxious crowd, along with the wonderful words "She's alive! She's alive!"

He turned her over and gathered her against his chest and whispered, "Lizzy . . . God, Lizzy . . ."

"Wes . . . ," she choked in a broken voice. "I'm . . . so c-cold . . ."

"Get a blanket!" he yelled to someone. "Now!"

"Wes . . ."

Her voice was so thready, so thin, he had to lean his ear to her mouth to hear her. "What, darlin'?"

Her eyes shut, and she lifted a hand to his cheek. "I'm . . . so . . . sorry I h-hit you."

His composure slipping, he swallowed several times, his throat burning, while he smoothed her cold, matted hair back from her brow. Then, giving up the battle, he dropped his head to her throat and wept.

Abigail fell to her knees beside him. Crying silently, she placed an arm around his shoulder and held fast to one of Elizabeth's cold hands.

Aaron looked on, his relief soon changing to a feeling of puzzled embarrassment at the emotional scene. In all the years he'd known his brother, he'd never seen him react in such a demonstrative manner.

Bradford and David watched from behind. They looked from Aaron to Weston, then Bradford stepped forward, knelt beside his friend, and took Elizabeth's free hand. He gazed down at Elizabeth. "We're all glad she's all right," he said calmly, attempting to diminish the intensity of Weston's actions. He leaned close to Elizabeth and whispered into her ear, "You needn't worry, Elizabeth."

Her heavy lids parted slowly. Understanding dawned. She looked up into his steady gold eyes and gave him a tremulous smile.

David and the others joined the small group.

Aaron knelt beside his brother. Weston lifted his head. Their eyes met and held. Then, very slowly, Weston eased Elizabeth off his lap and into the arms of his brother.

"I'll get the sleigh," he said, rising, his voice unnaturally tight, his eyes haunted. "We'd better get her home."

*   *   *

"Please, Ab," Elizabeth whispered hoarsely from her bed, "I want you to go."

"Don't be a ninny," Abigail said, her chin set stubbornly. "I want to stay here with you."

Aaron stepped close to Abigail's side. "Truly, Elizabeth, we'd much rather stay here with you."

Elizabeth coughed twice, clearing her throat. Struggling, she managed to sit up in her bed, arranging a pillow behind her back.

Abigail bent to aid her, but Elizabeth waved her away. "Abigail," she said impatiently, "the doctor says I'll be fine. There's no need to fuss over me."

"You almost drowned!"

"But I didn't."

"But you're feverish—"

"Slightly feverish," she corrected, "only slightly. I'm not dying, for heaven's sake! I'll be fine in a few days." For good measure she added, "You don't see Papa hovering over me like an anxious mother hen, now, do you?"

"That's because you won't let him."

"He's not even here, is he?"

"Well, I don't care." Abigail crossed her arms over her chest. "I simply do not care to attend a Christmas Eve service or a party without you."

His expression set, Aaron nodded. "I agree."

"Now you're both being ridiculous," Elizabeth said wearily. "The children will be looking for you to lead them through their program in tonight's service, Abigail. You can't let them down. They'll be lost without you. And Papa will be looking for you, also. You both know how very disappointed Gabrielle will be, too, if you don't show up for her party." She gazed at both of them, her eyelids heavy. "To be perfectly honest, I'm very tired. All I really want to do is sleep. So you see, I'd be rather poor company for you both. And I could rest much better if you went and enjoyed the evening." She reached out and took their hands, gently placing Aaron's over Abigail's. "Aaron, please take Abigail to church this evening and be her escort to Gabrielle's party." With a tired smile, she added, "It would make me very happy."

Abigail stared at Elizabeth for a long, quiet moment. She turned to Aaron and met his gaze. But her eyes flicked away almost instantly. A deep blush stole over her face. She shook her head. "Oh, Elizabeth . . . I don't think . . . I simply couldn't . . ."

"Please." Elizabeth snuggled beneath the quilt, lifting plaintive eyes. "Please go."

For a moment Aaron seemed about to object. But instead he tightened his hand around Abigail's, turned to her, and said, "It would be my pleasure to be your escort tonight, Abby. What do you say?"

"Elizabeth, I—"

"She says yes." Elizabeth smiled and yawned. "Now good night."

A persistent tapping invaded her sleep.

Elizabeth snuggled deeper beneath the quilts, willing it to stop, and tried to reenter her dream world.

The tapping continued.

Groaning, she lifted heavy, achy lids. Her throat hurt; her mouth was parched. She felt disoriented.

Tap! Tap! Tap!

She raised herself up on an elbow and tried to focus on the sound.

Tap! Tap! Tap! Tap!

She narrowed her eyes and peered through the dark room toward the sound. The fire in the fireplace had burned down to glowing embers; the night was dark, the moon well covered by thick clouds. But a faint wash of light from the new snow shone through the window.

Tap! Tap! Tap!

She sat up slowly. Her head aching, she eased off the bed and made her way toward the window. Reaching it, she bent, pressed her nose to the cold pane, and squinted. Outside, the snow fell softly to a quiet, snow-shrouded world. The snowflakes were large and thick and lacy and fell so slowly that they seemed to be suspended in midair. She tried to focus on the large, dark shadow in the tree. She finally did, then drew back quickly, certain she was indeed still dreaming.

Perched on a snowy limb, directly in front of her, was Weston. He wore a strange-looking cap on his head, and in his arms he held a large bundle.

He was grinning like a fool.

Tap! Tap! Tap! "Let me in, Beth!"

Weak, she sank to her knees before the window and rested her hot forehead against the wonderfully cool pane. "You can't come in, Wes. Everyone's gone, and I'm so . . . tired . . ."

"Beth, it's freezing out here!"

"Dreams can't freeze to death," she murmured, her eyes drifting shut.

Tap, tap, tap, tap, tap!

"Oh, for heaven's sake," she muttered, forcing her eyes open. She looked out the glass to find two eyes staring back at her.

"Let me in, Beth!"

She forced her head off the window, then willed the rest of her body to stand.

"C'mon, Lizzy!" he pleaded. "Open the damned window before I fall out of this tree!"

Too tired to argue, fearing he wouldn't relent, she eased the window open. From outside, his hands reached in and joined hers, forcing the window up the rest of the way. Then he was in her room—bag, hat, over six feet of grinning man, all covered by a thin frosting of snow.

He dusted his shoulders off, shook himself like a great hairy dog, then bowed before her and with a lazy smile said, "Merry Christmas, Beth."

Speechless, she stared at him, her mouth gaping open. The winter air blew in, bringing with it the lovely unified sound of Christmas chimes as they reverberated throughout the city.

"Ohhh . . . ," she said softly, pressing her fingertips to the pane, forgetting him for a moment, "how beautiful they always sound on this night. It seems I forget somehow . . ."

A tremor passed through her. Seeing it, the smile died on his face. He dropped his bag and bent to close the window.

"Leave it open just a bit," she begged, lifting her eyes to his. "I want to hear them."

He hesitated a second, then relented. "All right, darlin', but back into bed with ye." He took her arm and steered her toward her bed.

"What are you doing here?" she croaked, angling a suspicious glance at him.

"Getting ye back into bed."

She shook her head and sat down on the bed. "You can't stay . . ."

He picked up her legs and set them on the bed.

"Papa . . ."

"Won't be home for some time yet."

"But Gabrielle's party . . ."

"Will do fine without me." He covered her with the quilts and tucked them snugly around her.

She sank down onto the pillow, too weak to fight him. "Wes," she whispered, "what are you doing here?"

He paused, studying her. Her dark red hair was spread out on the pillow, her cheeks flushed bright with fever. He realized how fortunate he was to see her lying there alive, and found himself momentarily overcome with emotion. He dropped to one knee and captured her hand. All traces of teasing were gone when he said, "I'm spending Christmas Eve with ye, Beth. There isn't anywhere else I'd rather be."

She gazed at him silently, her eyes filling with tears. Her lids sank shut. He leaned over the bed, his breath fanning her cheek, while his hand rested against the side of her throat. With a touch as light as gossamer, his lips met hers. Briefly, for only a fraction of a moment, he continued the fragile contact, then reluctantly he drew away.

She opened her eyes.

He smiled.

To Elizabeth, the room was no longer dark.

He was quite a sight, with his comical knitted cap, his hair mussed beneath it, his blue eyes bright and earnest.

"Silly hat," she scoffed.

"Stole it from a sailor," he answered honestly. "What do ye want for nothing?"

She smiled indulgently and reached a hand to his face. He took her hand, pressed a kiss into her palm, then released it and crossed the room to the fireplace. He added a log to the others, then reached for the poker and stirred the latent embers. His face reflected the amber light from the flames, and the room took on a warm glow. "I brought us dinner." He found his bag and hesitated as he pulled out a bottle. "And something to keep us warm."

He approached the bed, dragging his bundle, then shed his coat. "Move over, Lizzy. Let me in."

"No, you can't," she objected.

But he ignored her. The bed sank under his weight. He pulled his boots off and dropped them to the floor with a thump. "There," he said, lifting the quilts and arranging himself more comfortably at her side, "that's better." He pulled off his hat and dropped it beside his bag.

Though not surprised at his temerity, she shoved against his hard shoulder. "You can't share a bed with me." But he didn't budge.

His eyes found hers, the smile gone. He blinked once. "I've shared more than a bed with ye, Lizzy."

There was no arguing with that truth.

A meaningful silence followed, then, "I'm thirsty, Wes," she finally admitted.

He pulled his bag up beside him. "Here." He uncorked the bottle and handed it to her.

She tipped the bottle into the air and took a long drink. It burned all the way down. She coughed. But a moment later, a satisfying warmth began to build within. "The Devil's brew," she said dryly, eyeing the bottle skeptically.

"So they say." Concentrating on his task, he dug deep into the bag and soon had a crusty loaf of bread, a small crock of butter, cheese, ham, and apple tarts laid before them. "A feast," he announced, a slow grin spreading across his face.

"Your mother's apple tarts?" She lifted an inquisitive eyebrow.

He shrugged and grinned sheepishly. "Always have loved those things. Are ye hungry?"

Motionless, she studied him. "Oh, Wes," she choked, touched by his gesture, yet struggling with her own awful confusion. She turned her head into the pillow and attempted to cover her face with her hands.

"Hey," he said, gently pulling her hands away. "What's this?" His thumbs wiped the moisture from her cheeks. "I know this isn't exactly the Queen's buffet, but—"

"It's perfect," Elizabeth whispered, reining in her emotions. She sat up, propping her back against the headboard. "Truly."

"Then let's eat."

They did, and in companionable silence, while the faint sounds of chimes rang out into the holy night and threaded through the window. For a little while, they let the future and the problems they would have to face therein rest.

When they were finally finished, she turned to him and smiled. "What else do you have in that sack?"

"Just memories."

"Of?"

"Of ye . . ." He offered no further explanation as he lowered the bag to the floor. Reclining against the headboard, he pulled her into his arms and brought her head to rest against his chest. "Are ye going to be all right, Beth? I asked Aaron, but he hadn't been to see ye yet. What did the doctor say?"

Her head nodded against his warm chest, his flannel shirt soft beneath her cheek. "Yes. I'll be fine."

He held her close, her breasts pressed against his chest, while he stroked the hair from her temple, kissed her eyelids, and infused her with his body heat. Each gesture was intimate and tender, yet devoid of all lust or passion.

The moment brought another new awareness of him, to have him touch her in such a manner and want nothing more . . .

"Wes," she whispered at length.

"What, darlin'?"

"You were right."

Silence. The fire hissed and crackled.

"You were right about my father, my mother, about my baby brother . . ." She swallowed. "About Aaron, too."

He rested his chin on top of her head, one wide hand riding up and down her arm to her shoulder. "I know."

"I hate it when you're right."

"I know."

"I love you, Wes." Simple, beautiful words.

He didn't answer. He couldn't. But his arms tightened around her.

"I have to tell him," she acknowledged sadly.

More silence.

"Merry Christmas, Wes . . ." Her voice trailed off sleepily.

"Merry Christmas, Lizzy." He closed his eyes and rested the back of his head against the headboard.

A few hushed moments later, she was asleep.

The bells rang out three more lovely songs before he soundlessly left her, exiting the way he'd come, closing the window tightly behind him.

CHAPTER
16

The children at the hospital always waited anxiously for their visitors, but on Christmas Eve the very pine-scented air they breathed was ripe with magical expectations.

Their minds danced with tales of Christmas, and their eyes glowed bright with hope, for this night, above all others, brought them joy and a measure of the attention they so sorely needed from some of the city's kindlier, more compassionate citizens.

Tristan McRaney was one of these.

He stood outside the large brick building, lifted his face to the sky, and listened as the chimes shimmered through him. Years ago, on eves such as this, long after the final Christmas service, after their own children were tucked safely into their beds, he and Catherine used to slip outside at exactly midnight to listen to the last Christmas hymn.

Back then he thought she'd be with him forever.

He sighed heavily and despondently dropped his chin to his chest. A few moments later, he squared his shoulders, forced a smile onto his face, and entered the building.

He spent the next hour with the children, singing, talking, giving them the finest gifts of all: love and his attention. And when the hour grew late, he gathered his gloves, hat, and cane and bade Mrs. O'Rourke a very Merry Christmas.

"And to you, Reverend," she replied, her eyes kind. "Especially to you, sir."

He walked down the silent, deserted hall, bemused by the intense need to linger. When he reached the stairs, he paused, catching once again the familiar scent of perfume. Then he surprised himself. Instead of going down the stairs, he allowed his instincts to guide him and followed the scent up the staircase.

The upper hall was darker than the lower, lit with only the dim glow from a few sputtering gas lamps. Not quite sure what it was he sought, he wandered down the lonely corridor soundlessly, until finally he stopped before a door.

There were many doors, but a thread of light shone from beneath this one.

He stood stock still, his senses reeling. His eyes slipped shut while he breathed in deeply. The scent was stronger, clearer, dearer.

His heart did a painful tumble.

His breathing suspended, he lifted a hand to the door but couldn't find within himself the power to knock.

He didn't have to.

The door swung open.

Not expecting his presence, the tall, slender woman nearly collided with him. Surprised, her eyes shot to his, then widened in distress, as her name escaped his lips in a disbelieving whisper.

* * *

"Good night, Abby," Aaron said, taking her hand. "Thank you for a wonderful evening."

Abigail smiled, one hand on the doorknob. "I had a lovely time." She looked up into his steady eyes for two seconds, then discreetly dropped her gaze, her cheeks warming.

Touched by her shyness, he bent to place a kiss upon her cheek, but at the precise moment of contact, she lifted her head in surprise and his mouth grazed the side of hers.

Startled, she drew back. But he didn't. She pressed her fingertips to her lips, while he remained close and studied her thoughtfully.

"Merry Christmas, Abby," he said.

"And to you, Aaron," she whispered, then turned and quickly slipped into the house as if he'd suddenly become her nemesis, while he remained outside the McRaney door for a long, long time.

Slowly she made her way up the stairs to her bedroom. The house was quiet.

She took her time, for she wanted to recall every memory of every moment she'd experienced these last few hours, and keep them safely locked within her heart forever.

In her bedroom, she laid her muff and scarf aside. The fire had burned low, yet the room was comfortably warm. Quietly she approached Elizabeth's bed, to find her motionless and sleeping peacefully.

Gazing down at her, Abigail felt a deep rush of affection, leaned down, and pressed a kiss to her warm cheek. "Thank you, Beth," she whispered, "for giving me a most wonderful Christmas gift."

Straightening, she turned away and crossed the room

to the bureau. She paused a moment, then opened the
top drawer. She knew exactly what it was she sought.
It never took long to find them. From beneath a few
neatly folded items, she extracted two sad-looking, much
handled feathers and a very small makeshift splint.

She lifted the feathers to her cheek, held them there,
closed her eyes, and once again saw the young man
whose selfless act of kindness had captured her heart
so many years ago.

Tristan's throat worked soundlessly for several seconds. "My God, Catherine!" His hands opened and closed
at his side.

"Tristan," she whispered and swayed, almost falling
in the attempt to back into the room.

His hands came up to steady her.

"Is it really you?" His eyes drank her in: the wide
hazel eyes now marked by tiny lines, the swept-back
auburn hair now streaked with gray. Yet, for all these
differences, she was no less beautiful than she'd been
the day he'd met her.

"Yes . . ." There was no need to lie. "It's me."

They stared into each other's eyes. Time became suspended.

At length, Tristan broke the stunned silence. "All
these years," he accused softly, his eyes tortured. "I—
we thought you were dead . . . I mourned for you . . .
We mourned for you . . ."

Beleaguered, she shook her head. "Did you really,
Tristan?"

"Yes." His voice was an impassioned whisper. "Yes.
Of course."

"No," she challenged gently. "You may have mourned
for me, but I think you always knew I wasn't dead. I

think you knew when they didn't find my body. I think you knew then."

A long, tense silence ensued.

He raised his palms. "Maybe . . . All right, yes." He nodded slowly and became fully honest with himself. "Yes, I always felt you might be out there somewhere . . ."

"I thought so." A sad smile swept her face. "But you didn't look."

"I didn't know where to look!"

She shook her head. "It doesn't matter. You see, in my heart, I was dead." She said the words so softly he barely heard her. "Catherine McRaney was dead. Mary Grace was alive." She sighed heavily. "I suppose you're wondering exactly who Mary Grace is or was?" When he didn't reply, she continued. "Mary Grace was a very kind woman I met on board the ship when I left here. She was about my age, a widow with no children. She died when the ship went down. But I lived. When I was found alive, I fully intended to come home." Her voice cracked with emotion. "I wanted so badly to come home, but somehow . . ."

Chagrined, she dropped her gaze. Blinking several times to quell the tears, she took his hand and drew him into her room, closing the door quietly behind him.

The need to touch her was fierce. He reached out to embrace her, but like a shy kitten she backed away. "Please sit down, Tristan," she said.

He was stung by her rejection, and his eyes reflected his pain. He reached up slowly, took off his hat, then clasped it between his hands, feeling sixteen and awkward and uncertain. He watched her move about the mean little room, her graceful, familiar hands nervously rearranging things, touching things: her hairbrush and

comb, the embroidery on her bedspread, the mirror—
ah, the mirror, almost a replica of the very one she'd
left at home, now used by her daughters.

Tristan lowered himself into a hard chair and tried to
anchor the tumultuous emotions that were rolling inside
him. How could she have stayed away all these years?
How could she have caused all his suffering?

Refusing to look at him, she focused her attention on
the walls, the floor, the window, anything but him. "I
know what you're thinking. And feeling. And I understand. You're angry. I have no defense to offer you. But
there's one thing I want you to know, Tristan. Captain
Braxton offered me passage. Nothing more. He was a
good, honorable man who died with most of his passengers when his ship went down. When I returned to
Toronto, someone very dear to me told me that it had
been rumored that I had run away with him." Her eyes
lifted, meeting her husband's. "The rumors were false,
Tristan. I've never been unfaithful. You've always been
the only one for me."

He shook his head, stunned, pained. "Then why? I still
don't understand."

"I would ask you if you remember the day I left."

"Yes," came his bitter response. "How could I ever
forget?"

"Our baby . . ." Her voice wavered. "Our precious
little Jacob had been dead only a week. I tried to talk to
you that day. I needed you. I needed you so badly, but
you had to go. Others needed you more than I. Always
more than I. You'd become so busy those days."

Tristan swallowed thickly. Guilt became a bitter pill.
He wanted to go to her, to take her in his arms, tell her he
was sorry, but her rigid stance held him away. How was
it he'd forgotten the way she'd seemed that morning—

despondent, desperate, lonely?

"I know how much it meant to you to have a son." She smiled in remembrance. "And we finally did. He was so beautiful, and we loved him so. All of us did— Elizabeth, Abigail. He was such a happy little boy. And then we lost him . . . because of me."

Tristan bolted from his seat. "No!"

She put out both palms to keep him at bay. "We almost lost Elizabeth, too."

His eyes sorrowful, Tristan shook his head vehemently. "No, Catherine! It wasn't your fault!"

"Wasn't it?" she asked calmly, aggrieved. "What kind of a mother takes her children out on a ferry and doesn't watch them?"

"You can't watch children every minute. You were only talking a minute."

Her eyes filled with tears. "A minute too long. A minute long enough for our baby to fall into the water and drown. A minute long enough for our brave little girl to jump in and try to save him and almost drown along with him."

"It could have happened to anyone."

"But it didn't. It happened to us."

"Catherine . . ." The name was a bereaved whisper.

She gave a small, sad laugh. "It's funny, Tristan, how differently you see things now."

Faced with the truth of that statement, the impact hit him with the force of a lightning bolt. My God! He'd blamed her! Oh, he hadn't said as much, but his actions had spoken more clearly, more eloquently than any words ever could have.

"Catherine, I . . ." Bereft, he shook his head helplessly. His gray eyes misted and sought hers. "It wasn't your fault."

She shrugged a slender shoulder. "It doesn't matter any longer, Tristan. I'm happy now. I've found my peace."

"Here?" He lifted his arms out at his sides.

"Yes," she said softly. "Here with the children."

"But Abigail and Elizabeth . . ."

"Have grown into fine young women. I watched them do so over the years. Benjamin has told me much about them. You've done a fine job."

Tristan furrowed his brow. "Benjamin?"

She smiled and dropped her gaze, carefully smoothing the wrinkles from the front of her black silk dress. "When they built the Lakeside Home out on the island, he found me. He's quite a regular visitor throughout the summer months. The children love him." She paused, then said, "They love you, too."

"He never told us about you." His voice echoed hurt and confusion.

"I asked him not to. I made him promise that he wouldn't. I thought it best that way."

"But why?" He took a step toward her.

She tipped her head. "How does the wife of a Methodist minister, thought to be dead, miraculously become resurrected and return to the family she abandoned?"

He studied her, his heart full of a host of unspoken words. The faint sound of the chimes ringing out the last of the Christmas hymns came from outside. Nostalgia swept over them. He slowly crossed the room to stand before her.

Hat in hand, he gazed down into her eyes. "Christmas is a time for miracles, Cathy. Surely you know that."

An eloquent chime-filled silence in which she could find no words to utter filled the night.

"I've been so lonely without you," he whispered fervently. "I have never stopped loving you, Cathy." His voice was deep and masculine, his eyes—the ageless, ardent eyes of the young man who had spoken vows to her over twenty years ago—spoke to her now, of love and hope and forgiveness. "I've wanted no other. There's been no other. Not even once."

"Oh, Tristan," she whispered brokenly, and dropped her chin to her chest, her eyes slipping shut.

He reached a finger to her chin and lifted it. "Forgive me, Catherine. Forgive me for allowing other things to take precedence over you and me. Forgive me for blaming you for what you could not have prevented. Forgive me for allowing myself to become a stiff, close-minded fool. Forgive me for all the wasted years—all the years we've been apart . . ." He paused, then said, "Come home, Cathy. Come home where you belong."

"Oh, Tristan," she repeated, turning her face into his hand. "What will people say?"

"Whatever they could say would not be enough to keep me from you now that I've found you once again."

"It will be so difficult—"

"But we'll be together. The way we were in the beginning."

The chimes rang out their last crystalline notes while the reverend dropped his hat to the floor and gathered his wife to his breast.

For Catherine McRaney, life began again, and Mary Grace drifted into the past, along with the loneliness of far too many years.

On Christmas morning, Elizabeth awoke to thin gray light threading its way through her window. It was barely dawn. She glanced over at Abigail, who instead slept soundly.

From below came the soft murmur of voices.

Elizabeth swung her legs over the bed and stood. During the night, her fever had abated, and though she was weak, she felt much more like herself. Something on the floor caught her eye. She bent and retrieved it.

Silly hat, she thought, holding it to her face and breathing deeply of the beloved scent it still held.

She walked to the bureau and tucked it safely into the top drawer, then donned her wrap and found her way toward the voices downstairs.

They came from the kitchen, along with the enticing smell of fresh coffee and bacon.

She entered the room, but stopped just inside the door, confusion nailing her feet to the floor. A woman in dark clothing, wearing one of Elizabeth's aprons, sat at the table with her father. Hands joined intimately, their eyes were locked on one another. Sensing her presence, their voices halted, and their gazes lifted to hers.

"Elizabeth," Tristan said, slowly rising from his chair.

The woman rose, also.

Dazed, Elizabeth stood in a tense, uncertain silence. She felt a prick of uneasiness as she gazed back at eyes so familiar, so very much like her own. She felt as though she were staring into a mirror.

"Hello, darling," the woman whispered softly.

The years swept away.

"Mama?" Elizabeth questioned in a small voice.

"Yes, sweetheart." Catherine extended her hands and cautiously closed the distance between them.

"Mama?" Elizabeth asked again, her brow knitted tight, her thumb working her cuticle.

Catherine lifted her arms. "It's me . . ."

"Y-You're alive?"

"Yes, darling. I'm alive." She reached Elizabeth and

embraced her tentatively, while Elizabeth stood stiff and unyielding in her arms.

"You're alive . . . ," Elizabeth repeated disbelievingly. Time became motionless as she tried to fully comprehend the implications of this truth. All these years, she thought, all these sad, lonely years. Weston was right. Her mother had indeed purposely left them.

The unfairness of it all hit her with the force of a hammer. She wrenched herself free from Catherine's arms. "Don't touch me," she hissed, her eyes filling with hot, angry tears. "Don't you ever touch me." Tears raining down her cheeks, she turned and ran from the room.

"Elizabeth!" her father called after her and took a step to follow. "That's no way to talk to your mother!"

But Elizabeth paid him no heed.

With gentle hands, Catherine halted him. "Let her go, Tristan," she said, gazing after Elizabeth. "She needs time to work this out for herself."

Abigail accepted Catherine's return much differently from the way Elizabeth had. Unlike Elizabeth, Abigail barely remembered their mother and the death of her brother; she recalled nothing at all about the circumstances of Catherine's unexplained departure or the specter of gossip that had clung to it all these years.

Elizabeth had protected her sister well.

Though Abigail tried to empathize with Elizabeth's distress and animosity, she could not. Her joy at having her mother home greatly overrode any other emotion, or any of the many underlying questions.

Abigail was simply glad to have her mother alive and her family intact. There was a new light in her father's eyes. Christmas had indeed brought a miracle.

Elizabeth felt differently.

"Beth," Abigail said worriedly from the door of their room later that same morning, "don't you think you're being a bit unfair?"

Elizabeth evaded her sister's eyes. "You wouldn't understand," she said as gently as she could.

"I don't see how you can be so angry when God has given us such a wonderful gift. She's here with us now. Does it matter so very much why she didn't come home sooner?"

Elizabeth met her gaze squarely. "Yes. To me it does." Still, Elizabeth wanted more than anything to see Abigail happy. Abigail looked at the world differently from the way most people did—with innocence and hope, trust and goodwill.

Elizabeth forced a smile. "I know you don't understand. I don't expect you to. You're not responsible for how I feel. So go on. Go on downstairs with Papa . . ." The name stuck in her throat like a rock. "And with Mama. It's Christmas."

"I don't want to leave you."

"I want to be left alone for a while. I'm all right. Truly."

Elizabeth spent the remainder of the morning silent and unrelenting, staring out the window of her room at the pureness of the frigid winter world. The houses were crested with snowy caps, while ribbons of smoke curled upward into a steely gray sky. Her throat burning with stubbornly restrained tears, she sorted through myriad conflicting emotions, trying to find a place and reason for them all, a justification for each and every one, and wondered why she could not accept this gift, this phenomenon, with the same sweet, complacent attitude as her sister.

Some of her emotions were so intense they frightened

her. She felt betrayed and angry, needy and alone. There was a part of her that wanted to fly down the stairs, kneel at her mother's feet, and lay her head in the gentle shelter of her lap.

But she didn't. She couldn't.

For there was that other part of her that wanted to hurl angry words of accusation: *You can't just come back like this! It's not that easy! You left us! You weren't dead! And you didn't come home! You could have, but you didn't!*

There came a knock on her door a few hours later.

She ignored it.

"Elizabeth?" It was her father. "Are you all right in there?" His voice was low and full of concern.

"Yes, Papa. I'm fine."

"Can we talk?"

God, how she loved him. She wanted so much for him to be happy. She swallowed the knot of misery in her throat and said, "Not now, Papa. Maybe later."

He left without pressing her further; his footsteps in the hall sounded heavy and forlorn.

She left the window and forced herself to dress. A short time later, another knock sounded. After a few silent seconds, the door tentatively swung open.

"Elizabeth?" It was Catherine. "May I come in?"

Her eyes glacial, Elizabeth compressed her lips, refusing to grant permission.

Catherine closed the door softly behind her and stood uncomfortably uncertain before her eldest daughter. "I'm so sorry," she said. "I'm—"

"I don't give a bloody damn what you are!" Elizabeth flung the words at her heartlessly. "I don't care anything about you!" But the voice that wavered and the tears that rushed to her eyes belied that statement. "Papa and

Abigail might be happy you've come waltzing back into our lives as if it were only yesterday you left, but I'm not them and I'm not happy!" She lowered her voice to a fierce whisper. "And don't you expect me to be!"

Catherine gazed at her daughter, her heart breaking. "My poor darling . . ."

Elizabeth snatched up her cloak, scarf, and muff and whizzed past her mother, almost knocking her down. She jerked the door open, whirled, and looked through her as though she were nothing more than the thinnest wisp of smoke. "I'm not your darling," she said. "I never was."

Elizabeth strode through the cold morning. Her steps long and determined, she often slipped along the snowy path while she swallowed her hurt and nursed her confusion into a much more tolerable self-righteous indignation. She walked for hours, away from Ashbridge Bay, down Queen Street, on to King, past the corner of Yonge, below the windows of the Temperance and General Assurance Company, on toward the Hub Hotel—all the while searching, searching for answers.

The city was relatively quiet this day. The streetcars were silent, and the streets were almost empty. Every now and then, a sleigh led by large-footed horses, draped with sleighbells, would pass, packed with merry occupants on their way to visit friends and relatives.

The sights and sounds left her feeling even more lonely.

Eventually she found herself at the wharf. She looked out at the ice and watched the snow shift across the pale surface like thin layers of misplaced desert sand.

She thought of the horror of being beneath that ice. She thought of the man who'd pulled her from it, and of last night—Christmas Eve spent in his arms, his tenderness toward her—and knew, if she was sure of nothing else, that she loved him.

She loved Aaron, too. She could not deny it. But it was a different love, much like what she felt for Abigail—protective, quiet, warm. Love for a sibling.

She lifted her eyes. In the distance she saw the island and the lighthouse and she thought of Benjamin.

She missed him.

"Merry Christmas, Benjamin," she whispered.

Feeling very tired, her lips cold and dry, her fingers growing numb, she turned toward home.

By the time she reached her house, it was late afternoon and snowing once again.

Before she could open the door, it was opened for her. Abigail gently pulled her in, her expression somber. "It's Aaron," she said quietly. "He's in the parlor." She paused for a moment. "He needs you, Beth."

CHAPTER
1 7

Sometime during the night, while Christmas chimes heralded in the birth of a holy child, Catherine McRaney had regained her life, and Everitt Munroe had quietly resigned his.

Elizabeth found Aaron sitting in the parlor with her father and mother.

When she entered the room, he stood. His shoulders drooped despairingly. His young, handsome face was lined with sorrow. A light stubble shadowed his usually smooth jaw.

Quickly forgetting her own pain in the face of his, she divested herself of her cloak and closed the distance between them. "Oh, Aaron, I'm so sorry," she offered sincerely, taking both of his hands.

He swallowed and nodded.

"How is your mother?" Elizabeth asked. *How is Weston?* she also wanted to ask.

"She's doing well. She's a strong woman." He paused. "We all knew it was only a matter of time."

"And Daniel?"

"It's hardest for Daniel. He's young . . ."

"Yes, of course." Elizabeth squeezed his hands. "What a sad thing to have happen at Christmas . . ." The words seemed inane, simple, useless. But they were uttered from a truly sympathetic heart that reached out to a person she dearly loved.

Aaron nodded again and offered her a doleful smile. "But you"—he looked from her father to her mother— "you've had a wonderful Christmas indeed."

Elizabeth made no reply. While Aaron had lost a parent, she had regained one. She lifted confused eyes to her mother and felt an almost painful urge to say something. Something kind, something welcoming? She wasn't sure. Instead, she averted her gaze and turned to Abigail. "Come, Abigail. Sit with Aaron while I make us some tea."

"I'll make the tea," Catherine offered, rising from the settee.

"No," Elizabeth insisted firmly. "I'll do it."

The Munroe house was filled with mourners. Men in dark suits, women in black dresses, all coming to pay their final respects to a dignified member of their circle.

Unknowingly, Everitt Munroe's last deed had been most noble.

He would have been pleased to know that he'd rescued Elizabeth, as well as Catherine, from the acidic tongues of some of their crueler acquaintances by tempering the shock of Catherine's return and diverting their attentions to this other, more somber event. Catherine McRaney's return somehow seemed less spectacular in the face of Everitt Munroe's death. Tongues that would have twittered perversely about the mystery were hushed, at least for now, dutifully silenced by respect for the man who lay within his coffin.

Early in the day, Tristan and Catherine arrived with their daughters. Amid the many speculative glances, Tristan kept his hand at the small of his wife's back at all times, supporting her with his strength, upholding her with his love.

They all came: Gabrielle, David, Bradford, Franklin, Enid, and many of the city's merchants and business-men—Timothy Eaton, Robert Simpson, Russell St. Clair, Ned Hanlan—all with sincere condolences, many arms laden with pies, puddings, hams, casseroles, and breads.

Abigail and Gabrielle proved indispensable. After set-ting Sarah Munroe and a forlorn Daniel into chairs beside the casket, they stood at the Munroe door, quietly greeting neighbors and friends, taking coats, directing them into the parlor, while Elizabeth and Aaron stood at the end of the coffin and clasped the hand of each who passed.

Weston was absent.

Tongues did twitter about that. "Disrespectful young whelp . . ." "Never did get along with his father . . ."

But Elizabeth knew better.

It wasn't disrespect that held Weston away. He was off alone somewhere, nursing his grief, probably wishing he hadn't waited quite so long to come home.

She felt irreverent.

Standing beside Aaron, it was Weston she longed to seek out, Weston she longed to comfort. She missed him terribly. But Aaron needed her more.

It was late in the day when Weston finally came through the door. The house was almost empty.

Elizabeth's heart swelled at the sight of him. All the pent-up emotion of the day called for release. She watched Gabrielle step forward, greet him, take his coat and hat, then touch his hand before turning back to offer the items to Abigail. The simple, sympathetic gestures sent spears straight to the center of Elizabeth's heart.

His eyes found hers.

Her heart strained toward him.

I'm so sorry, Wes.

I know.

I love you.

I love ye, too.

He closed the distance between them. "Wes," Aaron said. "I was beginning to worry about you."

"I'm sorry, Aaron, I . . ." Weston shook his head helplessly, unable to voice the words. His Adam's apple bobbed. Elizabeth's heart ached.

"There's no need to explain." Aaron clasped his shoulder. "It's all right."

Weston took his place on the other side of Elizabeth.

She wanted nothing more than to turn to him, pull his head down to her breast, touch his face, hair, neck. And once, while she stood there, smelling him, loving him, her heart pulsing silently toward him, she lifted downcast eyes to find her mother's sympathetic gaze upon her.

Feeling guilty, Elizabeth quickly glanced away.

When finally the last of the mourners left, Tristan, Catherine, and Abigail paid their last respects.

"Thank you for coming," Aaron said earnestly. Then he said to Abigail, "Thanks, Abby. You were a wonderful help to Mother today. I don't know what we would have done without you and Gabrielle."

"I was glad to help," Abigail answered. It was the first time she'd had a moment to speak to him since he'd come to their door Christmas day with the sad news. "I'm so sorry about your father, Aaron. Truly."

Aaron clasped her hand and squeezed. She was the noblest and most selfless person he knew.

She withdrew her hand and moved down the line.

Catherine McRaney stood before Weston. His smile was restrained but sincere when he said, "Welcome home, Mrs. McRaney."

"Thank you, Weston."

His grief momentarily forgotten, his blue eyes danced wickedly. "Be careful not to place any apple tarts out on your windowsill."

She narrowed her eyes suspiciously. "So, it was you who stole my tarts all those years ago."

"Yes, ma'am, I did. And they were the best I ever had then or since."

Her smile was warm and forgiving. She tapped his forearm. "I'll bake you some soon."

"Weston," Tristan said, stopping before the taller man. So blessed was he by Catherine's return, he felt an intense need to offer the olive branch. "If you need anything, to talk . . ." He lifted a shoulder. "Someone to just sit with for a while . . ."

"Thank you, sir," Weston said. "I'll keep that in mind."

Dusk had fallen. Every guest had gone. The food was put away, the chairs placed back where they belonged. Aaron helped Elizabeth with her cloak, while Weston and Daniel steered their weary mother toward the wide, polished staircase.

"Good night, Mrs. Munroe," Elizabeth said from the door.

"Good night, dear," Sarah returned somberly.

"Good night, Daniel, Wes . . ."

"See you, Lizzy," Daniel said, his young voice fatigued.

Weston's gaze captured hers.

I wish I could stay with you, her eyes said.

But you can't, his answered, while at the same time they told her all the other things he dared not speak aloud.

The new year arrived. Two weeks passed, three. A month.

Aaron visited, but not quite so regularly. When he did come, he seemed reserved and quiet. Elizabeth attributed his mood change to a need to adjust to his father's death.

He refrained from his usual conversations about their wedding and future. And though Elizabeth felt wicked, she was secretly relieved.

How did a woman break an engagement to a man who'd just lost his father? How could she tell that man she loved his brother, had always loved him instead?

Yet she knew she must tell him. Pressured by this knowledge, she had trouble sleeping and began to lose weight. Still she remained silenced by an almost maternal compulsion to protect him from another source of pain so soon. After all, he'd protected her so well, so often, throughout the years.

She let the problem fester, her worry sometimes diverted by the changes that were taking place in the McRaney household.

Catherine took on more and more of the church and household responsibilities. Abigail gladly welcomed the reprieve.

Tristan did, also.

Catherine's return did not go unmarked by questions and a fair amount of gossip from Mrs. Caufield and her ladies. But there were others who remembered Catherine well and had loved her. They found they could love her still, for they adored their reverend and wished only the

best for him. Judging by the twinkle in his eye and the
lightness in his step, his wife's homecoming had made
his life complete once more.

As for Elizabeth, she ignored her mother as much
as possible. Oh, she was civil toward Catherine, but
it was more for her father and Abigail's sake than for
Catherine's. Heartbroken and confused, she held herself
aloof, maintaining a very cool distance between herself
and her mother at all times.

Winter drew on. January faded. The snow turned dirty.
Some days were gray and bleak, others snowy, a few
sunny, bright, and cold.

On one such day, Elizabeth followed her heart and
made her way down to the wharf.

She'd seen very little of Weston since the funeral.
He'd conspicuously stayed away.

And she missed him so much she ached.

He attended Sunday services with his family. But what
she did see of him was from a distance. Often during
Prayer, while all heads were bent, she would turn to
find his eyes upon her. But his gaze was vague and
impossible to read.

So today, despite a mind that told her to be patient,
she obeyed a heart that could wait no longer.

The streets leading to the wharf bustled with activity.
Even in the dead of winter, Toronto was a busy place.
Horses pulling sleighs and wagons sloshed through
plowed roads, while little boys strategically aimed snow-
balls at drivers. The streetcars rocked noisily along the
rails, while merchants stood in their doorways, passing
the time of day by calling out the latest bit of news to
one another.

The docks hummed with vibrancy. Men in heavy coats
and knitted caps milled about, intent upon their work.

A large number of the workers were immigrants who spoke very little English. They, and many other foreign families, gravitated toward harbor cities such as this, where work was plentiful for those with strong backs and willing hands.

Barrels, crates, and sacks of produce—grains, cotton, coffee—lined the wharf. Workers dug steel hooks deep into the sides of plump sacks, to heft them into wagons that would go to warehouses throughout the city. Other men, wearing heavy belts laden with tools, stopped their tasks to watch Elizabeth pass.

The wharf was not at all a place for most genteel ladies. Elizabeth was an exception, however. The open stares and coarse language went unmarked by her. Truth be told, if she had had a mind to she could probably have cursed as ribaldly as any man present.

She halted her trek behind a large warehouse and stood before the great structure of a modern ship.

Weston, David, and Bradford's new ship.

Gabrielle had told her much about it. But not having seen it before, she felt a sudden jolt of pride at viewing their efforts taking shape so magnificently. It sat proudly on a flat piece of land, very near the water, on a series of heavy timbers. By spring, she supposed, it would be almost finished and in the water, awaiting its engine and finishing touches.

"He's inside."

She whirled to find Bradford at her elbow.

"Oh, Brad, hello." Blinded by the sun, she squinted up at him and pushed a strand of hair from her eyes.

"Hello, Elizabeth."

They stood in silence, their cheeks ruddy, the wind lightly ruffling their hair, their breath curling out from their nostrils in smoky streamers.

She glanced away, past him, out toward the ice. Overhead, the gulls screeched, not deterred by the frosty air. After a few moments, her gaze returned to him. "Brad . . . I . . . ah . . ." She took a deep breath and straightened her shoulders. "I wanted to thank you for saying nothing about Wes and me . . . About the night you saw us together." Though she found it difficult, she tamped down her embarrassment and forced herself to hold his gaze.

He shrugged, his eyes vague, confused. "Of what night are you speaking, Elizabeth?" His voice was a low monotone.

Silently she studied him. Slowly he smiled. She expelled her breath. She needn't worry. He would never say anything at all about what he'd seen.

"You'll find him inside," Brad repeated, his gaze no longer vague, but knowing and kind.

"Thank you," she said, returning his smile. "Thank you, Brad." She turned toward the warehouse.

"Elizabeth . . ."

She pivoted.

"Things have a way of working out."

"Yes." She nodded. "I suppose they do. Well . . ." She motioned toward the warehouse.

He gestured with his head and pocketed his hands. "You'll find him near the back."

She entered the building and walked through the bustling warehouse, unmindful of at least a dozen curious stares.

But then she saw him. She halted, her heart tripping over her feet.

He could have been any other worker, dressed as he was, the sleeves of his checkered shirt rolled up over

muscled forearms, his golden hair covered by a dark
knitted cap.

But he wasn't any other worker.

He was the man she dreamed of, ached for, loved.
The man whose children she someday hoped to bear. He
strode toward her, his gaze downcast, oblivious to her
presence. On his shoulder he balanced a large crate.

Her shoes came into his line of vision. His gaze
shot upward. His heart quickened into galloping beats.
He stopped so suddenly that the crate rocked precariously, then tumbled from his shoulder and thumped
to the floor, on top of the toe of his left boot. He
cursed and hopped on one foot, mumbling another colorful obscenity while his cheeks grew red with embarrassment. "Dammit, Lizzy!" he exclaimed crossly. "Ye
ought to give a man warning!"

"About what?" she asked, a smile tugging at the corners of her mouth.

"Ye know damn well what I mean! What the hell are
ye doing here? Ye shouldn't've come down here alone!
Rough characters work these docks! It's not safe for a
woman!"

Stung, she felt her smile vaporize instantly. She
lifted her eyebrows, her expression growing stubborn.
"Gabrielle St. Clair has been down here many times.
She told me so herself." It was a silly, jealous statement.
Almost immediately, she wished she'd held her tongue.

"Only with her father!"

Her eyes grew frosty. "I don't need you to tell me
what I can and can't do, Weston Munroe!" she shot back.
Why, he didn't even seem glad to see her!

His jaw hung open for a few seconds while he searched
his mind for a quick reply. "Ah, the hell with it," he
muttered under his breath. "C'mon." Shaking his head,

he took her arm and led her toward a small office in the far corner of the building, out of earshot of any listening workers. "We can talk in here." He drew her in and closed the door.

The room was masculine and plain, containing only a small stove, a rough-looking desk strewn with papers and books, two large lamps, a few hard, tall-backed chairs, and a coffeepot sitting beside a couple of well-used cups. The room smelled strongly of cigar smoke and male sweat.

"Do ye want some coffee or tea?" he asked tersely over his shoulder.

"No." Her tone was just as clipped.

He pulled the cap from his head, flung it into a corner, pulled off his gloves, discarded them also, then pushed all of his fingers through his hair. Didn't she know what she did to him? The moment he laid eyes on her, the urge to touch her grew unbearable. He'd reluctantly stayed away, promising himself he wouldn't touch her again until she'd broken her engagement to Aaron. Loving her was bad enough, touching her, bedding her . . .

He turned to her. "Do ye want to sit down?" He seemed increasingly irritated and tense.

"No." Her anger faded into a web of hurt that was growing by the minute. Pick, pick, pick. Hidden inside her mitt, her thumb worked her cuticle. "I'm sorry about your father, Wes. I really am," she said in an effort to mend the breach between them, not at all understanding his coldness toward her. He seemed like a stranger, not the man who had loved her so tenderly.

He nodded.

"I know there were times you felt distanced from him. But I know he loved you."

"Yes. I suppose he did."

An uncomfortable silence stretched between them.

He broke it abruptly by asking, "Why are ye here, Lizzy?"

She swallowed and blinked twice before answering. "I was worried about you. I wondered how you were doing—"

"I'm doing fine."

"I haven't really talked with you since the funeral. I . . . I thought you might come . . ." She left off. Dropping her eyes, she felt uncertain and self-conscious.

He took a deep breath and searched his shirt pocket for a cigar. Finding one, he sat on the desk, dangling one leg over the edge. The silence grew rife as he lit the cigar. He inhaled deeply, then expelled the smoke slowly while he studied the wooden wall behind her head. At length he said, "I'm getting mighty tired of hanging outside yer window, Elizabeth."

Elizabeth again. His use of her full name always seemed to magnify the intensity of the moment. "I see," was all she could think of to say.

"Do ye?" he asked, his eyes finding her. "I take it ye haven't told him about us?"

She shook her head, her gaze still downcast. "No. Not yet."

"Do ye intend to?"

Her eyes shot to his. "Yes, of course."

"When?"

"When the time is right."

"When will the time be right?"

"Weston," she said patiently, her voice imploring him to understand, "he just lost his father—"

"And so did I!" His voice rose as he shot to his feet. His head jutted toward her. "You seem to be overlooking that small fact!"

"No. No, I'm not. I've wanted to come to you so many times. But I couldn't. And you've always been so different from Aaron. Stronger. More capable of handling—"

His brows met in a slash over his eyes. "Am I?"

Her confusion grew. Unable to answer, she shook her head, her eyes misty.

Then, with brutal precision, he fired his next question. "Are ye pregnant, Lizzy?"

The question hit her with the power of a well-aimed bullet. "What?" The word escaped her in a strangled whisper.

"Ye heard me!"

She dropped her muff, and her hands fell to her sides. "What would make you think such a thing?"

He narrowed his eyes. Slowly his gaze rode her from top to bottom. "Ye're looking pale. Ye've lost some weight. I'm told that happens in the first few months of pregnancy."

She stared back at him, speechless. Stubbornly she held back the tears.

"Well, are ye?" he questioned accusingly, dropping his gaze to study his boots, feeling awkward in the face of his thoughtless attack on her.

Anger ignited and rippled through her veins. Her tear-filled eyes spit sparks. "No! Damn you! I am not pregnant!"

"Would ye tell me if ye were?" He stared at his toes with intense interest, while his words cut her deeply.

"Of course I would! Do you really think I wouldn't?"

His gaze flew up to hers. "I don't know what I think!" He jabbed an angry finger in her direction. "All I do know is I don't want ye carrying my baby, marrying him, and passing it off as his!"

Her mouth dropped open in bald astonishment. When finally she found her voice, it was fraught with pain. "Well, at least he asked me to marry him," she said low.

His eyes grew wide as silence hovered. Then, "What in the hell do ye mean by that?" he barked, affronted. "I asked ye!"

"No," she said, "you never did."

"Well, I shouldn't have to ask ye! You know how I feel!"

Her hurt fled in the face of her rage. "Damn you to bloody hell, Weston Munroe! No, I don't know! Not anymore! And right now I wouldn't marry you even if it meant spending the rest of my life as a spinster!" She blinked hard to hold back a flood of tears. "How could you even think I'd do such a thing to you or your brother?" She spun toward the door, yanking it open. "I never should have come here."

Immediate remorse hit him. His heart constricted.

Jesus, Munroe. Do you have to be such a bastard?

"Aw . . . Lizzy." He stabbed the cigar into a metal tray on the desk, reached her quickly, and spun her around before she could make good her escape. Kicking the door shut, he jerked her into his arms, and crushed her up against him. "I'm sorry. I'm sorry," he said gruffly into her scented hair.

She held herself stiff in his arms, her anger and hurt too new, too raw for her to forget so quickly. "Let me go, Weston," she insisted, her voice muffled by his hard shoulder.

But he ignored her. With one hand he forced her jaw upward and covered her mouth with his. Starved, he kissed her with an almost desperate passion. He was purposeful and ardent, a master at the art of seduction. In time, loving him as she did, her lips softened beneath

his. With a small whimper of acquiescence, her arms
lifted to his neck, and she kissed him back. Their kisses
were hungry, greedy, impatient, speaking of their need
for each other. They pressed together as one, his aroused
body sheltered against her stomach.

"I think about you all the time, Lizzy," he said against
her mouth. "Sometimes I wake up in the middle of the
night missing ye so bad I can't stand it."

"I know . . . it's the same for me."

"I love ye, Beth."

Still injured by his accusation, she asked, "Then how
could you think I'd do such a thing, Wes?"

Abashed, he pressed his forehead to hers. "I don't
know. I imagine all sorts of things these days. I'm crazy
when it comes to ye."

This she understood. She'd done the same when thinking about him and Gabrielle. "I'm not pregnant, Wes."
Her palms rested against his chest. Through his shirt she
felt the heavy thudding of his heart. "But I wish I were."

Passion became a splendid thing. He dipped at the
knees and pressed his hips flush against hers, adapting
a movement that was reckless, rhythmic. "We could
fix that."

"Oh, I want to."

"Soon."

"Soon."

"And will ye be turning our daughters into little hoy-
dens like yerself, climbing trees and swimming naked
with boys?" he asked with a smile.

She chuckled softly, threading her fingers through his
hair. "Oh, no . . . no. Our daughters will be perfect ladies
like their Aunt Abigail."

"Ah . . . well . . . We'll see about that," was his
amused reply.

He dipped his head once more. Their tongues touched, and their breath mingled. They welcomed the reality, the depth, the warmth of their love for each other.

She relished the feel of him, the roughness of his cheek, the hardness of his hands.

Pushing her cloak apart, his hands came searching, roving over her ribs, her waist. Her body responded in kind.

"The days are so long," he whispered, tortured.

"The nights are worse." She hugged him tight.

"When?"

"Soon."

Her arms raised over his shoulders, she waited, anticipating the touch she longed for. His hands found her breasts. He cupped them gently, caressing her through the material of her blouse. Her eyes slipped shut. She moaned softly, savoring the moment, welcoming the heat that sluiced through her.

"I love you so much I ache with it," she conceded softly.

"I know. It's all I can do not to tell Aaron myself." He pulled back to search her face.

"Please don't."

"I don't know how much longer I can take this."

She breathed him in, kissed his cheek, held him close.

"Ah, Beth." The name was muffled and hoarse. "I've even thought of going away."

Alarmed, she drew back. "No, Wes. No. I couldn't stand it if you did."

"Maybe . . . just for a little while."

"No!"

Linking hands, they gazed at each other, both thinking of Aaron, Elizabeth thinking of Gabrielle and her father, also.

"If it were anyone other than my own brother," Weston said. He laughed mirthlessly, dropped her hands, and leaned his shoulder into the door, the picture of a man torn by his emotions. Wearily he wiped a hand across his face, then pinched the bridge of his nose, while his eyes drifted shut.

Saddened for him, Elizabeth ached. Wishing it were possible to ease his pain, she felt singly responsible for what he was experiencing, and what Aaron and Gabrielle would experience in the near future.

Time passed, offering neither of them an escape from the inevitable course they had to take.

At length he opened his eyes and said, "I can't stand the thought of him with ye—touching ye in any way. Yet it kills me to hurt him."

"I know," she whispered. Finding no other consolation to offer, she pressed her palm to his jaw and quietly admitted, "But it's you I love, Wes. It's always been you."

With a soft groan, he pulled her up against him and said, "Then marry me, Beth."

CHAPTER
18

Catherine snuggled against her husband.

She rested her hand in the center of his chest, felt the blessed cadence of his heart, and knew a joy she'd once thought she would never experience again. Complete, she sighed and softly remarked, "She doesn't love him, Tristan."

Silver moonlight beamed through the window and fell across the bed, lighting their room in a pale wash of winter light.

"Mmmm?" Tristan mumbled sleepily, tightening his arms around his wife.

"Elizabeth. She doesn't love him."

A few seconds passed. He rolled over to face her, pulling her body flush against his length. "You mean, Aaron?"

"Yes . . ."

"Of course she does."

Catherine hesitated a moment before responding. "In some ways, yes. But not in the way she should. She doesn't love him in the way that makes a marriage real . . . lasting."

For a long while, Tristan remained quiet, digesting his wife's words. From outside came the muted sound of a dog barking, followed by the angry howl of a cat. "What makes you think this?" he asked finally, caressing her back.

She gave a soft, indulgent laugh. "I may not have been here with her all these years, but I'm her mother. And a woman. I see things. Maybe I see them a little more clearly than you do. Her love is there if you look close enough. It's in her voice when she speaks of him. It's in her eyes when she looks at him." She paused. "It's especially in her eyes."

"But why would she agree to marry a man she doesn't love?"

She rose up on an elbow and gazed down at her husband. "For you. She's doing it for you because she thinks it's what you want her to do."

He gave a short disbelieving snort. "That's ridiculous. She doesn't do anything she doesn't want to do. Elizabeth is the most stubborn, headstrong woman I've ever known."

"And the most loving. When it comes to things that matter, she would do almost anything for those she loves, even if it means sacrificing her own happiness."

Tristan mulled his wife's words over silently.

"It's Weston she loves, Tristan."

"Weston," he scoffed, knitting his brow. He rolled onto his back and ran his fingers through his hair. "He's not for Elizabeth."

"You're wrong, Tristan. So very wrong. He's exactly right for Elizabeth. He's always been for Elizabeth. I don't see how you could have missed it all these years."

Tristan closed his eyes and grew silent. He sighed—

the deep, heavy sigh of a man burdened. Denial, it seemed, had become a common practice for him over the years. It had become easier for him to smother the truth than to face it. Had he faced it years ago, he never would have lost all those precious years with Catherine. He opened his eyes and grudgingly admitted, "I didn't miss it, Cathy. I . . . just sort of ignored it. I suppose I hoped in time her feelings for Weston would fade."

"Did yours for me?" Her question was soft, evocative.

"No . . . never."

Catherine touched his cheek. "Then please talk to her, darling. She needs to hear you tell her you understand. She needs to know that you'll accept her, no matter who her husband is. Aaron's not the one for our Elizabeth. A union between the two wouldn't be fair to either of them. Besides," she said softly, her smile secretive, "there's another who loves Aaron very much. In all the right ways. And I think in time he'll come to notice her, and possibly to love her, too."

Tristan gathered Catherine close. For several heart-beats, he gazed at her through the shadows, then very tenderly he touched his mouth to hers. "I've missed you over the years," he whispered huskily, "more than you'll ever know."

"And I you," she reciprocated softly. In the hour that followed, she showed him how very much that statement was true.

The next morning, when Elizabeth entered the kitchen for breakfast, Tristan was waiting. She sat down across from him at the table.

He stared at her a full two minutes before quiet-ly requesting, "Ride with me to church this morning, Elizabeth."

"But, Papa, I have so much to do today." She shook her head, reaching for the teapot. "I simply can't—"

"I could use your help with something."

His tone was gentle, but it was a tone he'd often used with her over the years when he wasn't requesting her obedience but expecting it.

Her gaze found his. "Well . . ." She hesitated, confused by his insistence. "All right, Papa. If it's that important to you." She turned to Abigail. "I promised Mrs. Summers I'd stop by this morning to check on her. Since she had the new baby, she hasn't been feeling well at all. I thought I'd take the older children out for a walk—"

Catherine set a dainty flowered plate, a small crock of butter, and a platter of warm scones on the table. She touched Elizabeth's shoulder lightly. "Abigail and I will visit Mrs. Summers first thing today. We'll take care of the children. You needn't worry."

Abigail reached for a scone. "Of course we will, Beth. Go with Papa."

"Well . . . ," Elizabeth replied reluctantly, looking from Catherine to Abigail, trying to quell her resentment at the affection that was obviously growing between the two women. "If you're quite sure."

"Quite," Catherine answered kindly. "Go with your father and enjoy the day."

The March morning was cold and bleak. After Tristan attached Henry to the sleigh, he and Elizabeth rode through the snow-packed roads together, each uncharacteristically reticent.

Sleigh bells jingled in the early morning air, adding a measure of music to the awkward void left by their lack of conversation.

A blanket covering her lap, a muff warming her hands, Elizabeth was not physically uncomfortable. "Hello, Mrs. Taylor," she called out as they passed another sleigh.

Elizabeth turned to her father. "She looks well, don't you think?" she asked lightly, trying to ease the tension she felt emitting from him.

Nodding, Tristan stared straight ahead. "Yes, she does indeed."

They fell silent once more.

What is it, Papa? she thought. *What have I done?*

It was Tristan who finally spoke. "Elizabeth . . ."

"Yes, Papa?" She turned to him expectantly.

He took a deep, fortifying breath. "I know it's been difficult for you to accept your mother's return."

So that's it. Elizabeth dropped her gaze and said, "I'm glad she's alive." That much was true.

He went on, "There are some things you don't understand about your mother and I—"

"I know having her home makes you and Abigail very happy," Elizabeth cut in, her voice a respectful monotone.

"Yes, it does."

"Then that's all that matters to me."

Tristan gradually steered Henry to the side of the road. "Whoa, Henry!" He pulled the reins, stopping the sleigh.

Elizabeth cautiously looked at him.

He turned to her, his gray eyes gentle. "That's not all that matters to me, Elizabeth." He reached over and pulled one of her hands from her muff. "You matter to me. You and Abigail and your mother." He squeezed her hand. "Surely you know that."

An awful knot formed in Elizabeth's throat.

"And though you may not believe it, I know your

mother loves you very much. Every bit as much as I do."

"Papa, please," she whispered, pained. "I don't want to talk about this with you."

"Then maybe you should talk about it with her."

She dropped her eyes and shook her head. "I can't."

"For me, Elizabeth."

In silence, she listened to the sounds of the awakening city while she considered his request. *Oh, Papa, don't ask me to do this. I know you've forgiven her, but I can't. I just can't. You don't know what it did to me when she left us, when I thought she'd died.*

"At least think about it," he urged in sad resignation. After several moments, he drew a deep, ragged breath. "There's something else, Elizabeth. Something we should have talked about a long time ago."

Her eyes remained downcast.

"You don't love Aaron, do you?"

Her eyes shot to his. He had changed the subject so abruptly. Within seconds her cheeks blazed a condemning red.

"You don't have to say anything." He smiled and touched a gloved hand to her cheek. "I see it's true."

"Oh, Papa," she whispered miserably, closing her eyes to block out her anguish.

"Ah . . . now, sweetheart. It's all right. You can't always control your heart." He shrugged. "The mind, maybe. But the heart, well . . . that's another matter. You need to know that there's no sin in loving another. The sin," he continued softly, "would be in marrying a man you don't love."

Her eyes opened, and two plump tears leaked out. She felt a weight lift from her chest. Gratitude for her father's compassion overcame all her doubts.

"Do you understand what I'm saying, daughter?"

She nodded, and a smile trembled upon her lips.
"Yes."

"Good," he said, drawing her close and crushing her
in a powerful hug. "I love you, sweetheart."

"I love you, too, Papa." They held each other tight,
rocking from side to side, while emotions churned and
acceptance became a sacred thing.

In time they parted, and Tristan reached for the reins.
With a snap, he set the sleigh in motion and pulled back
out onto the road.

"Papa," Elizabeth said after several minutes.

"Mm-hm?"

"How did you know?"

Smiling, he turned to her. "I guess I've always
known. But stubborn fool that I am . . ." He paused,
shaking his head. "Well . . . your mother made me
understand."

Oh, Mama, she thought, as another wave of intense
gratitude swept over her. *Thank you.*

A week later, Elizabeth decided it was time to face
Aaron.

She wore a white, high-necked blouse and a dove-gray
skirt with a matching fitted jacket.

Abigail was out this morning, so Elizabeth's hair,
defiant as always, was less controlled than she wished,
but she arranged it as best she could, covered it with a
fashionable charcoal-gray hat, then draped her shoulders
with a matching cloak and set off to do the task she'd
been dreading with every fiber of her being.

She didn't know what to do about Gabrielle, but her
first concern was Aaron. Regardless of what the future
held for herself and Weston, she knew marrying Aaron
would be a mistake.

The large warehouse that was the heart of Everitt Munroe's importing and exporting business sat along the wharf, not so very far from the building that housed Weston's venture.

Elizabeth entered the front door and made her way past the long row of offices. She found Aaron in his father's office.

It was a large, opulent room with gleaming paneled walls, a bookcase lining one wall from floor to ceiling, and the floor covered by an unusual but inordinately beautiful oriental carpet. In the very center stood a large mahogany desk.

Aaron sat behind the desk.

When she entered, he rose quickly from his chair and came around to greet her.

"Elizabeth, hello!" he said, taking her hands. "What a pleasant surprise." His smile was warm and genuine. She felt a sharp sting of regret that she had come to tell him something that would wipe away that smile.

He bent to kiss her, and she automatically offered him her cheek. He kissed her lightly, without passion, his mustache barely brushing her skin. They had not shared a deep kiss since before his father's death.

"Come," he said, indicating a wing-backed chair placed near the crackling fire, "sit down for a while and warm yourself."

"No." She shook her head and smiled stiffly. "I just came for a short visit."

"Can I get you something? Some tea, perhaps?"

"No, thank you." She crossed the room to the bookcase and studied the countless leather-bound volumes with intense interest.

"Well, what brings you down this way?" He leaned his backside against the desk, admiring the attractive picture she presented.

She took a deep breath. "Actually, I came to talk to you." She continued to gaze at the books.

"I'm flattered," he said, sincerely pleased she had sought him out. "It's been a long time since we've had a chance to talk alone."

She nodded, wondering how one went about broaching the subject of breaking an engagement. "Aaron," she said softly, drawing another deep breath. Turning, she sought his gaze.

Something about her tone triggered an immediate warning.

"Yes, Elizabeth?" He sounded concerned.

Her brow knitted with the complexity of her feelings. She swallowed before continuing. "You know I care for you very deeply."

He nodded. "And I for you, Elizabeth."

"You've always been . . . so good to me. So loyal . . . There were so many times I don't know what I would have done without you." She shook her head and dropped her gaze. "Aaron . . . I . . . I don't know how to say this."

He rose slowly and crossed the room to stand before her. "Say what?" he asked cautiously. But he knew.

She looked up and met his guarded gaze. "That I can't marry you."

An awful silence built between them. Every sound within the building seemed magnified.

"I'm sorry." The words escaped her in a hushed whisper. "Truly I am."

He remained quiet, his expression controlled.

She plunged on, hoping to ease the impact of her betrayal, knowing the worst was yet to come. "But you see . . . Though I love you dearly, my feelings are not what they should be. I am not the woman who should be your wife." She saw the pain in his eyes, and she reached a hand to his cheek. "You deserve so much better, so much more than I could ever give you."

He blinked once, his jaw hardening, and brushed her hand away.

"I know you don't understand—"

"Oh, I understand all right." He laughed, but it was a harsh, mirthless laugh. "That's a lovely speech, Elizabeth," he said, his voice colder than she ever remembered hearing it. "Why did you wait so long to use it?"

"Aaron, I—"

"It's Weston, isn't it?" He flung the accusation into her face.

Silence.

She dropped her gaze and stared at the varied pattern on the carpet.

"Isn't it!" he demanded, while her guilt grew more unbearable by the moment.

"It's him you love!" he accused.

"Yes. Yes. I love him," she admitted, her voice a tortured whisper. "But even if I didn't, it would be wrong for us to marry, Aaron. Surely you can see that."

"Damn him!"

Her eyes downcast, she felt the heavy burden of having driven a wedge between two brothers, both her friends, both men she loved. "It's not Weston's fault." She tried to salvage a measure of their relationship. "He loves you."

The air reverberated with unspoken accusations.

"Damn you both!" he whispered fervently. He spun and strode across the floor to stare out the window at the busy docks.

She lifted her head and stared at the unrelenting line of his back. He stood draped in cold silence. "I'm sorry, Aaron . . ."

"Save it, Elizabeth."

"I'd like to try to explain . . ."

"I don't want to hear any useless explanations," he said tersely. "Nor do I care about how sorry you are." Tense seconds passed. After a while, he pocketed his hands and sighed deeply. His voice much quieter, more controlled, he added, "I knew the minute he came back this would happen. I was a fool to think you'd ever gotten over him."

She took a few tentative steps toward him, emboldened by the need to comfort, by the need to offer some sort of balm to his wounded spirit.

But sensing her presence, he wasted no time in rebuffing her attempt. "Just go, Elizabeth," he ordered softly. "Please."

She touched his shoulder. "I am truly sorry, Aaron."

He shook her off without looking at her. "Get the hell out, Elizabeth! Now!"

Crestfallen, she left.

She hurried through the streets, oblivious to the people she passed, fighting an endless barrage of conflicting emotions.

"Elizabeth!"

She turned toward the voice. Gabrielle waved from her sleigh, headed in the direction of the wharf.

Elizabeth waved back and turned toward home, feeling even more dejected.

She stood outside her door, trying to balance her emotions before entering. Impatiently she swiped at her tears. *Good God, Elizabeth,* she inwardly taunted herself.

*You've done more crying these past few months than
you've done in your whole life. You're turning into a
sniveling idiot!*

When at last she did enter the house, she found
Catherine in the kitchen, bent over the table kneading
bread dough, flour up to her elbows.

"Hello, darling," Catherine said, offering her a welcome smile.

"Hello," Elizabeth answered softly. She stood uncertainly, watching her mother perform a task she'd seen her
perform countless times in her earlier years. The sight
unleashed a rush of nostalgic memories. She thought
about her father, about what he'd said, and felt an over-
whelming urge to draw comfort from those flour-dusted
arms. Instead, she turned, divested herself of her wrap,
and hung it behind the door. "Is Abigail home?" She
struggled to stabilize the quaver in her voice.

"No. She had several errands to run today," Catherine
answered pleasantly, "I don't expect her back for quite
some time yet."

"I see." Elizabeth crossed the room to stand before
the cast-iron stove. Fire hissed and sputtered within. She
held her hands out toward the warmth and over her
shoulder quietly asked, "Would you like some help?"

Catherine's arms stilled. Her hazel eyes lifted. Elizabeth turned. Their gazes met and held. "I would like that
very much, Elizabeth."

Elizabeth nodded. "I'll wash my hands."

They worked together, side by side, mother and
daughter, in a warm, cozy kitchen, while the years
slipped away.

"You used to help me with this when you were but a
little girl," Catherine said, reminiscing, sinking her hands
into the large mound of dough.

A small smile touched Elizabeth's lips. "I remember."

"As the reward for helping, I'd give you a piece of dough. You would play with it for hours. You'd sit at this table and shape it into different things—a snowman, your father, a ship, Abigail." Catherine chuckled. "You had a monster of an imagination for such a small child." She grew silent, while the tender memories hovered.

Time ticked by.

In the reflective intimacy of the moment, Elizabeth's hands grew still. Without looking up, she whispered, "Mama . . ." That one soft word expressed all her need for assurance and love.

Slowly Catherine's head lifted. "Yes, darling?"

Silence. More seconds passed.

Catherine stopped working and wiped her hands on her apron. "You told him today, didn't you?"

Elizabeth nodded.

Catherine reached across the mound of dough and covered Elizabeth's hand with her own. "It'll be all right, Elizabeth. You did the right thing."

Staring at the dough-encrusted hand, Elizabeth shook her head. Tears threatened to fall. "He'll never forgive me. He hates me. He was so cold to me . . . so . . ."

Catherine turned and took her daughter by the shoulders, despite her messy hands. "No. No, darling, he doesn't hate you. Aaron doesn't hate anyone. It's not in his nature. Surely you know that. He just needs time to work this out in his heart. That's all. Someday, he'll look back on this and know you did the best thing for both of you. He'll forgive you, and you'll be friends once again. For now, you'll just have to be patient. It's difficult . . . I know."

Elizabeth stared into her mother's familiar hazel eyes.

Sadly, she realized, she'd treated her mother in exactly the same manner as Aaron had her—hatefully, coldly. She had refused to allow Catherine an opportunity to explain herself, refused to listen to any kind of an apology.

As though reading her mind, Catherine quietly offered, "Go ahead, Elizabeth. Ask me whatever it is you need to ask. I'll do my best to give you the answers."

Then they came, all the angry, hurtful, painful questions bursting from her in a jumbled rush. "Why, Mama? Why did you leave us? How could you? Didn't you know how I would feel? All these years I blamed myself for your death."

"Oh, Elizabeth," Catherine interjected.

"I thought it was my fault," Elizabeth rushed on. "I thought if I'd only been able to save Jacob, you wouldn't have been so sad. You wouldn't have left." Elizabeth's voice cracked and broke. "You wouldn't have died. All those years, I needed you. Especially when Weston went away, and people said all those awful things about me. I needed you then. You could have come home at any time. Yet you didn't." She lowered her chin to her chest, a sob ripping from her throat. "You didn't."

Catherine pulled her into her arms, embracing her tightly. "Oh, my poor, poor darling," she whispered. "My poor darling. I didn't know. You were so young. I didn't realize you felt responsible." Her tears spilled over. "I'm so sorry, Elizabeth. I never stopped to think that you were feeling guilty, too. I went away because I couldn't deal with the guilt of having lost Jacob and almost losing you, too, due to my own negligence . . ."

Very slowly Elizabeth's arms rose and closed around her mother's waist.

"Your father . . . I didn't know if he would ever be

able to forgive me. Even if he could, I wasn't sure I could ever forgive myself. But I've always loved you, Elizabeth. You and Abigail and your father," Catherine said, her voice full of tenderness. "You must believe that."

They stood locked together for a long time, letting healing and forgiveness begin while old wounds faded.

After a long while, they separated, and Catherine began to explain to her grown-up daughter what she could not have explained to the child she left behind.

Elizabeth opened her heart and listened. "Did you love him, Mama?"

"Your father? Oh, yes, darling . . ."

Elizabeth shook her head. "Not Papa. Captain Braxton."

Catherine smiled softly. "Ah . . . ," she said thoughtfully. "I see you've heard the rumors, too."

"Years ago."

Catherine's hands tightened on Elizabeth's shoulders. "Listen to me, Elizabeth." She paused. "He was a friend. Only a friend. There was nothing between us other than that. When I left here, I had no money with me. He offered me passage. That's all, nothing more. Did I love him?" She shook her head. "No, darling. I loved your father. I've always loved your father."

They gazed at each other with a new, mature understanding.

Then, very softly, Catherine added, "Just as you've always loved Weston. Just as someone else we know has always loved Aaron."

CHAPTER
19

Later that afternoon, Elizabeth lay on her bed, staring up at the ceiling. Beyond her window the wind sighed softly, while within her heart there was a satisfying peace she'd been lacking since the day Catherine left all those years ago.

It would take time, she knew, to build this new relationship with her mother. But the foundation of their unity had been laid in forgiveness and cemented with the birth of understanding and acceptance.

From below came the comforting sounds of Catherine moving about the kitchen, preparing dinner, while the wonderful smell of baking bread drifted throughout the house.

Abigail and Tristan hadn't returned yet. Though Elizabeth had offered to help with dinner, Catherine had sent her upstairs to rest.

So Elizabeth lay, lazy and languid, on the quilts, her head resting upon her linked hands, while her mother's puzzling words echoed through her mind: "I've always loved your father. Just as you've always loved

Weston. Just as someone else we know has always loved Aaron."

She mulled the last sentence over and over in her mind, trying to guess the possibilities. "Who, Mama?" she'd asked. "What are you talking about? What do you mean?"

But Catherine had only smiled and told her she would find out in time.

When at last dusk began to darken her room, Elizabeth swung her legs over the edge of the bed. Rising, she lifted her arms and stretched tall, then crossed the room to the bureau and lit a lamp. She opened the top drawer and began rifling the contents, searching for a fresh handkerchief.

But instead of finding a handkerchief, she found Weston's cap. Smiling, she picked it up and held it to her cheek, remembering the night he'd worn it. Her eyes slipped shut while she relived the sweetness of that evening over again, yearning for him in ways that made her ache in almost every region of her body.

"Soon," she whispered. "Soon."

Opening her eyes, she tucked the cap back into the bureau. She was about to close the drawer when an object peeking from beneath a pair of Abigail's pantaloons caught her attention.

Curious, she moved the garment aside.

A feather?

Bemused, she picked it up and turned it over, studying it for several moments. Her gaze shifted back to the area from which it had come. She lifted the pantaloons and saw another feather lying beside a couple of thin sticks.

Bewildered, she continued to stare at the items, trying to place them, while a vague memory teased at the back of her mind.

And then it dawned on her.

The splint was the one Aaron had made and used on the injured bird she and Abigail had found all those years ago. And the feathers . . .

Why would Abigail keep such things?

But even as Elizabeth asked herself that question, she knew the answer.

Her eyes closed. Her eyelids trembled.

Abigail. Abigail loved Aaron.

All these years she'd kept these things safely hidden, while she'd kept her feelings for Aaron every bit as carefully hidden in her heart.

"Oh, Ab," Elizabeth whispered. "How sad you must have felt all this time. And yet you never let your feelings show." Elizabeth tucked the items back into the drawer, and for the first time since she'd broken her engagement, she knew, without a flicker of doubt, that she'd done the right thing for everyone.

The house was quiet. Elizabeth lay in the dark, watching the shadows dance across the walls, while she listened to Abigail's steady breathing. The fire popped and hissed within the grate, a lulling sound but hardly sufficient to lull Elizabeth to sleep this night.

Late into the evening she'd wondered and worried about whether to reveal what she knew to her sister. She'd held her tongue and retired for the evening, not quite sure what it was she wanted to say.

Finally, when she could stand it no longer, she rose, lit a lamp, crossed the room, and knelt beside Abigail's bed. "Abigail," she whispered, shaking her sister's shoulder gently.

Silence.

"Abigail."

"Mmmm?" came the sleepy reply.

"I need to talk to you."

Abigail's eyelids parted. "Can't we talk tomorrow?"

"Not if I want to sleep tonight."

"Oh, Elizabeth," Abigail grumbled, raising herself up on an elbow. "What is it?" She rubbed the sleep from her eyes.

Several moments passed while Elizabeth searched her mind for the right words.

"Beth?" Abigail asked worriedly, waking further. "What is it?"

Elizabeth reached across the bed for her sister's hand. "I talked with Mama today."

Abigail's voice grew mellow. "I could tell. You both seemed happier. I'm so glad."

"I'm glad, too," Elizabeth said honestly, then paused.

"There's something else, isn't there?"

"Yes."

"About Mama?"

"No. About Aaron." After a short silence, she added, "I broke my engagement with him today."

Another pause.

"You did?" Abigail's tone was carefully controlled, guarded.

Elizabeth noticed and wondered how she could have been so blind to the signs of her sister's feelings. "Yes, I did."

Abigail held her breath, trying to balance her joy against the deep loyalty she felt for Elizabeth. Finally she released her breath in a soft sigh. "But why?"

"Because of Weston," Elizabeth admitted. "It would be wrong to marry Aaron, feeling the way I do about Wes."

"Yes," Abigail agreed. "It would be."

"You always knew, didn't you?"

"Yes . . . I knew."

"Why didn't you ever say anything?"

"Because it was your decision to make. Besides . . . I did sort of say something. You just weren't listening."

Elizabeth released Abigail's hand and sat down on the floor, stretching her legs out in front. She leaned her head back against the wall.

Abigail slipped off the bed and joined her. "How did he take it?" she inquired softly.

"He was hurt and angry."

"Yes, I imagine even Aaron would feel that way at first. Did you tell him about Weston?"

Elizabeth gave a soft laugh. "I didn't have to. He already knew."

"I see," was all Abigail could think to say.

They sat together for a long time in companionable silence, in the dim light of one flickering lamp, while the flames of the fire warmed them and cast their faces golden. Each tried to determine what changes would occur in her life because of the happenings of this day.

"How do you feel?" Abigail finally asked.

"Free." That one simple word said it all.

Abigail nodded. "Good."

Outside their window, the tree branches clawed at the house, and the March wind, which had sighed earlier, now moaned.

"Abigail?" Elizabeth whispered at length. Her brow furrowed in concentration, she lifted her hands, interlaced her fingers, and made animal shadows bounce across the wall.

"Yes?"

"How long have you been in love with Aaron?"

The silence grew pregnant. An odd-looking rabbit hopped along the wallpaper.

Considering her answer, Abigail's hands created a bird in flight. Without looking at Elizabeth, she said, "Since the day he tried to doctor the bird for us."

Elizabeth smiled, remembering. "Why didn't you ever tell me?"

Abigail's bird swooped downward and landed lightly on the ears of Elizabeth's rabbit. "Because I loved you first," Abigail said simply.

Aaron picked his way along the wharf.

As March eased into April, all that was left of the winter's heavy snows were a few not so white patches and several gray, murky puddles.

It was Sunday evening at twilight. Usually he would have been attending services with his mother and Daniel, but church was not the place for him tonight. Not in his condition. Instead he'd gone down to the office, stared at contracts absentmindedly and drank far too much brandy, while he thought far too many unkind thoughts. No, the Lord's house was not the place for him this night.

Most of the time Weston accompanied the family to morning services, also. But he hadn't attended any of the services for the past several weeks. Now Aaron knew why. Guilt was a most effective deterrent.

The wharf was quiet. There was little activity on a Sunday evening. Only a few workers and those whose professions left them little choice ventured out on such evenings. His steps slow and methodical, he passed a young, fleshy prostitute, who made a crude gesture followed by an even cruder offer. Absently he dug into his pocket, flipped her a coin, ignored her thanks, and continued on his journey.

More than two weeks had passed since Elizabeth had broken their engagement. He'd carefully avoided his brother while he'd worked to fuel his injured pride into a slow-burning anger.

The odd thing was that if he were to be truthful with himself, he'd have to admit that he really didn't feel all that badly. Not nearly as badly as he would have expected. After all, he was a man spurned, in favor of his younger brother. Oh, at first he'd felt quite injured. But after he'd recovered from the initial sting of rejection, he'd begun to feel an almost amazing sense of relief.

More and more in the past several months he'd been thinking of another—a girl with soft gray eyes, chestnut hair, and a shy smile. But being the gentleman he was, he'd felt such terrible guilt at his errant thoughts that he'd denied the existence of any such attraction. Yet lately he'd begun to wonder if maybe, just maybe, his love for Elizabeth might be very similar to what she claimed hers was for him.

Still, being the honorable man he was, he could not take this personal injury sitting down.

Certainly not!

Weston must be confronted with his betrayal.

It occurred to him that his own thoughts and actions bordered on hypocrisy, since he had begun to question the wisdom of a match between himself and Elizabeth on his own. But then again, no one knew that but him. As for his brother, well, he was nothing more than a Judas who had to be confronted with his dishonorable actions. If nothing else, the cad would do right by Elizabeth this time.

He approached the ship, paused, and studied the huge vessel, trying to refuel his anger, wondering why, now that he'd decided to face Weston, he suddenly felt reluctant to cause a breach between them that would possibly never heal.

Then he thought of Elizabeth once more and found the motivation he needed.

Walking aboard the vessel, he ignored the curious stares of the few workers who milled about. Most were finished for the day and were headed toward an establishment where they could find food and companionship.

"Where's Munroe?" he asked one burly fellow in a black knitted cap.

"Below deck," the man answered and gestured toward the stairs.

Aaron nodded his thanks.

He strode to the staircase, his anger momentarily abated by his admiration of the vessel. Almost complete, and partially furnished, the ship was one of the finest he'd ever seen. As he descended the stairs, he noticed fine examples of cabinet work and carving on the sideboards to his left and right. All the woodwork, metalwork, glass, furniture, upholstery, and carpets were similar in design and most elegant. He felt a stab of guilt that he'd never come to see the vessel before. Father would have been quite proud of Weston.

That thought brought another spurt of animosity.

He found Weston in the engine department.

It was a large, poorly lit area. But by the light of several lanterns, Weston worked on the steering gear, lost in deep concentration. At first he didn't hear Aaron's approach.

"Hello, Weston." Aaron's tone was low and tight.

Surprised, Weston pivoted. "Aaron, hello."

They studied each other for several moments—two brothers, each so different, one dressed in workmen's clothing, the other dressed as one of Toronto's leading young businessmen.

From the deck above came the heavy clump of workers' boots and the light hum of their conversation as they left the ship.

The silence grew uncomfortable.

Weston fixed Aaron with a questioning gaze. "What brings ye out this evening?"

Aaron broke eye contact and turned his attention to the steering gear. He shrugged and lied. "I thought it was time I saw what you've done with your ideas."

Weston pulled a rag from his back pocket and wiped the dirt from his hands. "They're more Brad's ideas than mine. He's the designer, the brains behind all the work."

Aaron carefully studied the gears, the space that would hold the engine, Weston's shoes, the wall, anything but his brother's face. "You know, Father would have been proud of this—of you." There was a certain sad acceptance in his tone.

"No." Weston shook his head and smiled skeptically. "Father was never proud of me, Aaron."

"Yes, he was," Aaron insisted. "After you left, he missed you. Then . . . when he had the stroke, and I took over at the office for him, all he ever did was remind me of how you would have run things had you been here." Aaron shrugged and thrust his hands in his pockets. "I wasn't you. That was the whole problem. You were the son he wanted to follow in his footsteps. The one most like him. Not me. Not even Daniel. You have all the charisma and drive we lack."

Weston stared at his brother in disbelieving silence.

Aaron gave a soft laugh. "Don't tell me you never realized he felt that way."

Sensing Aaron's mood of dejection, Weston honestly answered, "No . . . I didn't. I'm sorry, Aaron."

Aaron smiled cynically. "For what?"

"That ye felt that way."

"Ah, well . . ." Uncharacteristically, Aaron belched loudly.

Weston leaned his backside against a thick beam and crossed his arms over his chest. He eyed his brother suspiciously. "Ye've been drinking."

Affronted, Aaron shrugged. "And if I have?"

Weston narrowed his eyes. "More than a little, I'd say."

"Maybe."

"There's something else ye came here to talk about, isn't there?" Weston pinned him with a shrewd stare.

Aaron met his gaze. "Yes. We both know there is."

"Elizabeth," Weston said somberly.

Aaron nodded. "Yes," he answered, his voice just as somber.

"Neither of us wanted to hurt ye, Aaron."

Aaron's face stiffened.

Weston lifted himself away from the beam and closed the distance between them. Empathy rose within. He tried to reach for Aaron's arm. "Ye're my brother—"

Aaron twisted away. The phrase set off an explosive trigger. "Damn right I'm your brother! Funny you remember that now! Stealing a man's fiancée is a hell of a thing for one brother to do to another! Or didn't you ever even think of that, Wes?"

"Yes . . . I did . . ."

Aaron's next move was unexpected and forceful. All the pent-up emotion he'd nursed came boiling to a head. He lunged and caught Weston in the ribs, slamming him backward.

Weston's breath left him in a whoosh. His head struck the beam behind, and for a moment a buzzing sound filled his ears. He shook it off and tried to rise. "Come on, Aaron, I don't want to fight ye—" But another slam ended Weston's sentence and sent his head snapping back into the beam.

Aaron rose to his feet and stood over the stunned body of his brother. Balling his hands into fists, he yelled, "Well, you sure as hell better fight me, because if you don't, I'm going to break every bloody bone in your body!"

Cautiously Weston rose to his feet. Widening his stance, he held out his palms in supplication. "Aaron, listen—" But a blow caught him on the side of his jaw, jerking his head back. He stabilized, refusing to be goaded. "Aaron, damn it!" Another blow. Then another and another. In seconds, his nose bled, yet he held his ground, reluctant to lay an angry hand on his brother.

"How long did you wait before you bedded her, Wes?" Aaron sneered, regretting his slanderous attack on Elizabeth even while he initiated it. Yet he found himself unable to stop the bitter flow of words. "How well did she play the whore for you?"

Weston's eyes grew icy. He tightened his fists, while his jaw tensed. "That's about enough, Aaron."

"What's the matter, brother, don't you like to hear the truth? I should have known when you came home you'd waste no time in laying with her!" Though he didn't believe it for a moment, he added, "After all, you'd had her plenty before you left!"

Incensed, Weston lunged. "Damn ye, Aaron. You know she isn't like that—" The impact of his body against his brother's knocked the wind from them both as they fell to the ship's floor.

"Couldn't prove it by me!" Aaron choked out, wrestling beneath Weston's greater weight.

They rolled from side to side, Weston trying to still Aaron's flailing fists. "Keep yer mouth off Elizabeth!" Weston yelled. "If ye want to attack someone, let it be me! I went after her! I was the one who pursued! She tried to remain loyal to ye!"

"Then . . . all . . . the more reason for me . . . to beat you bloody!" Aaron gasped between breaths. "She won't . . . want you when I get done—" One of his hands broke loose and clipped Weston on the side of the head. The other hand came loose, and he grabbed Weston's neck, gripping his windpipe, squeezing with every ounce of strength he had.

"Damn it," Weston said in a raspy voice while he fought to break Aaron's grip. He'd never seen him like this. Enraged, Aaron was much stronger than he looked.

With a swift upward clip of his arms, Weston broke the hold. They rolled, one over the other, cursing, pummeling each other, both motivated by different factors, one by love and need, the other by damaged pride and a feeling of inadequacy.

They banged against a barrel and sent it flopping onto its side. Oil leaked out and spread across the floor. They struck a table leg, sending a lamp crashing down. Another one followed. Still the two fought on, oblivious to their surroundings, clouting each other as though they were mortal enemies, until finally they lay exhausted in a tangle of arms and legs.

"It was always you," Aaron got out, his anger suddenly gone. "You were first with Father . . . and with Elizabeth . . ."

"That's bullshit! Ye're a crazy bastard." Weston rolled off his brother.

"Oh, God . . . I'm going to be sick."

"Good!"

"You broke my hand." Aaron held his hand up in front of his face and tried to wiggle his uncooperative fingers.

"Me!" Weston exclaimed. "Ye're the one who hit me!"

Aaron flopped his head to the side and glared at him. His lips were swollen and bleeding. "You stole my fiancée! What was I supposed to do?"

"She was mine first!"

This Aaron could not deny. "Well, you ran off and left her—"

An ominous crackling sounded, and a moment later, the men smelled smoke.

Alarmed, Weston's head lifted off the floor. "Good God, Aaron! The ship's on fire!"

Forgetting their wounds, they struggled to their feet.

Weston tore his shirt from his back, ran across to the spreading flames, and beat at them. "Go on up!" he yelled. "Get the bloody hell out of here! Go get help!"

The smoke thickened. Across the floor, the flames leapt and grew. Coughing, Aaron quickly shed his coat and imitated his brother's actions. "I'm not leaving you down here!"

"Aaron, don't be an ass!" Weston squinted, his eyes burning. "Get out of here!"

"Go to hell!"

"By God, ye're a stubborn fool!"

"Like yourself!"

Side by side, they fought the oil-fed flames, but they were no match for the growing inferno. Flames licked their hands and reached for their trousers, but still the two refused to give up the battle.

From behind came voices. The burly man Aaron had passed earlier grabbed at Weston's arm. "Mr. Munroe! Ye got t'get above deck!"

"No! Take him!" Weston ordered, gesturing toward Aaron.

"C'mon, Mr. Munroe," said another stout fellow, reaching for his other arm.

"Go get help!" Weston shook them off and resumed his fight.

"We already sent the others," the bigger one said. Then both workers shared a meaningful glance, nodded, picked a brother, and threw a well-aimed punch.

On Richmond Street, Reverend McRaney's evening services drew to a close.

All were respectfully seated when they heard the commotion outside. A moment later, a young man burst through the door, shouting, "Mr. Latham! Mr. Stevens! Come quick. Yer ship's on fire!"

David and Bradford bolted from their seats and ran down the aisle toward the young man.

"Where's Mr. Munroe?" David asked worriedly, knowing Weston had planned to work late.

"He's in the engine room. Ben and George went down after him."

"Oh, God," Bradford whispered.

Outside the church, they stared out toward the wharf. An eerie orange glow lit the sky. His stride purposeful, Bradford led the way to a carriage. A second later, Bradford, David, and the young man were gone.

Elizabeth had listened to the exchange with her heart in her throat. "I'm going, too," she said to her mother and Abigail.

"Not without me," Abigail put in.

"Or me," Gabrielle said, following close at their heels, trying desperately to match their longer strides. They picked a carriage, anyone's carriage, lifted their skirts in a most unladylike manner, swung up into the seats, and within seconds, with Elizabeth driving, they, too, were careening down the street.

The clangs from the bells of the fire engines added to everyone's fear and dread. Elizabeth silently prayed, *Oh, God, please don't let him be hurt. Please let him be safe.*

When they reached the wharf, they found it a sea of frantic activity. Horse-drawn wagons and fire engines lined the docks. Men rushed to form assembly lines. Someone yelled, "Man the pumps! Get those hoses stretched out! Hurry, men!"

Another man yelled, "All right, now pump! Pump!"

The men worked diligently. After a few furious minutes, streams of water hit the ship.

The throng grew. Tristan arrived with Catherine. At least half the church followed.

Elizabeth scanned the crowd for Weston. She rose up on her toes, trying to see over the heads of the milling mass. Having no success, she took a step into the crowd but found her effort impeded by her father's hands. "Let me go, Papa!" she screamed and broke his hold. "I have to find him!"

She ran into the crowd, shoving her way toward the ship, smoke blinding her eyes. Water sizzled as it struck the flames. Steam lifted into the cold night air. The stench of burning wood, oil, and other materials grew thick. Heat radiated from the vessel. Elizabeth's heart beat furiously while she scanned the faces of all the men.

Chaos abounded.

Panicked, Elizabeth felt close to tears. *If I find him alive,* she thought, *if he has one living breath within his body, I'm going to kill him!* What kind of a fool would stay inside a ship and try to fight a fire?

But she knew the answer. Weston would. Especially when so much of his, Bradford's, and David's future had depended on his completion of this vessel.

And then she saw him. He stood in the midst of several others, his face streaked and filthy, his blond hair wet and darkened by soot and smoke.

Relief hit her in a wave so powerful, so intense, her knees threatened to buckle. "Weston!" she cried, shouldering her way through the crowd. "Wes!"

Weston, David, and Bradford stood together. Locked in solemn silence, they watched the foundation of their dreams crumble. Aaron stood beside them, feeling utterly dejected and guilty beyond measure.

David sighed heavily. "I feel like I just jumped off that damned roof again."

Weston laid a hand on his friend's shoulder. "I'm sorry, man. I'm so sorry."

"Aw, well." David smiled wryly. "At least I didn't get a broken leg out of this one."

Water poured onto the deck of the ship. The fire hissed; the flames diminished, but the three men knew that most of the vessel was in ruins. This would set them back months, possibly destroy them all financially.

Weston wiped a hand across his face. "She sure was a beauty."

"Yes," David agreed. "She was." He turned to Bradford. "By the way, Brad, what were you going to name her?"

Bradford looked at David as though he were the town simpleton. He said matter-of-factly, "*Gabrielle,* of course."

Aaron coughed.

David's eyes bulged. "*Gabrielle!*"

"Well, I'll be damned," Weston said with a chuckle. "Gaby would've loved it."

They fell silent once again.

"We can rebuild," Bradford said mildly, his brilliant mind already clicking, working over the details, computing a more capable, more innovative vessel.

David shook his head. "Our investors won't put up this time. They lost enough as it is. We haven't the capital."

"Yes, you do," said a quiet voice.

As one, they turned toward Aaron.

"No!" Weston shook his head adamantly. He pointed a blackened finger at his brother. "I don't need yer blasted money!"

Aaron looked toward the charred vessel. "Seems to me you do."

His chin set stubbornly, Weston's head jutted down toward Aaron. "The only reason ye want to help is because ye feel guilty, because ye—"

"Want to." Aaron's voice was a soft monotone. "I've wanted to from the beginning, but I was afraid to challenge Father. Father's gone, Wes. We could throw in together . . ."

"Wes," Elizabeth cried, reaching them, almost knocking him over as she crashed against his body. "Oh, Wes, you idiot!" She hugged his neck. Instinctively his arms closed around her. She touched his face, neck, hands, and chest, murmuring his name over and over.

Several moments passed before she even noticed Aaron.

CHAPTER

20

When she and Weston finally separated, Elizabeth saw Aaron. She didn't try to hide her surprise. "Aaron. You're here, too?" Puzzled, she took in his disheveled state, the swollen lips, the purplish eye, the soot-streaked face. "I wondered why I hadn't seen you at services this even—" She left the sentence incomplete while her questioning gaze returned to Weston. Perplexed, she glanced from one to the other, comparing bloodied noses, swollen jaws... Narrowing her eyes in suspicion, she asked, "What happened here?"

Flushing, Aaron dropped his head and studied his shoes.

Weston cleared his throat, his attention flicking away to the smoking vessel.

"What?" Elizabeth demanded, plunking her hands onto her hips.

Aaron's eyes lifted to hers.

"A lamp fell," Weston cut in brusquely, his gaze still averted.

"A lamp fell?" Confused, she studied the two for

several more uncomfortable seconds. "A lamp fell? Is that what started the fire?" Their silence was her answer. "How? How did it fall?" Then quite suddenly she knew. "You two. It fell because of you two!" Stunned, she digested the implication of her own words. "You've been fighting." Her voice was soft with disbelief. "My Lord . . . you've been fighting," she cried plaintively, her voice growing louder. "Oh, look what you've done to each other!"

The two men held their guilty silence.

"Over what?" she demanded. "What would cause you to bludgeon each other like this?"

David fidgeted.

Bradford coughed.

"Me?" she all but screeched, tipping forward and flattening her palm against her chest, while she glanced from one to the other.

The noisy crowd milled around them. She continued to study their faces for several tense moments. "You caused this . . ." Her voice grew louder while sparks leapt in her eyes. She pointed a condemning finger at the smoking wreckage. "This . . . this . . . carnage is because of me?" Pinning Aaron with her cutting gaze, she sniped, "You! I thought you had more sense." She threw her head in Weston's direction. "I might have expected as much out of him—"

"Me!" Weston bawled indignantly, palming his chest.

"But 'you'!" Elizabeth continued her tirade upon Aaron. Poking a finger into his sore chest, she stepped closer and sniffed. "By God! You're foxed!"

Beleaguered, Aaron shifted uncomfortably.

Watching the exchange, David felt a measure of sympathy for the brothers. "Aw, leave off, Elizabeth. They feel bad enough as it is."

"It's true," Bradford added. "They never meant for this to happ—"

"Shut up!" She turned on the two defenders like a rabid dog. "Just shut up!"

Chastised, David and Bradford snapped their jaws shut.

Drawn by the shrill tone of Elizabeth's voice, a crowd formed a circle around the small group.

"Look at your faces!" she exclaimed, turning back to the guilty. "Both of you, beat to a bloody pulp!" She crossed her arms over her chest, thoroughly disgusted. "What a couple of fools! You're mad! You're both mad!"

"Now, Elizabeth . . . ," Aaron began patiently.

"Don't—you—Elizabeth—me! All this time I've been feeling sorry for you, and here you are drinking and carousing and brawling just like this"—she gestured toward Weston—"this . . . idiot brother of yours."

Shamefaced, Aaron squirmed.

Weston scowled. "Now wait just a goddamn minute, Lizzy!" He straightened to his full height, towering over her.

But Elizabeth's fury was hot and unrelenting, fueled by her earlier fear of losing him. Her emotions cried out for release. And released they were. She whipped around to face him. "Don't you even dare talk to me, you . . . you . . ." Not able to think of a word evil enough, she thumped him in the arm. Hard.

He grunted in pain.

"Look what you've done!" She jabbed a finger toward the ship. "You've not only ruined this for yourself, but what about David and Bradford? Don't you care about them?"

Aaron cleared his throat.

Weston's face blazed. "Of course I—"

"Well you have a fine way of showing it. Just how do you plan to right this wrong?"

"I intend to help—" Aaron put in.

"Oh, no—" Weston interrupted, turning on him.

"Oh, yes," Bradford and David interjected.

Weston spun around to his friends, his brows slashing across his forehead. "I won't take his money!"

"Then don't!" Aaron snapped, losing his patience. "They will!" He pointed a finger at Elizabeth. "As for her, this time you're going to marry her and do right by her, if I have to hold a gun to your head."

Weston hooked his hands on his hips, his expression black. He leaned over his brother. "I bloody well intend to!"

"I should hope so!" Aaron yelled up into his face.

Incensed, Elizabeth's cheeks flamed. "Who do you think you're talking about here?"

"You!" Weston's nose practically met hers, as he bellowed down at her. "We're getting married!"

She stared up at him, outraged, her eyes filled with leaping flames of their own. "The bloody hell we are! What do you think I am? Some cow you two can barter back and forth?" She whipped around to Aaron and pinned him with her scathing gaze. "How dare you presume I want to marry this bas—"

"Now, Elizab—" Aaron began.

"And you stay away from my sister!"

Startled, Aaron jumped back.

Behind Elizabeth, a recently arrived Abigail moaned in abject misery.

But Elizabeth was oblivious to Abigail's or anyone else's discomfort as she raged on. "Despite her feelings for you, any man who didn't have the character to see her worth years ago needn't come knocking on our door! Ever!"

When she had finished with her reign of terror, a silence as thick as the smoke that shrouded them descended. Dismissing them all, she pivoted and, without a backward glance, huffed off into the crowd, leaving her sister mortified, much of her audience stunned, others amused, one brother thoroughly browbeaten—and the other, madder than hell.

"I'll be damned," said the big man who'd carried Weston away from the flaming ship. He scratched his heavy beard reflectively. "I never saw anyone take Mr. Munroe to task like that little lady just done."

"No," said his companion. "Can't say I 'ave either."

"When do ye suppose the weddin'll be?"

"Well . . ." The smaller man ran five thick fingers through his hair. "I'll wager two shillings it'll be before the next sculling match."

April brought rain and warmer temperatures. The days lengthened. Trees budded. The snow disappeared into frosty memories, while the ice melted and streams ran free. Spring was heralded by an abundance of wildflowers, bringing bright splashes of color to the mainland as well as the island.

The ferry service resumed.

Ontario's placid lake waters beckoned, blue once more.

Within weeks, Weston, David, and Bradford, along with Aaron, were back in business. Young and resilient, they rebounded. They salvaged what they could of the old *Gabrielle* and began to build the new one. The fire caused them the loss of several of their investors, but a brave few remained, and with Aaron's financial support and newfound enthusiasm, the future looked bright once more.

At least in the business realm.

One mild April morning, Weston stood on the wharf. He looked out toward the island, reflecting on the changes that had been wrought in his life during the past year.

He'd come home, embarked on a business venture, almost lost his hide but not been defeated, lost his father but found his brother.

And most importantly, there was Elizabeth . . .

But Elizabeth hadn't just happened this year. No, she had been a part of him for as long as he could remember.

Memories of a wintry night taunted him, bringing a hot surge of desire and a mixture of needy emotions he'd suppressed for far too long.

He wanted her. He needed her. He loved her. And dammit! He was going to have her! He was tired of sulking!

He'd been sulking for three weeks now.

He pocketed his hands and shook his head. Damn that woman for her viperish tongue! Dressing him down in such a manner in front of the city of Toronto!

But she's right, Munroe, he admitted. He was a fool! With all the women in the world, he had to love one who could flay him to the bone with her tongue. He deserved everything he got!

And he missed her. He was as tired of waiting as he was of sulking.

What had she been doing these past weeks? Did she think of him? Could it be that maybe she meant what she'd said the night of the fire? Could it be she really didn't want to marry him?

He looked up and squinted. Against a cloudless azure

sky, gulls screeched, then swooped low over sun-dazzled waters.

Setting his jaw, he made up his mind. He was going to marry her even if he had to gag her to do it, even if he had to keep her gagged every day of her life afterward!

He returned to his office and wrote the note. He passed it on to Aaron, who passed it on to Abigail, who passed it on to Elizabeth.

Sitting on her bed, Elizabeth read his words:

Meet me on the island tonight.

W.

Very carefully she folded the small sheet of paper and handed it back to Abigail. "Tell him no," she said quietly, confusion and pride barring her from voicing her agreement with his directive.

"Oh, Elizabeth." Abigail plopped down on the bed beside her sister. "You tell him."

Elizabeth angled her a sly glance. "Most diplomatic of you, Ab. But I don't wish to see him."

"I don't believe you. You love him," Abigail responded impatiently. "You always have. What's holding you back now?" For two weeks, Abigail had steamed over the way Elizabeth had revealed her feelings for Aaron. But eventually she'd come to view the disclosure as a blessing. Aaron had called on her twice since that night and had been most attentive. He told her that although he cared for Elizabeth deeply, he was no more in love with her than she had been in love with him.

Abigail couldn't have been more pleased. But she was no fool, and she was not won quite so easily. Though she loved him, he would have to earn her devotion, and when he did, well . . .

"No." Elizabeth dismissed the subject of Weston tersely, still angry at both brothers, still unsure of how to handle Gabrielle's earlier revelations of her emotions about her one true love.

Maybe Weston could ignore Gabrielle's feelings, but Elizabeth could not. Gabrielle could be empty-headed at times, but she was still Elizabeth's friend.

If Elizabeth was to be honest with herself, she would have to admit the anger she'd felt toward Weston was quickly fading, and she ached for him, for his smile— his touch. And he had said he wanted to marry her. He'd declared it in front of everyone the night of the fire. Yet her stubbornness prevailed in the face of her loyalty to her friend. So, with those thoughts in mind, she glanced over at Abigail and lied. "I simply do not wish to see him."

"At least think about it," Abigail pleaded, desperately wanting to see her sister happy. "You're being most unreasonable."

"And you," Elizabeth snapped, "are being a busy-body!"

Abigail sighed. "Elizabeth," she began uncertainly, while absently picking at a loose thread on her skirt. "You . . . you . . . aren't upset because of Aaron and me, are you?"

Remorseful, Elizabeth's irritation fled. Her expression softened. "Oh, no, Ab." She laid a comforting hand over her sister's. "Please don't think that. I'm not upset in the least. Despite what I said to Aaron, I think he's perfect for you. My only regret is that I didn't see it sooner."

On an especially fine day during the first week of May, Elizabeth ventured out toward Victoria Row. Abigail's birthday was fast approaching, and she wanted

to give her something special. In all of Toronto, there
was no grander place to shop for such a treasure than
Victoria Row.

Birds sang out a spring greeting, while the gentle
wind whispered of warmer days to come. She strolled
by Howard's Block, past the many luxurious restaurants,
past rows and rows of elegant shops, gazing into spacious plate-glass windows, admiring glittering jewelry,
stylish clothing, elaborate china, and bric-a-brac.

"Elizabeth! Hello!"

Elizabeth turned. "Gabrielle!"

Gabrielle hurried to her side. "How very wonderful to
see you! I was planning on a visit, but I simply haven't
had the time!" As usual, she was dressed fashionably
and was bubbling with excitement. But today, Elizabeth
noticed, there was something different about her, a glow
that almost seemed to radiate around her.

"It's good to see you, too," Elizabeth returned sincerely. "You look well."

"Oh, Elizabeth. I am! I truly am! I'm more than well.
I'm wonderful!" Gabrielle hooked arms with her. "Walk
with me for a while. I have so much to tell you."

Elizabeth smiled and fell into step, finding it easy to
quell any lingering resentments, despite her estrange-
ment from Weston. "So tell me," Elizabeth said as she
looked down at the shorter woman, "how have you really
been?"

Gabrielle lifted shining eyes. "I'm better than I've
ever been in my life, Elizabeth." She paused for a
moment, almost holding her breath. "Are you ready
for this?" Not waiting for an answer, she plunged on.
"I'm getting married!"

Elizabeth's heart and feet stopped dead. "Married."
The word was but a stunned whisper.

"Yes!" Gabrielle threw herself against Elizabeth, hugging her tight. "Isn't it wonderful? I'm so very happy! I want you there, of course. At my wedding. You and Abigail! My very best friends. Can you imagine? Me, married? I nearly died when he asked me. Well," she corrected in a rush, "he didn't exactly ask me. He just sort of marched up to my door, knocked, and when my father answered, he calmly announced his intentions! I almost fainted dead away right at that very moment, right in the parlor! My mother did! Poor Mama. Can you believe it?"

"No . . ." The quiet word escaped Elizabeth's lips unnoticed.

The two separated.

Gabrielle laced her hands demurely in front of her tiny, nipped-in waistline. Her eyes grew misty, her voice soft and fervent. "I love him, Elizabeth. I love him so much it hurts."

Her world teetering, Elizabeth stared down at the glowing young woman. Though Gabrielle had always been lovely, there was a maturity, a newfound beauty that had been absent in her until now. She was genuinely in love this time. There was no doubt about it. The selfishness and avarice that had always marked her character were all but gone. After viewing the result of what that true emotion had wrought, Elizabeth ran through a gamut of conflicting feelings.

"Do you know what I mean?" Gabrielle asked. "About loving someone that much?"

"Oh, yes." Elizabeth found she could answer that question quite easily. "Indeed I do."

"Then be happy for me, Elizabeth. Please. I've never wanted anything as much as I want this. I want to be his wife. I want his children—ten children." Her bright green eyes grew wide. "At least ten. He's so . . . so . . . beautiful . . . and tall. Not short and . . . and round like me." She looked down at her own curvy figure, then back up at Elizabeth. "I hope all our children look exactly like Brad!"

Brad! Elizabeth's mind reeled, while her eyes nearly popped from her head. Finding her voice, she tipped forward and whispered, "Bradford . . . You're marrying Brad?"

"Yes," Gabrielle went on, so lost in her joy, she didn't discern the shocked surprise so evident in her friend's eyes.

"But I thought you and Weston—"

"Weston!" Gabrielle exclaimed. "Humph! Hardly!" She dismissed the assumption with an airy wave of her hand. "I'm not for Weston, and Weston is not for me. I've known that for quite some time. Besides," she said, her voice softening, "everyone knows how you two feel about each other." She paused, captured Elizabeth's hand, and with a touch of genuine regret said, "I'm sorry if I hurt you, Elizabeth. I know there were times I led you to believe there was more between Weston and myself than there truly was. Please . . . forgive me."

Elizabeth blinked. "Oh, Gaby . . ." was all she could find to say as relief became full blown. Finding her voice, she widened her eyes and exclaimed, "But you and Brad!"

"Yes. Can you believe it? Me and Bradford Stevens! Even my parents were surprised. We're such opposites. At first, my father was worried about his ability to take care of me. After all, he's just getting started, and the fire set him back. But I told Papa that once they get this ship finished and show this city how successful and prosperous their company is going to be, we'll be just fine."

"Yes," Elizabeth answered, her joy reverberating throughout her body. "I'm sure you will." She threw her arms around her friend and squeezed until Gaby gasped for air.

"Elizabeth, pleeeeze! I can't breathe!"

"Oh, Gaby!" Elizabeth cried, laughing. Then quite suddenly she released her. "I can't wait to get home and tell Abigail and Mama!" Without another word, she spun around, eagerly breaking into a run.

"I'll come by soon!" Gabrielle called after her. "I want Abigail to help with my wedding dress. She's ever so much finer a seamstress than Mrs. Grogan!"

"I'll tell her," Elizabeth said over her shoulder. "She'll be delighted."

Early the next afternoon a note was delivered directly to Weston by a young dockworker he didn't recognize.

> Dear Weston,
> Not feeling well. Please come at once.
>   Benjamin.

Without hesitation, Weston headed for the ferry docks.

CHAPTER
21

Hurrying from the ferry, Weston set off along the sandbars. The great globe of the sun dipped low over the horizon, angling red and gold shafts of light across the waters, creating sparkling prisms upon the still surface. In the distance, a colorful sky met with the seemingly endless line of water.

Eli greeted him as he strode briskly along the shoreline. "Hello, boy," Weston said, bending to ruffle the fur on the dog's head. "Where's your master?" In answer, Eli leapt ahead, leading the way to the lighthouse.

Finding the door ajar, Weston knocked once before entering. "Benjamin!"

By the light of a single lamp, the old man sat at the table, his elbows propped on the surface, a book open before him. He looked up, his small round spectacles slipping down to the end of his nose. "Weston!"

With a worried expression, Weston crossed the room. "What's wrong?" He laid a hand on Benjamin's shoulder and dropped to one knee beside his chair.

"Aw, lad," Benjamin moaned, leaning back in his

chair, affecting a pained expression. He placed an open palm across his prominent stomach. "I think I've a bad case of indigestion."

Weston's brows drew taut. "Indigestion?"

"Aye." Benjamin nodded a bit too convincingly.

Weston studied him for several silent, discerning moments, until finally he narrowed his eyes and said, "I think you have a touch of something all right."

"Ah, now, Wes," Benjamin complained, squirming under the younger man's knowing gaze. "Don't be unkind to an old man . . ."

Weston rose. "What old man? You're as healthy as a mule!" Hands on hips, he glared down at him, shaking his head in disgust. "Benjamin Duncan, you old fox! You nearly scared me white! Why would you send me a note like that if—"

"Hello, Wes." Her soft-spoken words jolted him into silence.

He spun.

Partially hidden in shadow, she stood beside the bookcase he'd given Benjamin, her hands clasped in front of her dress, her thumb working her cuticle mercilessly.

Not bothering to mask his surprise, he took in with a hungry gaze the simplicity of her high-necked dress, the haphazard condition of her coppery hair, the healthy glow of her cheeks, the sweet smattering of freckles across her nose, and the sudden vulnerable expression in those wide hazel eyes. He found her lovelier than he ever remembered, and knew that Benjamin had sent the note for her.

"I would have come for you, Beth," Weston admonished gently. "There was no need to scare me out of my wits."

"I wasn't sure," she admitted. And she hadn't been,

especially after she had all but ignored his earlier request to see her. She had wronged him, and she knew it.

She drank in the sight of him as he stood loose and relaxed. A shaft of waning sunlight fell across his shoulders, giving him a golden, otherworldly glow, making him more attractive than he had any right to be. She struggled for composure, staring at his dear handsome face. Her emotions intensified, pelting her with a desire and longing that only he could elicit.

"I've missed you, Lizzy." Slowly he moved toward her.

"I've missed you, too, Wes." Her heart hammered wildly.

"Why didn't you come?" he asked softly, stopping before her, his face serious and intent. "Why didn't you come to the island when I sent you the letter?"

She shook her head, reluctant to voice her misapprehensions, which suddenly seemed silly and insignificant.

Bemused, he tightened his brows. "Surely you're not still angry about the fire."

"Of course not . . ."

"And Aaron and I . . . ," he added, widening his stance and hooking his hands on his hips. "We've made our peace . . ."

"I know."

"Then what?" he asked, staring at her intently.

Embarrassed, she hesitantly began, "I thought . . ." She paused for a moment, taking a deep breath. "You and Gabrielle . . ." She dropped her gaze, her face lighting like a torch. "Last winter she told me she was in love. Not knowing about Brad, I assumed it was you. I didn't want to hurt her . . ." She found herself unable to continue.

But there was no need for her to do so, for knowing her as he did, he understood. Though he was touched by her loyalty to her friend, he couldn't resist the opportunity to bait her. "Why, Lizzy Beth," he said, "I'll bet you were jealous, too."

Her eyes shot to his, anger instantly sparking—anger toward him for teasing her and toward herself because the words he spoke were so true. Faced with that truth, she wondered how she could have been so foolish.

As though bored with the exchange, Benjamin rose, turned, and ambled toward the door. "Come, Eli. Captain Avery's holdin' dinner for us."

Elizabeth reached out a hand in supplication. "Don't go, Benjamin. Please. Not yet." She took a step toward him, but Weston caught her arm, halting her.

At the door, Benjamin turned and leveled his gaze on her. "It'll be all right, Lizzy. Ye'll see." Then he was gone.

Weston tightened his grip, his eyes dancing wickedly.

Her indignation flared. She whirled, creating a small tornado with her skirts, and tore loose from his grasp. She lit for the door, her face flaming, her pulse throbbing. Jealous! Ohhhh, the conceited bore! Despite the fact that he was right, she'd never give him the satisfaction of gloating about it!

Her skirts slapped at her legs, and she bolted from the lighthouse, into the dimming rays of sunlight and down to a quiet strip of beach.

"Elizabeth!" Within seconds, he caught her from behind. He jerked her to a stop, both wide hands hugging her waist. "Dammit, Lizzy," he muttered, pulling her back against his hardness, "don't ye think it's time we ended this game?"

His heart beat wildly against her back. She struggled within his embrace. "It isn't a game!"

He pressed himself into her backside, his hands riding her ribs up to her breasts. "No, Lizzy. It isn't. But we've fought ever since we were children, and I have a feeling we're going to be having battles long into our marriage." He laid his mouth against her neck, while he held her tight.

Angry tears smarted. She pinched her lids together. "I hate you, Weston Munroe."

"How bad do you hate me, Lizzy?" he asked, using the same words he'd used on her so many times before.

"Oh, Wes," she whispered, beleaguered. She swung to face him, stilling his hands. "It's not funny. There was a moment yesterday when I ran into Gabrielle on Victoria Row that I really did think you were going to marry her."

"Marry her!" The statement escaped him in an astonished bark. His eyebrows rose almost to his hairline. For several seconds he stared down at her as though she'd gone mad. Then, all control fleeing, he released her, anchored his hands on his hips, tipped his nose to the sky, and roared with laughter.

Incensed, she watched him through a red haze for what seemed like a very long time. "Ohhhh, you, you . . . ," she finally hissed, feeling angrier than she'd ever remembered feeling before. "You insensitive ass!" She took a step away from him, balled her fist, wound her arm back, and swung with all her might.

Out of the corner of one eye, he saw her arm coming toward him. He ducked. She missed his head by a mile, and the power of her swing sent her whirling in a wobbly circle. Though still disabled by laughter, he managed to catch her around the waist, steadying her. Swallowing his chuckles, he looked down into her face and asked, "Where the bloody hell did you get the fool idea that I wanted to marry Gaby?"

She narrowed her eyes into thin slits and yelled, "Oh, don't you try to tell me you never even thought about it!" She stabbed two fingers into his chest.

"All right," he admitted. "Maybe I thought about it for half a minute when you were engaged to marry Aaron. But it was never a serious consideration—"

"Nothing's ever serious with you, is it, Weston? Everything's just a game," she accused, "ship-building, sculling matches, climbing oak trees, everything . . ." She shook her head. "Everything."

"Not everything." His tone was suddenly quite serious.

Oblivious to his soft-spoken words, she lifted her chin a notch higher. Water lapped the shore, willows swayed in the wind, gulls sailed above, while her heart vacillated furiously.

Her eyes lifted to his. Seeking the reaffirmation she so desperately needed, she searched the deep blue depths.

"You're not a game to me, Lizzy. You never were." Finally understanding her need to hear his explanation, he said, "What there was between Gabrielle and me was over almost as soon as it had begun. I assumed you knew about her and Brad. They've been attracted to each other for quite some time now." As he watched her digest his words, he felt a wealth of love for her, so deep, so true, he found himself speechless. He felt a strong need to protect her—his little hoyden, so strong, yet so tender and vulnerable.

Elizabeth blinked. Fresh tears of joy and embarrassment burned her nose. Amid the return of her mother, the death of Weston's father, and her problems with Aaron, she'd missed all the signs of Gabrielle and Bradford's courtship. "No," she murmured in answer to his earlier statement. "I . . . ah . . . I didn't know." She dropped her gaze to the grass at her feet. "I'm sorry for doubting you, Wes. So very sorry."

"Aw, Lizzy . . . ," he said, touching a finger to her cheek, stilling the downward journey of a translucent tear. "Did you really think I'd play you false?"

She couldn't answer.

The silence echoed around them. Very slowly he reached into the pocket of his trousers, withdrew a small box, and silently held it out to her.

Her eyes snapped up to his.

His expression solemn, he waited, feeling incredibly exposed. "I'd planned to give it to you when I first came home. But . . ." He shrugged and left the sentence incomplete.

Her eyes still locked with his, she reached for the box and took it from his open palm. Then she looked at the box and held it wordlessly for several seconds. Very slowly she lifted the lid to view a small, lovely, pearl-encrusted emerald brooch. Emotion rocked her. She swallowed thickly, lifting the brooch from its velvet cocoon. "Oh, my . . . ," she whispered, overcome. "Oh, my . . ."

"Turn it over," he commanded softly.

She did. In the fading remnants of daylight, she made out the words he'd had inscribed there so very long ago . . .

Lizzy Beth, Forever In My Heart. W.

Her throat clogged. Her dark lashes trembled upon her cheeks. Such beautiful words from one who swore he could be no poet. To think he'd given such words to her. "Oh, Wes . . ." She found no expression eloquent enough to equal the one he'd had placed upon this treasure.

He watched the emotions play across her face and knew she understood. He stepped close and gently drew her against his chest. He looked down at her, and his voice grew earnest. "I love you, Lizzy. Don't you know that by now? I always have. I always will. But it wasn't until I left that I knew how to tell you. And then . . . it was almost too late."

Reading the truth in his eyes, she laid the past to rest with all its doubts, all its uncertainties. She clutched the brooch in her palm while her arms rose and circled his neck. "Oh, damn you, Weston Munr—"

His mouth cut off her words.

What began as a tender kiss became needy, hungry, impatient. His mouth swept hers. His hands rose to her throat. His thumbs formed a firm brace along her jaw, while his warm tongue washed the interior of her mouth, offering testimony to the depth of his love.

Then, very slowly, his hands lowered and began to work the buttons of her dress, from her throat down to her waist.

"Here?" she asked.

"Yes, here," he answered into her mouth. "Where else, Lizzy?"

Where else indeed, she thought, but here where it all began. "But Benjamin—"

"Won't be back this night. There's no one here. Just us."

And he was right.

The long line of beach was deserted but for the lighthouse, nature, and the shimmering lake. The violet shadows of twilight fell around them, shielding them, protecting them.

His gaze sober, he whispered, "Before we do this, I

want you to say it, Lizzy Beth. Say you'll marry me."

Her throat tight, she nodded and accepted the love that had always been hers, would always be hers.

He reached up and drew the pins from her hair one by one, dropping them to the ground, allowing the disorderly mass to fall past her shoulders in splendid disarray. "Say it," he ordered, his voice soft. He threaded his fingers through her hair.

"Yes," she whispered, emotions storming her senses as she felt his hands move through her hair, down to her shoulders. "Yes, I will. I'll marry you."

"You won't change your bloody mind, now?" he asked, a shadow of a grin working at his mouth.

"No." She returned his smile, her eyes glinting mischief. "Not tonight, I won't."

He separated the unbuttoned material of her dress, then drew it down over her shoulders, past her hips, to let it fall in a puddle at her feet. He dropped to one knee and slowly removed her shoes, then followed them with her stockings.

"My family . . . " she began, worried what they would think of yet one more lengthy absence.

"They aren't here," he said, looking up her slender form. He rose. "Soon we'll be married, and we can do this anytime we want." He grinned, his eyes dancing with merriment, while his hands cradled the hollows of her hips. "No corset," he observed with approval.

"No corset." She chuckled, knowing he'd always held blatant contempt for such binding garments.

"Don't ever wear one." He bent and touched his nose to hers.

"Not even when I'm fat?"

He rolled his forehead against hers. "Not even then."

Within seconds, she stood only in her brief white

undergarments, oblivious to the coolness of the evening air.

"Now you," she insisted. She placed the brooch into its case, stooped to lay it at their feet, and rose to reach anxious hands to his suspenders. She drew them over the broad width of his shoulders, let them hang in loose loops at his hips, then undid the buttons of his shirt, while he freed the buttons on his pants.

In moments, he'd divested himself of his garments and boots and stood before her, seemingly unaware of the magnificence of his form. With tender hands, he reached for her, spread her chemise wide, and laid his palms upon the bare skin of her breasts. A sigh escaped as a sweet rush swept her.

"Aw, Lizzy," he said, his deep voice husky, his gaze hot and ardent. "You are a beautiful woman." Gently he drew her down to the ground, to the carpet of their clothing, all the while offering her quiet words of encouragement.

He stretched out beside her, stroking her—with his tongue, his hands, ever the master tutor, teaching her more about the secret joys that passion and experience would bring to them both.

She closed her eyes while his tongue played across her throat, her breasts, her nipples, and she arched toward him when the sensations became so intense that the rest of her body ached for attention, until finally she could stand it no longer and quietly requested, "Here," and drew his hand to the place that yearned for him.

"Like this?" he asked, his eyes watching her face.

"Oh, yes," she whispered. "Exactly like that."

"It's good, isn't it, Lizzy?"

"Yes." She opened her eyes to find his beloved gaze on her. "It's very good."

"It's supposed to be." He chuckled low in his throat, pleased with the honesty of her response, thankful he was marrying this woman, this unconventional Victorian lady with whom there would be no staunch objection to this part of their life. He kissed a hot path from her neck to her hips, then removed her chemise and pantaloons and drew her naked form flush against him, fitting his hardness into the cradle she provided, reveling in the heat that ignited between them.

He took her hand and guided it between their bodies.

She found him firm and hot, and at her touch he went still as a shadow. But it wasn't long before he groaned and moved against her, adapting to a rhythm as old as time.

"Oh, Wes," came her strangled voice, smitten by the beauty of his maleness, overwhelmed by the fact that she, no beauty, would be wife to this fine man.

His control weakening, his tongue touched her lips, and he drew himself away from her.

As the night wind sighed and the moon shed silver beams around them, he moved over her, laying his long, hard length upon her. His hands sought her hips, bracketing them, holding her still, while, in anticipation, her arms gripped his damp, taut shoulders.

He slipped into her slowly, and she closed her eyes, receiving him, loving him, welcoming him.

"Stay," he whispered huskily, holding himself still within her. "I want to feel us together, like this . . ." He closed his eyes and gave himself up to sensation and pleasure. She was warmth and satin, femininity and strength—the embodiment of all he desired, all he would ever need. "This is what it's all about, Lizzy. Us together. You and me . . . this . . . ," he uttered softly, while he rose up slightly, opened his eyes, and looked down the length of their locked bodies. Then his control weakened, and he groaned, pushed deep, and began to move slowly within her.

"I love you," she whispered, matching his motions, glad she could speak the words so freely at last. "I love you, Wes." His heart beat like thunder against her breasts. She felt his breath on her chest, his weight on her body, the fullness of having his body encased in hers, and knew a wordless serenity. Life without him, without this, would have been a most abysmal, sad, and empty existence.

Their restraint dissolved. Young and demanding, their bodies partook of each other. His head dropped to her shoulder. His thighs tensed. She arched her neck and closed her eyes again. His breathing grew harsher, his thrusts stronger, swifter. The sensations within her intensified, and a moment later, Wes moaned, lunged one last time, pressed deep, then shuddered within her.

They lay exhausted, sated, replete at last. As the embers of their love mellowed, she clasped him to her breast and breathed in his scent, unaware of the wondrous gift he'd unknowingly placed within her. He was heavy but he was not a burden. His skin glistened with sweat. Moonlight crowned his silver-blond head. She kissed his shoulder, touched his nape, and found herself unable to voice the burgeoning emotions that swept her.

The music of the night embraced them, serenading them with perfect harmony. Far out across the lake, a ship's lengthy whistle joined the chorus. Above, cast against a wide onyx sky, a grand dusting of stars shone down upon them.

He eased from her body, rolled to his side, and pulled her into the protective circle of his arms. Their limbs entwined, he kissed her forehead, each eyelid, then lifted her hands and kissed each palm.

"Again?" she teased, reaching for the velvet box at her side.

"Soon," he promised, angling her a wicked glance. "What a greedy wench ye are, Beth."

"Indeed." She arched a brow, laughed, and settled back against him.

Locked together, they lay swathed in the luminescent light of the moon, two souls finally one, gazing out at the shining waters of Lake Ontario.

In those hallowed, precious moments, they looked into the past and knew this lake, this island, this city were a part of each of them, a symbolic part of their entwined lives. Their surroundings signified the history of their love—its birth, its awakening, its continuing essence. And looking into the future, they knew this was their home, would always be their home. A safe harbor for their love. A safe harbor for their children soon to come. They envisioned a life with countless evenings such as this. A lifetime of sparring, of passion, of hope, of enduring love that would only grow stronger as they grew older.

Content, she snuggled against the mat of golden hair on his chest. When at last she lifted loving eyes to him, she touched her fingers to his lips and quietly murmured, "Forever, Wes."

He drew her close, his expression one of profound tenderness. "Ah . . . yes, Lizzy," he said softly. "You're damn right . . ."

And then, with a sudden reckless grin, his lips found hers and sealed the vow for all time.